The Revelation Key

By F. L. Wylie

The Revelation Key
© 2017 Faith Lubben Wylie,
Wylie Communications, Inc.

Print edition published by Wylie Publishing
eBook edition published by Kindle Press

Cover Design by F.L. Wylie
Photograph courtesy Visit Meteora

For the architecture and history behind the story, visit
www.RevelationKey.com

ISBN: 978-0-9997507-2-8

Rachel — Good luck with your creative pursuites !

The Revelation Key

By
F.L. Wylie

Faith L. Wylie

Wylie
PUBLISHING

1

The Perfect Murder

Four Months Ago, Fort Worth, Texas

Bees slept in the dark space, waiting for sun and a return to foraging.

Robert Jackson plopped files on the desk—requests from the Classics Institute and the Nicene Foundation.

Light cracked the darkness, sending the bees into action. The first bee rushed to the opening.

Robert reached into the drawer, crushing her as he grabbed the stapler. She released a burst of pheromone, calling other workers into battle. They swarmed to attack the intruder, imbedding four barbed stingers into his flesh.

"Damn!" Jackson jerked his hand from the desk drawer, shaking off the bees. More lethal honeybees swarmed out.

He yanked the drawer open wider to retrieve his EpiPen. The contents spilled on the floor. He knelt to search for the life-saving injection.

His breath rasped as air squeezed through his closing throat.

Call 911.

He tried to reach the phone in his pocket. The fingers on his right hand had swollen like sausages ready to burst their skins. His right arm wouldn't move.

His vision blurred as his blood pressure dropped. He grabbed a

1

marker in his left hand and scratched out the words, "Be careful." He slowly started the third word. "B." The ink trailed off into illegibility. In his last moment of consciousness, he scrawled one more letter.

DAY ONE

"In the beginning God created the heavens and the earth."

Genesis 1:1

Numbers held special meaning for ancient and medieval people. In Biblical numerology, God is one. One symbolizes uniqueness and unity. The circle represents oneness and unity. *Alpha* is the Greek numeral for one.

3

Athens Airport, Greece

Sunday in June

I sucked in hot, dry Athenian air, clearing the aircraft atmosphere from my lungs.

Most passengers came to Greece for relaxation and tourism. Not me. This research trip was a lifeline to rescue my academic career after last semester's disasters.

Losing my mentor, Uncle Robert, devastated me. I struggled to bounce back after my boyfriend dumped me. Then I failed Greek. I never got an F. Ever. Hell, I rarely got Bs.

Focus on the mission. I scanned the signs held by cabbies and tour bus drivers.

"JACKSON." The traditional blue and red glow of the family name popped out—sort of like the Lone Star flag.

I caught the eye of the man holding our sign. The tall blond stood out in the row of Mediterranean types. He headed toward us.

Rev. Dr. Billy Sullivan, my traveling companion, set down luggage and dug in his pocket for a tip.

I shook hands with our driver. "Amber Jackson."

"Carl Helman. I'm the art history expert at the Classics Institute."

"Oh, I expected an old German with little wire-framed glasses."

Carl smiled. "No, just a Ph.D. candidate."

He turned to Billy, waving away the tip.

"Carl, let me introduce Rev. Dr. Billy Sullivan. His expertise is Early Christian manuscripts and Biblical Greek."

Billy gave his load to Carl. I stifled a giggle. The former preacher looked respectable in his monogrammed golf shirt. But he had snored his way across the Atlantic overnight, with a little trickle of drool on his chin.

Carl, on the other hand, looked like MacGyver The original MacGyver was my childhood hero. In the old reruns, he nabbed the bad guys by being smarter, not more violent.

"This will be a unique project for us," Carl said as he loaded the Toyota. "We don't normally study the Dark Ages."

Billy claimed the front passenger seat, a tight fit for his bulk. I folded my big feet into the tiny back seat.

Carl headed for The Classics Institute, where the two staff scholars would join Billy and me on our research team this month.

The Institute was in the *Plaka* neighborhood, settled by Greek merchants when Athens became the capital after the War of Independence in 1834. It now teemed with tourists on a Sunday afternoon, surrounding us with aromas of sweat and cafes. The Institute snuggled next to the Jackson Textile Importers building.

My aunt and uncle had launched their international operations here, turning a family cotton farm and cotton gin into a multi-national textile business before selling to a conglomerate a year ago. They were University of Fort Worth alumni and helped support the study-abroad facility next door.

This jaunt was my college graduation present, a month in Greece doing research with experts. A fun trip, Aunt Lydia said. But I knew better. This Early Christian study trip was a charity gift to get me back on my feet for graduate school in the fall.

Carl showed us how to use the Institute's international SIMM cards in our phones Billy grumbled as Carl carried Billy's bags upstairs to a student room.

I got my aunt and uncle's Athens apartment in the back of the Jackson building. The only thing missing was the homey atmosphere provided by my aunt and uncle. Aunt Lydia planned to come with me but backed out at the last minute.

On the entry table, I noticed a package.

Addressed to a dead man.

4

Classics Institute

His name had that familiar blue and red glow that emanated from the letters. "Robert Jackson." My uncle.

Carl brought another load of my stuff. "Just ignore that mail. We'll send it to your aunt since she decided not to come. Let's meet in an hour to go to Daphni Monastery."

"Sounds good."

I picked up the package. Postmarks showed it had been mailed to Uncle Robert at his overseas apartment just before he died. I returned it to the entry table beside the basket of unopened mail.

His bizarre death troubled me. Who died from bee stings in February? Inside the house? Honey bees don't swarm and attack unless they think the hive is in danger or you step on them while they harvest pollen from clover.

I glanced at his empty chair. I found myself waiting for him to come through the door and make the world right again. I snuggled into the worn leather, closed my eyes and imagined him beside me.

Uncle Robert never laughed at my questions or told me to hush up. He always treated me like I was smart, even when I was a clumsy kid following some crazy quest.

Was this research project another crazy quest? Early Christian art spoke to me about our heritage and history. But no one else seemed interested.

I showered away the flight across the Atlantic, then retrieved the Swiss Army knife from my checked suitcase and moved it to its usual pocket in my bag.

The package still beckoned from the living room. Bigger than a shoe box. Heavier, too. My fingers played with a loose corner of tape.

No. Opening a dead person's package would be like robbing a grave. I shoved it away. Surely I could control my curiosity out of respect for my uncle.

The box filled the entire room. I moved it to the kitchen. It whispered my name. The guest room was no better.

I tried eating chocolate as a diversion.

Why would my uncle have it shipped to Greece instead of his home in Fort Worth?

Did my aunt know it was here? Should I call her?

What would my uncle do?

He'd open the box. I grabbed my knife and slit the tape.

The phone interrupted.

"Amber, time to go over my plan for your studies," Dr. Billy Sullivan said.

"I'll be right there. I'm looking forward to it." Not.

Learning Greek was mission impossible. I'd rather open an exotic package from Paris.

I stashed the box in the guest room, swung my bag over my shoulder and set forth on my quest to break into the upper levels of academia as an art historian.

I joined Billy in the Institute library, the front room that served as the general hang out for students and faculty.

"What do you need to learn this month?"

"I have to get past my mental block on learning Greek. And I want to study Early Christian art."

"Teaching Biblical Greek is my specialty, so you're in good hands." He handed me an open book.

Strange letters looked like little black worms on the page. I scanned for letters from our alphabet. The first line looked easy. *"Ka-ta Map-kon."*

Billy frowned.

I looked again. P stood out in bright plum purple. Except p is r in Greek. I made the mental switch, but it refused to change color on the page.

"Ka-ta Mar-kon, "From Mark. This is the start of the Gospel of Mark."

"Can you read more?"

Apxn. What was *Apxn? Ap* would be the first syllable. No, make that *Ar.* But *xn* didn't have a vowel. The blue n taunted me. What was a lower case n in Greek? An e. But e should be yellow.

"Ar-xe?"

"Try again."

I scanned the letters. That white x should be an orange chi.

"Ar-che?"

"Lord, have mercy. You've had a whole semester of Greek?"

"Sort of ... I flunked the class."

Billy waited for more gruesome details.

"The Greek alphabet drives me crazy. My mind just can't switch between English and Greek letters. It gets confused. The letters are all the wrong colors."

"The wrong colors? What do colors have to do with it?" Billy asked.

Careless mistake. I knew better than to talk about the color of letters. I learned that in elementary school. Other students made fun of me. Teachers didn't like it. They told me that letters and numbers didn't have colors. Why did my brain insist on coloring my letters?

"I mean everything is wrong about the alphabet, the sounds and shapes."

"So you're still learning the alphabet?"

Billy frowned as he rested his chin on manicured fingertips. My eyes were drawn to his ring, three colors of gold braided together in interlocking bands.

He looked up. "You must copy the Greek letters and words as you read them out loud. It takes longer, but it helps master the alphabet."

He pulled a calligraphy pen from his pocket. "Use this. It has the thick and thin strokes of traditional writing." He demonstrated in controlled, neat strokes.

The pen produced uneven lines and blobs when I wrote a few characters.

"Revelation will be a good assignment since you like art history," Billy said. "It's packed full of Christian imagery."

"Ugh. I hate Revelation." I slumped lower.

He glowered over the top of his reading glasses.

Revelation made me feel like puking. The last book in the Bible is a prophecy of destructive punishment and resurrection. My stomach churned just thinking about arguments with my ex-boyfriend about that violent prophecy. Still, Billy was a potential mentor. I needed him if the grad school questioned the F on my final transcript.

"I had a bad experience with Revelation last year. My ex-boyfriend decided he was called to devote his life to the Lord and prepare people for the coming End Times."

Crying would be so embarrassing. Billy leaned forward to hear me.

"I wanted to study Revelation, ask questions. I like to dig into ideas. Because I didn't accept the church's set answer he told me I was lukewarm and would be left behind at the Rapture."

"Good to learn that you have different callings now instead of later."

"It's a humiliating way to get dumped."

"Well, I can speak from experience. It ruined my pastoral career when my former wife decided she didn't share my call and filed for divorce. I had to switch to teaching and writing. It took me years to get my career back on track," Billy said. "You don't want your crisis of faith to hold back his ministry."

"Yeah, Dustin was smart to get rid of me."

"Did you bring an interlinear?"

"Yeah."

"Cover up the English translation line, copy the original Greek words, then see how many you understand. Check it against the translation line. Start with the first three chapters of Revelation."

He sounded like my father, a high school principal.

Carl Helman bounded into the room. The art history teacher was anything but fatherly.

"Your rooms okay?" he asked.

"Mine's good." Except for missing my aunt and uncle.

"I had forgotten how Spartan student rooms are," Billy said. "I'm not used to twin beds and a shared bathroom down the hall."

Carl shrugged. "We aren't a resort. People come here to study."

Billy would love my accommodations, but I didn't intend to give them up.

"Time to go," Carl said. "Daphni Monastery was closed after an earthquake but it is now reopened after repairs."

Carl maneuvered the tiny car through the narrow streets that circled the Acropolis, then navigated a six-lane highway atop the ancient Sacred Way from Athens to Eleusis.

"Daphni was a temple to Apollo, but Christians built a church over the sacred place," Carl said.

His blue eyes caught mine in the rearview mirror. He winked. Was he deliberately provoking Billy? I crossed my eyes back at him.

Carl glanced toward Billy and cocked his head. "Christians plundered the temple columns to use in the church."

Billy looked up from a brochure describing our destination.

"Goths sacked the temple in 395 AD. I believe the Goths were a Germanic tribe."

No smart-ass answer? Carl turned to the impossible Athenian traffic, yelling curses out the window.

How did he switch so fast from English to Greek to German? I couldn't twist my Texas tongue around all those crisp, short syllables in Greek names and words. A Greek could say *"Thou-kyd-i-des"* faster than I could drawl "Daaaal-las."

5

The Macedonian Dynasty ends

August, A.D. 1056, Constantinople

"Save the key, Father."

The monk leaned in to hear the 75-year-old empress. "What key?"

Theodora pointed. "Stephen's key. It's in the Book of the Purple-born. I will not abandon it to these arrogant bastards."

Father Alexios opened the book. No key. Was it hidden in the binding? A key would be easier to smuggle. Perhaps the empress was delirious. He opened his robe and bound the book to his heart.

"Take my chalice, too. *Leave now*," she said.

Instead, he knelt by her bed and prayed, his tears bathing her restless hands.

Her scowl softened. "Oh, Alexios, if only I had borne a son as loyal as you. I should have married as my father ordered. But I was stubborn. I failed our empire."

The monk glanced around the purple granite room. For almost two centuries, Theodora's ancestors had begun or ended their lives here. Basil the Macedonian, Leo the Wise, Constantine VII Purple-born, and Basil the Bulgar-killer had shaped the Eastern Roman Empire.

The empress put his thoughts into words. "The Macedonian

Dynasty dies with me today. But you can save the key."

Voices of the patriarch and the leader of the senate echoed in the palace hallway.

The empress closed her eyes. "The vultures circle. Go while you can."

"The key will be safe with the holy brothers at Daphni." The monk slipped out.

"*Omega pi eta,*" Theodora whispered. "Lord, have mercy on me, a sinner."

6

Daphni Monastery

Present Day

Stillness enveloped us in the massive church. Light trailed from windows high overhead, revealing dust hanging in the air and swirling as we disturbed the abandoned space.

Culture's foes had stripped the marble panels from the walls. Naked patches revealed the rough stone bones of the structure.

Christ the Judge scowled from a golden mosaic high overhead. More than nine hundred years of turmoil and nature had not dimmed the artist's vision. It spoke past barriers of time, culture and language.

"The most awesome Christ *Pantokrator* ever conceived in Byzantine art," Billy read.

Pantokrator. All Strength. My *Koine* Greek was pitiful, but even I knew *Pantokrator*.

I stared up. Where was the nice Jesus, the gentle Good Shepherd of the Beatitudes? This Jesus, the angry judge of Revelation, gave me the creeps.

Light flickered across his dark, lined eyes as he glared into my soul. Instead of offering a blessing, his sinewy fingers pointed down to Hell. The room spun and then dissolved as I fell into the darkness, cast into Hell just like Dustin predicted.

Strong arms caught me. "*Fräulein* Jackson, don't lock your

knees when you stare up," Carl said.

"God spit me out," I mumbled.

"No, you fainted. I fail to understand why you want to study this primitive art."

I regained my balance and let go of Carl's arm. "The books say it's a masterpiece."

"If you like grim crap from the Dark Ages."

"But these were the early images of Christianity. We jump from classic Greek and Roman art to the Renaissance, skipping a thousand years. Aren't you curious?"

Carl shrugged. Billy glanced at his watch.

I turned to the mosaic. "Why are you angry? Why are you here?"

"I'm not angry, it's butt ugly," Billy said.

"I'm sorry, Dr. Sullivan, I was talking to the Angry Jesus. Why would an artist create the Angry Jesus in this holy place?"

"Jesus is angry because we don't follow His Word. We can't opt out of God's Law. Everyone faces the judgment of the Living God." Billy's voice boomed with the authority of twenty years of preaching.

"Eff your Angry Jesus." Carl flipped an obscene gesture toward the dome. "This is about power and domination. The unholy alliance of Empire and Church created the Angry Jesus to control people through threats of Hell."

The two glowered at each other. Billy had 30 pounds on Carl, but Carl looked like a soccer player. An image of a kick between the eyes popped into my head.

Just who I needed for my mentors—an intolerant atheist and a sanctimonious preacher. Aunt Lydia must have been desperate.

I walked away to listen for the story of this place, whispered by those who crafted the mosaics and walked these marble floors.

The thriving monks were filled with devotion when they built this church. Crusaders violated the holy space just a hundred years later. Finally, Ottoman Turks threw out the Latin interlopers.

The furious face of the *Pantokrator*, though, survived the assaults and earthquakes that rocked this sanctuary. Hair tingled on the back of my neck when I looked at it.

Carl followed me down a side aisle.

I flashed an apologetic smile. My dimples and long, dark blonde hair usually got me through tense situations. "Thanks for helping with our research. You must have your own project and class preps."

"We're between sessions. I teach one more class in July. After that I'm unemployed. The extra pay this month should get me through my doctoral research."

"I thought you worked for the Classics Institute."

"One-year position."

A mosaic showed two black-robed figures presenting a chalice and book to a nice Jesus.

"Who are these saints?"

Carl read titles set in the mosaic. "Holy Alexios and Empress Theodora. Obscure patrons, like donor plaques today."

We circled back to the central room. It opened into four arms of the cross through arches that stretched three stories high. Light flowed through the curving space.

I lay down to photograph the dome. Carl stretched out beside me and counted windows and columns.

"The architecture is unusual," Carl said. "Usually, four main piers support the dome. Here eight piers are arranged in an octagon. It spreads the weight and allows the central dome to be bigger."

"So this isn't a total waste?"

"Perhaps not."

I couldn't keep my eyes off the Angry Jesus.

"Dr. Sullivan, why is Jesus labeled IC XC?"

"It's an abbreviation," Billy said. "*Iota Sigma* for *Iesous* and *Chi Sigma* for *Christos*. Often, you just see *Chi*, like the X in Xmas."

"My brain refuses to read anything but IC XC. Today we'd label this picture OMG!"

Carl laughed. The *Pantokrator* frowned.

Billy looked down at me. "Your professor may be right. Some people just can't learn languages."

Ouch. "Maybe the book Christ holds is the key. Is it Revelation?"

"No, this has eight seals. Revelation has seven."

The *Pantokrator's* face grew dark as he clutched the book to his heart. Revelation's warning whispered: "Mess with these words and you'll be cut off from the tree of life."

We got up off the floor and escaped into the June warmth.

7

Forest at Daphni

"Let me show you my world, the Classical world," Carl said.

We climbed over foundations and stones, remains of the monastic community. An ancient forest shielded the ruins from modern Athens.

"This place gets its name—Daphni—from this forest. This tree is called *Daphne* in Greek, laurel in English." He picked a sprig and tucked it into my hair.

"Apollo's lover Daphne was turned into a laurel tree, so laurel is sacred to Apollo. The oracle at Delphi enhanced her visions by eating or burning the sacred leaves."

I pulled the sweet spicy sprig from behind my ear. "This smells familiar."

"You call them bay leaves—for cooking. The hallucinogenic properties are probably a myth. I've never tried smoking or eating them."

"A great factoid for my trivia bank."

"You collect trivia?" Billy asked.

"Yeah, I love interesting little tidbits. My family teases that I'm a wiki head who collects worthless knowledge."

As we walked the uneven path to the car, I tripped.

Carl laughed. "I warned you about eating those leaves."

As we headed back to the Institute, images of treasure spilling from a dusty box distracted me from the faith-versus-facts bickering in the front seat. Perhaps the box contained an old book, or maybe emperors' portraits on coins. Uncle Robert's final challenge —a message from beyond the grave—awaited me.

8

Jackson Textile Importers

I locked the apartment door. First step was photographing the address labels and customs stamps on the dusty box.

A nagging voice—that *Behave yourself, be a good girl* voice of my mom—told me *tape it up.*

Maybe just a peek, my curious, gotta-know-everything gut said.

Uncle Robert joined my mental debate. *That's a good question. Let's find out.*

Uncle Robert beat out Mom. I set aside a letter from the top of the box and eased out the bubble wrap.

Tissue opened to reveal pieces of an old goblet. Cloisonné enamel and pearls decorated the silver base. The bowl, carved from stone, was broken into two big chunks and some smaller pieces. A wad of tissue held loose pearls and enamel chips.

I tried fitting pieces together. Were the pearls real? I rubbed one against my teeth. It had an authentic gritty texture. Real silver? It was tarnished like silver.

"Are you a pile of junk or something valuable?"

The goblet remained silent.

I settled into Uncle Robert's chair with the letter. I felt him beside me, encouraging my curiosity.

Fortunately, the Paris antiques dealer had written in English.

"I trust you will be pleased with this artifact. The Greek letters around the base indicate a possible origin in southern Italy or the Eastern Mediterranean.

"I fear the provenance is not strong. I discovered this lovely goblet at a shop in Besançon, just northwest of the Alps near the Swiss border. Items from the East are found in the area since the Duchy of Burgundy participated in the Crusades.

"You said you might give this antiquity to Mme. Jackson as a present. I could arrange for a specialist in Crusader art to authenticate and restore it.

"I continue to seek Byzantine coins for your collection of emperors."

Huh. Maybe a Crusader drinking cup. Or a fake Crusader drinking cup.

"Why did you buy this?"

No answer. Instead Uncle Robert's last words: *Be Careful Bees.*

I returned the goblet to its hiding place, unpacked my laptop and organized the guestroom desk.

Time for a Greek alphabet poster. I wrote English letters in order, then put Greek letters under the equivalent English letters.

Some Greek vowels have two characters instead of one. An E can be *eta (H)* or *epsilon (E)*. An English O can be *omega (Ω)* or *omicron (O)*.

I debated about *chi (X)*. Does Ch go under C or under K?

Next, I color-coded the Greek letters with markers to match the colors they are in English. A is a gold letter, so I put a gold outline on *alpha*. E is a yellow letter, so *epsilon* and *eta* got yellow outlines. O is bright white, so *omicron* and *omega* didn't get outlines.

That helped. The wrong colors confused me when I tried to read Greek. Do other people really see in black and white when they read? I can't imagine.

The Greek alphabet finally made sense. I tacked my new poster to the wall.

The marker board looked too clean. "Uncle Robert?" and "Is it fake?" recorded my questions. I added a third: "What does Revelation mean?"

I had come to Greece to study images of Paradise. Instead, I was stuck in the hellhole of Revelation. Maybe my dream of becoming an art historian was silly. My parents thought I should get a graduate degree that actually led to a job. Or better yet, move home, teach high school and take graduate classes on the side to save money.

Talk about real Hell. Reading Revelation had to be better than teaching unruly teens. Or admitting to my parents that their daughter failed.

I opened Revelation, struggling past the crazy-colored Greek words to the message the Elder scratched two thousand years ago.

9

The Revelation of Jesus Christ

Island of Patmos, First Century

"Blessed is the one who reads aloud the words of the prophecy, and blessed are those who hear and who keep what is written in it; for the time is near." Revelation 1:3

John raised his palms to the sun. The island of Patmos under his feet felt insignificant, a mound of rock teetering between the cloudless blue of the heavens and the rolling aqua of the Great Sea.

It was the Lord's Day. The elder prayed for those who had lost so much, whose faith was shaken by tragedies.

He shuddered as if Heaven and earth shook. He put hands over his eyes, his body swaying against the hurricane wind of the spirit. How long did it last? Seconds? Minutes? Hours? He collapsed to the ground.

At last his universe calmed. He rose, gathered his cloak around his shoulders and stumbled down the dusty path to the village.

He filled a goose quill with lampblack ink. Unmindful of grammar, he scratched crude Greek letters on the papyrus. He must send a message to the seven churches. Jesus stood among them. God had not abandoned his people.

10

The Plaka

Hunger beat out worries of Hell. I went to find dinner companions.

Dr. Billy Sullivan and Carl Helman crowded around a map with Dr. Sophia Wright, the petite classics scholar who led the Institute.

Most academic types were casual. But Sophia always had her dark hair in a stylish short cut and dressed like she worked in an office.

Carl glanced up. "We go on a road trip tomorrow to see medieval manuscripts."

Billy, the Biblical scholar, beamed. "More than see! We're going to touch and feel and read and study and smell manuscripts. I'll hold in my hands the very Word of God as copied by men of God over a thousand years ago."

"Where?"

"Meteora, where monks lived suspended in the heavens," said Carl. "About four hours northwest of here. We leave before dawn."

"I told Lydia I wanted access to a monastic library with Greek manuscripts on this sabbatical," Billy said. "I've hunched over copies or peered through glass cases for too many years. I don't know how she did it."

"Mrs. Jackson maneuvered it through some junk dealer," Sophia said. "Your miracle is the result of a well-timed donation.

Lydia Jackson is good at that."

"She is remarkable. It's an answered prayer."

Sophia frowned. "Meteora is a tourist trap, so don't expect much. It will be a waste of time. Are you two up to the climb?"

"I was a distance runner for the track team, and I've hiked around campus for the last four years," I said.

"With God's help, I can climb anywhere. Significant documents are still out there," Billy said. "Today, most new sources are found in broken books and loose pages, or tucked in another book."

"Perhaps the scenery will be a nice diversion."

Carl winked at me. Billy was oblivious to Sophia's dim view of our mission and of Aunt Lydia's method to arrange it.

My stomach growled. "It's dinner time. Shall we eat at the *taverna* around the corner or in the *Plaka*?"

Billy looked up. "Amber, you'll be my photographer. I need sharp, well-focused, high-resolution image photographs of the manuscript pages I select for further study. None of this cell phone crap."

A chance to prove myself. "I'd love to. I'm a pretty good photographer."

Travel plans pushed aside thoughts of food. Finally we could seek sustenance. We snaked through tourists along Adrianou Street and snagged a table outside. Shops and cafes spilled onto the sidewalks and courtyards, blending inside and outside in a seamless flurry of activity.

After we ordered, Sophia turned to me. "Miss Jackson, what are your academic goals for this visit?"

I took a deep breath. "I have two. First, improve my Greek. Second, study Early Christian art. Perhaps find a topic for my master's thesis."

"Why? Why do you want to master the Greek language? Why examine Early Christian art?"

"I was in a Bible study group. The teacher talked about the

original Greek words. He said you couldn't fully understand the Bible unless you studied Greek. So I took Greek last semester. And my interest in Early Christian art is related. What are the early images of the church? How did those influence the development of Western Civilization? How have our beliefs changed since then?"

"How will you apply this knowledge?"

"Go to grad school. Write a thesis. Hopefully become an art historian."

"Yes, we discussed graduate school at your uncle's funeral. I am surprised you were accepted at such a prestigious school. I know the dean there."

I sat up straighter. "Great. That will give my work more credibility, knowing I studied with you."

"Your work must stand on its own. The program there is rigorous. It will be a challenge for you."

As I blinked back tears, the inquisitor turned her attention to Billy. "Is your title Doctor or Reverend?"

"Either is fine. I use Doctor, but I'm also ordained. I teach New Testament Greek at a seminary. I also speak and write for the Nicene Foundation. I may be at the Nicene Foundation full time. The founder is retiring and I'm a finalist for the top job."

"Dr. Wright, tell us why you are here." Billy said.

"I want to light a fire in my students about history, to get them to examine it anew," Sophia said. "That's hard in three 50-minute segments a week. Here, away from their regular world, we can shake their preconceptions and create true curiosity."

The sun slid behind the towering plateau of the Acropolis as Billy explained the difference between uncial and minuscule manuscripts. We dug out scraps of paper as he demonstrated changes in writing styles that scholars used to date manuscripts.

I had pegged him as a slow-talkin' Southern preacher. Tonight, he was a passionate scholar. No wonder my aunt liked him.

Sophia leaned over Billy's calligraphy. "That script is similar to the oldest manuscript of Plato's *Dialogues*, a tenth century

Greek codex I studied at Oxford."

"Yes, it probably came to Western Europe during the Crusades," Billy said. "Greek calligraphy is my hobby. I'm part of an Early Christian interpretation group."

"How amusing. Do you parade around in costumes and construct swords from duct tape?"

"Nope, no duct tape. We correspond in the language of the times and host living history events. We even use hand-made candles for worship."

What did Sophia have against duct tape? It came in great colors now.

The scholars lost me in the intricacies of letter forms. About all I got was that uncial is all caps (older), and minuscule means lower case letters (newer). Carl rolled his eyes at the minutia. We turned to appetizers, much better than my student diet of Ramen noodles and scrambled eggs.

I tore pita bread and scooped up creamy goat yogurt flavored with garlic, lemon, cucumber, and dill. "*Tzatziki i*s so much better than ranch dressing."

Carl laughed. I finished off our share, then helped myself to the rest.

A hand rested on my knee.

"So, *Fräulein* Amber, are you one of the Jackson heiresses?"

"Nah, I'm just a grateful recipient of my aunt's generosity. My folks are underpaid teachers."

"*Doch*, your aunt must think you are very special."

I guided his hand off my leg.

"Yeah, she's always treated me like a daughter. She and Robert don't have kids. My folks keep telling her not to spend money on us. They think we should work hard, get good grades and earn our own way."

"I say enjoy it."

Was he referring to his hand or my trip?

"Oh, the trip is awesome. I asked for an audio Greek language course for a college graduation gift. Instead, she gave me this research trip to Greece."

"Academics aside, what are your personal goals?"

"Compete on Jeopardy. Write 100 Wikipedia articles. Win the 'pub quiz' championship at the Wagon Wheel Brewery. Discover an important piece of art at a garage sale."

"I knew there was some fun behind that serious face."

Carl draped his arm across the back of my chair. This dress must look better than I thought. After a good meal and a potent potable I was willing to flirt a bit, but I didn't intend to be Carl's friend with privileges. I'm not into casual sex. No more trusting men and being humiliated.

We strolled back to the Institute, following Adrianou Street as it wound around the east flank of the Acropolis. Spotlights painted the fluted columns of Parthenon with gold. Temple ruins glowed against the deepening purple of the sky. Socrates and Plato walked these paths, but only modern lighting could create this panorama.

Carl linked arms with Sophia. He whispered in her ear as they walked ahead of us.

"They're an odd pair, aren't they?" I said.

Billy shrugged. "They seem to work well together. I suspect Sophia runs things with a firm hand. Carl puts on a show of rebellion, but does whatever she asks. That's what a graduate assistant is supposed to do."

The last tinges of sunset faded.

This was the birthplace of democracy and philosophy. The ancient Athenians had been filled with hope, with optimism. Perhaps Carl was right about ugly art. Old myths of apocalypse and judgment seemed out of place.

I shouldn't care about Revelation and warnings of the End Times. I liked Pope Francis. Who could believe St. Malachy's twelfth century vision that Francis was the final pope?

The Parthenon still glistened above, providing the protection of Athena to the residents of her city below.

Revelation Chapter 1 described a great image of Jesus standing with the seven churches, represented by lampstands. Why did the Angry Jesus still haunt me?

DAY TWO

"Let there be a dome in the midst of the waters, and let it separate the waters from the waters." Genesis 1:6

Two is the number of truth. The testimony of two witnesses establishes truth. Two is also the number of companionship and community. The Greek numeral for two is *beta* (B β).

12

Varlaam Monastery, Meteora

Noon Monday

The man-made beauty of the Parthenon paled beside the vista that stretched around us at Meteora. Giant fingers of stone thrust heavenward from the Plain of Thessaly far below.

Meteora means "suspended in the heavens."

I paused in the courtyard to absorb the vision. "We really are closer to Heaven here."

"Don't be ridiculous. God is found in scripture, not on a rock." Billy said.

I ignored Billy. Others before had felt the power of this place. The first holy men climbed the slender sandstone pinnacles to live in bleak caves carved by the winds. Later monks scaled 1,800 feet of terror to build retreats on top of the weathered stone pillars. The monasteries kept invaders out and treasures of the faithful safe inside.

We had been privy to those treasures for a couple of hours. Our host, Abbot Paulos, and his young assistant, Brother Iakobos, had shown us smoky icons and simple buildings.

The abbot helped me light a candle and pray before a 600-year-old icon of the Madonna and Child. The child looked like a two-foot-tall wise old man seated on her lap.

In the dining room, a fresco showed skinny black demons pulling monks down to Hell, where a comic-book beast lurked. I laughed.

A hundred photos resided in my memory card and we hadn't started on individual manuscript pages. We took a break from the medieval world and gathered in the courtyard for pictures.

Andreus Mikos, an antiquities dealer with old-fashioned manners, had arranged our visit and acted as the unofficial coordinator. Dr. Georgios Karmanos, an impatient bureaucrat, was our liaison from the Ministry of Culture. His assistant, Demetrius, looked bored. I bet they had seen all this before.

After group photos, I got a close-up of Billy presenting an autographed copy of one of his books to the abbot.

As we headed to the restrooms, I stopped the antiques dealer. "Mr. Mikos, you know my aunt and uncle, Lydia and Robert Jackson?"

He nodded. "I was so sorry to hear about death of uncle. I know them both for many years. Such a tragedy. I knew people could die from bee stings, but still, to have friend suffer like that."

"They knew he was allergic. He always kept an EpiPen nearby. But apparently it rolled under the bookcase and he couldn't get to it."

"So sad for your aunt."

"Yes, this has been very hard for her. At the Athens apartment, I found a present that Uncle Robert bought for Aunt Lydia but hadn't given to her yet. Do you think she would like getting it now?"

Andreus smiled. "That sounds like Robert. He liked to find little treasures for Miss Lydia. I'm sure one last gift would be meaningful to her."

"Can you look at it? I think it's a Crusader chalice. It's in pieces—silver with pearls and colored enamel. The bowl is carved from stone that looks like yogurt, translucent white with burgundy."

His eyebrows shot up. "This stone! I must see it."

"Could we have the goblet put back together for her?"

"Yes, yes. I come Wednesday to see it. You are sweet girl to think of aunt."

After the restroom, I walked to the edge of the courtyard.

The monastery cat had the same idea. He hopped up on the stone parapet and stretched in the warm rays. I found myself duplicating the sleek gray beast's motions.

Varlaam Monastery balanced atop one of the tall fingers of stone, raising the residents toward heaven.

On the plain below, fields formed a patchwork quilt of soft, lush greens encouraged by spring rains. I felt like I was flying over in an airplane.

The monks who built these ancient monasteries were determined. I would not have climbed into a hand-made net to be hauled up to the heavens. It was easier now. Bridges and stairways had been added to make the monasteries accessible to tourists.

Today, there were no tourists, just the cleaning crew, a handful of monks, and our group.

I leaned over the parapet to get a better angle. Steady the camera, breathe in and hold, squeeze the shutter. I changed angles. Steady ... breathe in ...

The image shifted. Something pushed from behind.

My camera fell as I grabbed for the railing.

I teetered as someone shoved harder.

I couldn't hold on. I pitched forward.

Nothing solid. Just air. For 1,800 feet.

No. Not me. I'm invincible.

It's not my day to die.

Images tumbled in my mind.

Monks falling from grace.

The raging fires of Hell.

The Beast, jaws open.

The Revelation Key

What *was* below?
I couldn't see down.
Only sky above.
I closed my eyes.
No soft fields.
Just the Beast.
Waiting for *me*.
A scream. My voice. Blackness. Silence.

13

After the Fall

No white light beckoned me to the afterlife? I deserved a white light. No oxygen. Only darkness.

Light and focus returned slowly.

I gasped. My lungs filled with the aroma of herbs—rosemary, sage, dill, garlic. Hell's Kitchen or the Garden of Paradise?

A long white beard framed an ancient face. *"Kyrie Iesou Christe, Yie tou Theou, eleison me ton hamartolon."*

Over and over, St. Peter chanted the prayer as he knelt over me, squeezing my hand.

"Lord Jesus Christ, Son of God, have mercy on me, a sinner."

So *this* was Heaven. The *Pantokrator* didn't send me to Hell after all.

St. Peter prayed in Greek instead of Latin as he welcomed people to heaven. He even dressed like an Orthodox monk. The Pope was in for a surprise.

Clarity emerged. I saw clumps of herbs, warm dirt and solid stone wall. My landing spot was the herb garden, jutting out on a tiny ledge a few stories below the main courtyard.

Sit up, my mind ordered. The body refused.

Numbness faded. Wet stickiness seeped down the back of my neck. Plastic butterfly clips had tucked up my long hair under a modest scarf. Now, those plastic teeth were embedded in my scalp.

I looked up to the railing, about 40 feet above. The gray cat stared back.

A blond head popped over the courtyard wall high above me. "*Shiza*," Carl yelled. "Come help. Amber fell. She's hurt!"

Sophia and Abbot Paulos soon peered over the parapet. Karmanos' bald head appeared. He started yelling in Greek.

The elderly monk released my hand and pulled down my skirt. He would be praying for weeks in penance for touching a woman and seeing ... well, who knew what had been exposed.

Paulos emerged from a tiny door partway up the wall and climbed down an ancient folding ladder. "You are hurt?"

"Scraped and bruised mostly. I don't think anything is broken."

He helped me sit up and take a sip of cold water. I jerked as he dabbed the mess on the back of my head.

Old St. Peter inched up the ladder and disappeared into the dark doorway. The abbot's assistant, Brother Iakobos, clambered down and squeezed on the ledge with us as he jabbered into a cell phone. A monk with a cell phone?

The monk was either calling an ambulance or reporting me to the police.

I grabbed Paulos' arm. "Don't call anyone. I'm okay, really I am."

Carl found his way through the maze of passages to the scene of my humiliation. The men in black hoisted me up like a sack of potatoes with dangly legs as Carl pulled from above. Carl picked me up and started up a narrow whitewashed stairway.

I squirmed. "You don't have to carry me. I can walk."

Carl panted from exertion. "Hold still, Amber. This is tough enough without you wiggling around. If you bleed on my shirt, I'll drop you."

The stairway led to the refectory, furnished with long stone tables and benches where the original monks ate.

I cringed. "Don't you dare lay me out on a stone slab. That would be too, too creepy."

"*Ach, du Scheiße!*" Carl plopped me in a wooden chair at one end of the room, then sat down himself.

The room was ghoulish, the walls covered with grim religious scenes. Monks fell to Hell in the biggest fresco, stretching from floor to high ceiling. Black demons grabbed the monks off a ladder and pulled them into the gaping mouth of the beast below.

I had laughed at the fresco earlier. After my fall, the images were horrifyingly real. But I hadn't been pulled into the jaws of Hell by demons below. No. I had been pushed from above. By human hands.

14

Dining room at Varlaam

I stared at demons as Sophia and the gang checked me over. The monks provided first aid supplies and scattered. Brother Iakobos lurked outside the door, probably eavesdropping.

The other monks had long white beards and walked with an aura of serenity. Iakobos was younger, faster. Bushy eyebrows, heavy glasses and a beard covered most of his face, leaving just a band of high forehead visible beneath the round black monk hat. He wouldn't meet my eyes.

Sophia picked shards of broken plastic clips out of the back of my head. "I can not believe you fell. I instructed you not to do anything that would embarrass the Institute. Undergraduates are so irresponsible."

Just my luck to have Dr. Snooty Witch as my nurse.

Billy paced. "I should have watched you instead of lingering in the library. I promised Lydia I would keep an eye on you."

"A demon pushed me."

Carl laughed. "Good joke. There are no demons."

"No. I'm not joking. I was pushed by a person with demonic intent."

"Someone pushed you? Who? No one is here."

"That's *ridiculous!*" Sophia returned to her task. "There is no reason anyone would push you."

Billy put an arm around my shoulder. "Why do you think that?"

"I don't know. I was steady to take pictures. Then I was pushed. I lost my balance and couldn't hold on to the railing."

"Could it have been a gust of wind?"

I tried to recall the seconds before the fall. "I don't remember wind blowing my hair in front of the camera, or fighting to keep my skirt down."

"Just relax. It will be okay." Billy patted my hand—like I was 12 years old and had fallen on the playground. But at least he cared.

My scalp suddenly burned. "Agggh, that stings."

"Be quiet," Sophia ordered. "I'm cleaning it with rubbing alcohol. This will need medical attention. You may have suffered a concussion."

Yeah. If I had a concussion, I didn't know what I was talking about.

Billy left to gather our things from the library and persuade the abbot to let us come back the next day. Monks minimized contact with women. During regular tour hours, the holy men retreated to their private areas. Karmanos had warned me and Sophia to blend modestly into the background on this insider visit. I blew that. I bet the monks were glad to see me leave.

Carl helped me down the hundreds of steps snaking around the side of the pinnacle. He held my elbow as I tried to move my feet. The steps were too steep; the railing was too low. I couldn't look down.

Carl paused. "Do you want me to carry you?"

"That would be really scary, being carried down all these horrible steps." Not to mention embarrassing.

"That's good, because you aren't easy to carry. I wasn't sure I could squeeze your big feet up that narrow staircase earlier. And you are rather heavy."

"Are you saying I have a fat ass?"

"No, I like your curvy ass. But you are not a small woman."

I contemplated going it alone. Nope. I was too shaky. Much as

I hated to admit it, I needed Carl's help.

"Just let me hold onto you. Go slowly."

"When I saw you lying in the dirt you looked so funny."

Carl entertained with tales of my humiliation as I clutched his arm and tried not to look down. Jerk.

At last, the bottom. Blessed safety. I looked back. Ancient buildings clung to the heights. Either I was incredibly lucky or an angel had been watching me.

Someone else was watching me, too. A black-robed figure followed our progress from atop the towering walls.

I felt arms around me.

"Amber, you're trembling," Carl whispered. "Do you need to sit down and rest?"

"I ... I ... no, just get me out of here."

15

The Macedonian Dynasty begins

December, A.D. 886

Church of the Holy Apostles, Constantinople

Leo the Wise studied his brother's face as priests dressed the 19-year-old in the ceremonial robes worn by the leader of the Orthodox Church. Stephen's smooth face shone with youthful piety. Leo had named him patriarch just a few weeks ago. Could Stephen deliver the support of the church to the 21-year-old new emperor? The two waited in the sacristy.

Leo placed a firm hand on Stephen's shoulder. "I once called you brother, but now I address you as Holy Father. You are strong in your faith. We will be criticized for our actions today, but this is the Christian thing to do."

The patriarch nodded. "Today, Michael III will take his rightful place among the rulers of the Roman Empire. His remains have lain in shame for 19 years. Any emperor deserves respect."

Leo remembered the elaborate imperial funeral for his father, Basil the Macedonian, just a few months ago. Leo glanced at his brother.

Stephen's eyes met his. "When we studied together, did you imagine that you would be emperor and I would be patriarch?"

"I knew you would be patriarch. That was our father's plan, and he always got what he wanted."

Leo paused. Basil claimed piety when he had his third son castrated, setting him aside for life in the church. But it also eliminated an unwanted heir.

"Our childhood study of church numerology has inspired me to write a series of homilies about the Psalms," Stephen said.

"My court scribes are gathering Plato's works. I ordered them to stop re-writing history to glorify our father and vilify Michael the Drunkard."

"Do you remember Emperor Michael?" the patriarch asked.

"No, but Mother spoke kindly of him. I was a year old when Father assassinated him."

"I was born two months after that night. He never saw me."

It was time. The brothers followed the clerics with their glow of candles and cloud of incense down central aisle as whispers rustled through the gathering.

At the tombs of their parents, Basil and the Empress Ingerina, Leo lit a candle for his father and knelt for an appropriately-reverent time. Despite their stormy relationship, Leo admired his father's political skills. Basil got a position in the stables of the young Emperor Michael III and quickly became Michael's trusted chamberlain.

Leo rose. He and Stephen lit a candle at their mother's tomb.

The pale beauty of the daughter of the Viking Inger, captain of the emperor's personal guard, caught 15-year-old Michael's eye. But Ingerina's mother was an icon-hater. The regent empress feared Ingerina could fuel that old heresy. She picked a different wife for Michael.

The procession moved down the nave. He heard whispered insults from those attending the funeral. "Bastard." "Peasant." Leo ignored the rumble. "Sons of a whore." Leo saw a flush rise in Stephen's cheeks.

The coffin for Michael III was simpler than Basil's carved purple granite casket. Leo listened as Stephen chanted the liturgy in his high, strong voice.

Leo had been raised on Basil's propaganda. But he also heard the gossip. Michael had not deserved to be assassinated.

The young emperor had made two mistakes: loving his mistress Ingerina and trusting Basil. Michael and his wife were childless. Michael persuaded Basil to divorce his first wife and marry Ingerina. He adopted the older Basil as his son, setting up Ingerina's children as Michael's adopted grandchildren and eventual heirs.

But Basil would not be emasculated and pushed aside.

Leo delivered his eulogy carefully to squelch speculation about personal matters or undermine his rule. He and Stephen would never know for sure which emperor was their father.

Leo remembered the insiders laughing at Basil, with his coarse Armenian accent, claiming to be a Macedonian Greek, but history would respect him for re-establishing the great Macedonian tradition of Alexander the Great and Justinian. Basil had the last laugh.

Perhaps Michael was laughing today.

16

Kalambaka

Five stitches and a tetanus shot later, we checked into a hotel. Sophia insisted on sharing a room to keep an eye on me. I washed off dirt, blood, rosemary and dill in a warm shower. Interesting scent.

Sophia gave me a prescribed pain pill and heaped on ice bags as I stretched out.

"I can't sleep. I almost died today."

"Shhh. Just rest and let the pain medication do its job."

I replayed the event. Only this time, I didn't fall. I floated on a cloud above the monastery, watching the activities below. Far in the distance, voices mumbled. "Foolish accident ... Amber ... irresponsible ... menace ... send her home."

It was so restful on the cloud. I could float there forever.

A skeletal black hand snatched my arm and jerked me down. The cloud gave way. I screamed.

"Amber, wake up. You're dreaming. Wake up." Sophia looked in my eyes, checked my temperature and removed the melting bags around me.

I took a few test laps around the room. All parts still worked. "Where's my shoulder bag? I can't find my cell phone."

"Billy gathered everything. He must have them," Sophia said. "But you need to rest."

"I need my billfold. I have nothing to wear to the monastery tomorrow. My good church dress is ruined."

"That silly cotton peasant dress was your good dress?" Sophia shook her head. "Never mind. No need to return to the monastery tomorrow. Rest here at the hotel while we finish."

It took a minute for that to sink in.

"No, no. I have to go. Billy asked for my help. I can't let him down. This is important research."

"He is giving you busy work. He will do just fine without you."

She finally gave in and called Billy, who delivered my bag to our room. The compartments held camera, mini-tripod, notepads and a sketchbook in addition to all the normal stuff like my Swiss Army knife and a small roll of duct tape.

Billy had jumbled everything together. I dug around. Where was my camera?

"No! My camera. My wonderful camera. It's gone."

My precious camera had slipped from my hands as I grabbed for the railing. My SLR digital camera. It was an extension of my body and my brain, a part of my being.

"What is your problem now?" Sophia asked.

"I lost my camera and today's pictures. I can't live without my camera."

Who cared that I was cut and bruised? I would heal. But I could never afford a camera like that. Aunt Lydia got it for me last summer when I helped inventory and document her artifact collection in Fort Worth.

"I need to shop for a new dress and a cheap camera."

Sophia didn't even look up from her book. "Just use your cell phone camera. You do not need to go traipsing around."

"But how will I know I'm okay if I don't move around?"

"You can not go alone. You would probably hurt yourself. Take Carl."

I winced. Maybe I deserved to be treated like a child.

Heat radiated off stone and concrete as Carl and I joined the restless stream of sweaty tourists. Nazis burned old Kalambaka during World War II. The modern town wasn't much architecturally, but who needed beautiful buildings when surrounded by natural beauty like this? Some visitors came for the monasteries; others were drawn to the weathered stone peaks for rock-climbing and hang-gliding.

We stopped for halva cake at a sweet shop. Can anything be better than baklava? Maybe halva cake. I scarfed one down to celebrate being alive, then selected goodies to take to the monastery in the morning.

We strolled past the usual shops: gold jewelry, cheap modern icons, reproduction Greek pottery, leather goods, tee shirts, cafes and bars. I selected a plaster bust of Pericles for my dad.

Carl pointed at a dress shop window. "You would look good in that dress."

"But that's so bare on top."

"It's sexy."

"Burka is the goal, not sexy."

Actually, I could see his point. I hated little black dresses that barely covered your ass. But this was almost a maxi dress with a long flared skirt. With a jacket and dark stockings, it would work.

I looked at the price tag: €200. "I can't afford this. Do they have a Walmart here?"

"In a tourist town? It's all overpriced. Just use your aunt's credit card."

I hesitated. Carl winked at me as the clerk came over to us.

"This is too much. We'll give you 50 euros."

After dickering, Carl agreed to pay €90. I reluctantly handed over Lydia's card.

"I'll think naughty thoughts tomorrow when I see that dress." Carl's eyes crinkled.

"Oh, stop being such a flirt. You'd get turned on by a burka."

"*Doch.*"

It was tougher buying a camera. I started with the cheap point-and-shoots. Before I knew it, Carl and the clerk were down at the expensive end of the store.

"What did you have before?" Carl asked.

"That awesome Canon."

Carl bargained with the clerk. Only a sap paid the price on the tag, he said. He led me out of the store as the clerk swore Carl's offer was impossible.

As we walked away, I felt a touch on my arm.

"Come back," the clerk insisted. "My boss says okay."

Carl's talents greatly reduced the dent on Aunt Lydia's charge card. Thanks to him, I could return to action.

Did I want to return to action?

17

Patmos

First Century

"These are the words of him who holds the seven stars in his right hand, who walks among the seven golden lampstands." Revelation 2:1

The elder worried about his seven churches. What word of encouragement from Christ would help them all? They were so different.

First, his home church at Ephesus. "You have abandoned your first love," he wrote in warning. "You will eat from the tree of life in Paradise," he promised.

Trials were coming for the church at Smyrna. "Do not fear what you are about to suffer. Be faithful unto death and I will give you the crown of life."

The believers at Pergamum were strong, but they allowed heretics in their fellowship. "Repent, or I will make war against them," he warned. "I will give you hidden manna and a new name."

Thyatira. If only that Jezebel were gone. "I will strike her children dead," he promised. "Hold fast until I come, and I will give you the morning star."

The church at Sardis looked good, but the elder knew how they acted away from the fellowship. "If you don't wake up, I will come like a thief."

The believers at Philadelphia had so little. The city still showed signs of the devastating earthquake that had destroyed it. The other Jews rejected those who followed The Way. "Hold fast to what you have," the elder wrote. "I will make you a pillar in the temple of my God."

The brothers at Laodicea were seduced by the city's wealth. John hated everything about Laodicea—a person couldn't even get a cool drink of water. A Roman aqueduct brought water from hot springs six miles away. By the time it reached the city, it was tepid. "I know your works; you are neither cold nor hot. So, because you are lukewarm, and neither cold nor hot, I am about to spit you out of my mouth."

18

Kalambaka

Carl pointed at me with his fork. "You're doing your research all wrong."

I chewed slowly, devising an answer. "I haven't started my research yet. I'm still evaluating what I see, looking for inspiration."

"Wrong, wrong, wrong. You've spent two days visiting sites and taking pictures like a tourist. You've wasted two days if you aren't working a plan."

"So you tell me. What should I do?"

"Use your four weeks here to gather and organize data. You love photography. Do a survey of Christian art of a particular time period. Then analyze. What's the phrase, 'inspiration is 99% perspiration'?"

"Carl is correct," Sophia said. "Too many students and scholars start with a conclusion and seek evidence to support it. Like Dr. Sullivan. He seeks evidence to support his beliefs."

Ah, pick on Billy time. He skipped dinner to write up his notes, making him an easy target.

After dinner I escaped to the coffee shop next door for dessert and phone time without Sophia looking over my shoulder. Demons were pulling monks down to hell, and I wanted to know why. I couldn't imagine why *that* horror would be in the monastery dining room. Surely the internet could tell me.

I'd be on my own on the tougher question. I put it in Jeopardy style.

"This demon pushed a student off a monastery balcony."

"Who is the one known as... 666."

I scanned my email first. Better read Aunt Lydia.

How did your day go at the monastery? Did Billy see any interesting manuscripts? I hope reality wasn't a disappointment for him. Was the art inspiring? Any problems?

Had someone told her about my fall from grace? It was early afternoon back home. She might get my answer right away.

Interesting day. I took a tumble but I'm OK. Just a few stitches. I had to buy a new dress and camera on your credit card. Sorry! Dr. Sullivan looked at several manuscripts. He will go through the cache of loose pages and scraps tomorrow. The icons and liturgical items are totally awesome. Thanks again for the amazing experience.

Should I tell my parents? They expected me to behave and follow the rules. If Aunt Lydia knew about my fall, though, they also might know. I gave them the same tale about a tumble and a few stitches.

I didn't have to censor my text to my friend Kira.

I had the most frightful day. I thought I was a goner. Monastery is on top of a mountain, the Greek version of El Capitan at Yosemite. I fell off the balcony. If a ledge hadn't stopped my fall, I would have been a pancake 2,000 feet below!

Someone pushed me. I have five stitches in my head and I totally ruined my good church dress. Don't tell my folks.

Carl, the graduate assistant, is hot and talks like Arnold Schwarzenegger. I'm sending a photo I took to test my new camera. Don't worry. I remember my vow to swear off men. After Dustin, I've had enough.

A guy slung his backpack beside me and sat down with a cup of coffee.

I worked down the email. Better read the weekly prayer list from church. The usual list of people were fighting cancer, looking for jobs and struggling with family conflicts. Then I saw it:

Dustin requests prayer for Amber to find God's purpose for her life as she studies in Greece this summer.

"That twit! It's none of his damn business."

Oops. I didn't mean to say it out loud. How could he share my personal issues with the entire congregation? I could never show my face there again.

I turned to my research, muttering over the Greek attributions. Another angry word or two may have slipped out.

A voice asked, "Are you okay?"

I turned for a better look at my table mate. American accent, about my age. Baggy jeans, loose cotton shirt, unruly bangs hanging in his eyes, scruffy beard, puppy dog eyes.

"Fine. Just pissed at men." I turned back to the screen.

"Well, Ms. Pissed-at-Men, are you here to visit monasteries or climb mountains?"

I didn't bother to turn. "Monasteries and manuscripts. I'm researching a gloomy fresco I saw today."

"You look like you lost a rappelling duel to the mountain."

"I took a tumble at Varlaam this afternoon. I study art history."

I kept typing. Mr. Scruffy-Beard didn't take the hint.

"My area is Orthodox spirituality, so we are kindred spirits. The image is a key part of Orthodox life." He pushed his hand into my space. "I'm Jim Sampras."

I guess I could at least shake hands. "Amber Jackson."

I extracted my hand from his firm grasp. He did have nice brown eyes. And Jim was a pleasant name—an intriguing blend of lavender and caramel brown.

"So what image are you looking for? I work at Meteora this summer, so I may know it."

"The demons pulling the monks to Hell in the dining room at Varlaam."

"That's 'The Ladder of Divine Ascent.' An abbot wrote a book comparing the monk's journey to heaven to Jacob's ladder. The monks are supposed to master 30 steps of virtue to climb to perfection."

"But Jacob's ladder was more a safe wormhole between heaven and earth. This looks like an obstacle course with the demons trying to pull the monks off the ladder and toss them down to the beast."

"What can I say? God's apparently more forgiving than the abbot. The book was required mealtime reading during Lent, so the fresco is in the refectory in a lot of monasteries."

"Byzantine images are weird. They're mysterious and captivating, like they're telling me something. If I could figure out Greek, I might understand."

"My family is Greek American; so weird is normal," Jim said.

"So why cover all the surfaces in the church with images of obscure saints?"

"We call that style, 'Invasion of the Saints.'"

"I'm serious."

Jim shook his head, adding further chaos to his disheveled dark hair. "We follow the words of Paul. We're surrounded by a great cloud of witnesses to give us strength and encouragement. For Greeks, it's like surrounding ourselves with pictures of our aunts, great-grandparents and cousins."

"The only thing missing is a New Orleans funeral band playing, 'When the Saints Go Marching In.'"

"Well, it also provides jobs for artists and gives us something to look at when the liturgy gets boring," he said. "Give me your email and cell number. I know some good sources about spirituality and the image."

I paused. What would it hurt? I needed all the help I could get.

"So are you really okay after your tumble today?"

"Yeah, I just fell in the garden and had to have a few stitches."

Jim ordered more coffee.

"There's a great story about the gardens at Varlaam. At first, individual monks lived in the caves. The first formal monastery, the Great Meteoron, was built on the tallest stone pillar. Another group of monks built Varlaam on a neighboring pillar.

"The newcomers hauled up top soil and tended their fruits and vegetables. The monks of the Great Meteoron looked down on the thriving garden of their lesser neighbors for three years.

"On Easter Monday, they armed themselves with 40 axes, rickety ladders, nets and ropes, and assaulted their neighbors' garden. Led by the abbot, they 'hacked it remorselessly to pieces,' the history book reports."

I smiled. "The moral is 'You shall not covet your neighbors' garden.' Don't worry, I just broke a few herbs."

Carl found us giggling over monastery tales. He didn't talk to me as we walked back to the hotel.

"Sophia, I brought back our missing girl," Carl reported.

"What were you thinking? You can sleep in, but the rest of us must be at the monastery early," Sophia said. "The monks finish *orthros* prayers at dawn."

We got organized and turned in. I would not let Sophia leave me behind in the morning.

I couldn't get comfortable. If I rolled on my back, the stitches hurt; the right side had a skinned knee; left was a bruised shoulder and elbow. My mind wouldn't turn off.

Who attacked me? Did someone want me dead? Would that demon try to kill me again tomorrow?

I could just sleep in. It would be safer and less humiliating. Would Aunt Lydia be disappointed if I gave up?

What was I thinking? I couldn't give up. Failing Greek was bad enough. I couldn't fail again. Aunt Lydia had given me a second chance. I would not destroy her faith in me.

I would be at the monastery tomorrow, demons or no demons.

DAY THREE

"And God said, 'Let the waters under the sky be gathered together into one place, and let the dry land appear.' and it was so."
Genesis 1:9

In the Bible, three is the divine number.

Three men visited Abraham—it was really God calling on him.

God came down to Mount Sinai on the third day. God redeemed Jonah from the belly of the whale on the third day. Christ rose on the third day.

The symbol of three is the triangle. The Greek numeral for three is *gamma* (Γ γ).

20

Tuesday at Dawn

Suspended in the heavens at Varlaam

We traveled the switchback road into the mountains as sun broke over the horizon. The towering stone pinnacles, soft in the pre-dawn glow, gained sharp, slanted edges in the angular rays. The leaning spires of weathered sandstone seemed to break off the mountain ridge, ready to tumble into the mist-blanketed plain below. They looked dangerous, threatening. Unsteady.

I gritted my teeth. Fear would not stop me from a chance to earn Billy's respect.

The Rev. Dr. Billy Sullivan looked like a Southern preacher in a black suit, monogrammed white shirt and sincere red tie. It fit with his name—somber and solid in black, gray and red. I wondered if he had a gold tooth to go with the combed-back hair.

"You look like you're ready to give the sermon," I said.

"I'm always ready to share the good news of Jesus Christ. I have a good feeling about today."

Dr. Georgios Karmanos and Demetrius didn't share Billy's enthusiasm. Karmanos restlessly checked his watch.

Carl Helman wore his usual tight jeans paired with a shirt the color of his eyes and an Italian silk sport coat. Freaking sweet, if I was the sort of person to notice.

Dr. Sophia Wright pinned a black lace scarf over her dark hair in deference to our locale.

I focused on my feet as we crossed the bridge, avoiding looking down into the crevasse or up to the heights. My heart pounded. I forced myself to breathe deeply and relax my shoulders. Demetrius hovered by my side.

The cool silence of early morning wrapped around us. Billy bounced ahead as we snaked up the side of the mountain. Stone steps had been added to bring bus-loads of tourists and their euros to the ancient hideaway. My bruised muscles protested. Modesty aside, I was glad for the warmth of my jacket. The balconies and overlooks made me shiver even more. I vowed to watch my back-side.

The caretaker unlocked the gate. We bypassed the ticket booth, gift shop and other atrocities. The chant of morning prayers whispered in the courtyard from the *katholikon*, the main church of the monastery. We waited by an eight-sided fountain.

Worn wooden doors opened as the holy men filed out, stretching and blinking after standing for an hour of prayer and liturgy in the candle-lit sanctuary. Monks didn't sit during services. Instead, the church had little stalls with arm rests along the walls where they could lean.

The cat's eyes narrowed to slits as he slipped from the dim church into the bright, slanting rays of dawn.

"Evlogite," we asked. The traditional greeting meant "Give your blessing."

A chorus of *"O Kyries"* was the response. "The Lord," meaning "May the Lord bless you."

Strong Greek coffee brewed in the refectory as we gathered around a wooden table at one end.

St. Peter, my savior, was actually Father Gabriel, a retired monk who tended the gardens. The other monks addressed him as *gheronda*, elder. He shared a bowl of fresh fruit as I passed the basket from the bakery. A few other retired monks who lived at the monastery joined us for breakfast.

"I am glad this is not fasting day," *Archimandrite* Paulos told me as he helped himself to a second triangle of baklava.

Most of the conversation was in Greek in deference to our hosts, with a few English comments thrown in for me.

People were more relaxed today. Was it sharing table fellowship, or had my disaster the day before broken the ice? Gabriel, my saving angel, nodded at me several times. Maybe today would be a better day.

Abbot Paulos had been a Biblical scholar and teacher before taking over the historic monastery. He and Billy gestured and jabbered in Greek about their shared passion.

Demetrius, who struck me as a cold fish yesterday, tried to make conversation. Had Karmanos told him to keep an eye on me?

Brother Iakobos circled like a vulture in his black robes and hung back in the shadows. When I offered sweets he turned away and shook his head.

After breakfast, a few scraps remained in the pastry basket. Father Gabriel gathered the pieces of bread, kissed them, and knotted them in a cloth napkin.

"Why does he do that?" I asked Demetrius.

"Bread is gift from God and reminder of Last Supper. The kiss is 'thank you' to God for providing daily bread to us. Bad luck to throw away bread."

The scholars couldn't wait to get to the manuscripts. Billy lugged a stack of notes and reference books to the library.

I had other work. Yesterday's pictures were somewhere on the mountain. Had that been the purpose of the attack? As if a little shove could stop a wiki-head.

Carl and I started at the front gate and worked our way around the courtyard in a more methodical way. Carl took a few GPS readings, sketched a map and noted the location of each major image and architectural feature as I shot. With Carl's help, this project just might work.

Demetrius, Gabriel and the cat chaperoned us.

Through Demetrius, I learned the cat's name was *Skia*, Shadow.

Skia was no fat, pampered cat of the West. Oriental cats were long and sleek. His big round eyes saw everything around him as his narrow head turned quietly on his long thin neck.

We ended with the *narthex* and *katholikon*. It stopped me cold again today. Hell filled the lobby into the main church.

Roaring Hellfire stretched from the *Pantokrator*, enthroned on a sea of glass at the top of the wall, all the way down to the fang-lined jaws of an enormous scaly reptile.

I turned to Demetrius and Elder Gabriel. "Why do we face Hell as we enter the church?"

"Painting is Last Judgment," Demetrius said.

"But why is it here, welcoming us into the church?"

After vigorous waving of hands and rapid Greek, Demetrius had Gabriel's answer.

"Father Gabriel says it shows choice between life inside church and life outside church," Demetrius said. "Life outside holds evil and death. Inside is salvation by God. Image is here to remind worshipers as they enter into eternal life in church."

"Curious." I started taking pictures, focusing on one image at a time to steady my mind and stop the horrifying swirl.

Below the heavenly court, an empty throne awaited the Second Coming. John the Baptist and Mary prayed before the empty throne in intercession for the souls gathered below.

In the center, naked souls waited their turn on the scale. Angels watched the balance as a demon jumped on the pan to tip the scale. The demons dragged the condemned to the vortex of fire or to dank gray cells of Hell on Christ's left. I zoomed in with the camera. Those flickering flames were human souls being sucked into the jaws of the beast.

"Don't waste time on this." Carl pointed to a scene. "This is done after Dante. Those people being chewed on by worms, Dante got that from the Apocalypse of Peter, not Revelation. Choose an earlier period before this Western European influence, before the Crusades." He walked out.

Demetrius yawned and wandered off.

"What were you telling these monks?" I waited for the artist's message.

Skia rubbed against my legs. I picked him up and scratched behind his big round ears as I studied the various levels of Hell. Carl was right; the condemned were crawling with worms in one of the cells. Wormy!

Gabriel slipped a black knotted cord out of his left pocket and softly chanted the phrase that brought me to consciousness the day before. I recognized a word: "*Kyrie.*" Lord. I found myself repeating it as I stood once more under the judgment of the *Pantokrator*. Somehow, it didn't seem so scary with my black-robed angel at my side.

Carl's voice broke the spell. "Amber, Billy needs you."

21

Library at Varlaam

Tuesday morning

I winced as I slung the backpack over my sore shoulder. Demetrius grabbed my gear and carried it to the library. Karmanos's assistant was starting to grow on me.

"I need good, detailed photographs," Billy ordered. "We'll work on this table."

I analyzed the light. Windows lit the reading tables in the front, but the back shelves were illuminated only by high clerestory windows. Frescoes—paintings done in fresh wet plaster on the wall surface itself—showed Old Testament prophets between the high windows. The four gospel writers supervised us from frescoes on the ceiling.

"We want as much light as possible without direct sunlight. Can we put this table closer to the windows?"

Sophia grumbled about being pushed aside and demanded help moving a philosophy manuscript—the works of Plato with commentary by Leo the Wise—that she was reading.

Iakobos, Demetrius and Carl man-handled the large, hand-hewn table into the prime position. I directed as they lifted chairs onto the table. Paulos fetched white liturgical linens to drape over them as reflectors. With a little ingenuity, we had a passable copy stand.

Billy selected the books and pages to shoot. Karmanos fretted and paced as the monks positioned each codex, supporting the covers and spines of the ancient handwritten books. I stood on a chair and shot down using both available light and flash. After recording key pages of several manuscripts, we turned to scrap pages from the cache of broken books and loose pages. Paulos positioned the first fragment in our makeshift copy stand. The flat loose pages were easier.

As I took pictures, Billy leaned uncomfortably close.

"There's one fragment that is important," he whispered. "I'll need great pictures of it."

I nodded.

We fell into a routine as we worked through the stack. I jumped when Billy touched my leg. Ah, the crucial page. I snapped as many pictures as possible and bracketed the exposure.

Still more manuscript fragments paraded in front of the camera. My arms protested, but I refused to wimp out.

Iakobos lurked behind us. If I didn't know better, I'd say he was staring at my ass. Hey, I didn't ask to be standing on a chair leaning over a tripod.

Billy joined Paulos in positioning the fragments. "I'd like to spend more time studying a couple of these fragments. Can I borrow them?"

The *archimandrite* looked agreeable to sharing with a respected colleague. Karmanos and Iakobos turned dark as they vigorously shook their heads.

"Historic artifacts cannot be in private hands," Karmanos said. "They belong to the government of Hellas. We will move pages to the Byzantine museum in Athens. You may put in request to study them there."

The abbot and Iakobos let loose with a string of Greek. Do monks swear?

Carl explained. "They're telling Karmanos that these fragments belong to the monastery in particular and to the Orthodox Church in general. Apparently, ownership is an on-going battle."

Karmanos tried to outshout the two monks. Sophia ranted at

Billy about embarrassing the Institute and overstepping his authority. Voices rose in a grand opera crescendo.

Billy raised his hands in surrender.

"Hold on! I can see that dog won't hunt. I'm not trying to take anything. We'll just get good pictures today. If I need to see them again, I'll come back. Forget that I asked."

Forget? Fat chance. We worked efficiently, but the collegial atmosphere was gone.

Karmanos challenged Paulos on how the fragments should be stored. Before, the broken books and loose pages had been stacked casually in boxes in a back bookcase. Billy's interest changed that. No way would Karmanos let the disputed scraps be tossed back into boxes.

"I have a tablet of acid-free art paper in my backpack," I offered. "You could use that to interleaf the fragments."

Karmanos and Iakobos accepted my donation. The abbot found a wooden box and removed a purple silk cloth.

Heck, maybe these fragments really were valuable. Donating some archival paper was the least I could do. As Iakobos and Karmanos interleaved the fragments with protective paper, I took a closer look at the purple silk.

"Can I take some pictures of this?"

Abbot Paulos waved his hand without looking up from the fragments. I took that as yes.

The original burgundy wine color was still strong in the folds. Some of the purple had faded to browns, mauves and pinks. The white woven pattern of octagon medallions had darkened to ivory.

Carl lounged over the table where I worked. "Purple dye was very expensive and exclusive in ancient times."

"Aunt Lydia would love this ... She's a textile designer." I adjusted the angles slightly. "I'm going to make a print for her."

"The purple dye is made from snail spit. Vats of rotting snails stank up the Port of Tyre, ancient writers say."

I heard a soft voice speaking Greek to me. Father Gabriel led me to the back of the library. As the prophet David looked down from the fresco above, Gabriel gently coaxed a book from its spot in a glass-fronted bookcase. The book's thick wooden covers were covered with silver and embossed with an eight-pointed star that reminded me of the Nativity star.

Gabriel opened the boards, revealing the same purple silk lining the inside covers.

He spoke directly to me.

Carl translated. "He says this is a Psalter with commentary, so it is less important than complete scriptures. It was written by Constantine Purple-born for his son."

I stroked the fine texture of the silk. Oh, I knew better; don't touch. But I couldn't resist. The Byzantines appreciated fine things —colors, textures, ornamentation. Even with water stains and frayed edges, the silk was awesome.

Gabriel turned through a few pages. Full page illustrations of classic images, churches, and King David dressed as a Byzantine emperor filled the manuscript. It was a masterpiece.

"Thank you so much, Father Gabriel. You're right. I love it."

Carl didn't bother to translate. Gabriel smiled and responded in Greek while I answered in English. Somehow, we communicated.

Why had I dreaded coming here? I had done good work, and no one had tried to kill me.

Paulos locked the fragments in the monastery's treasury. We returned the library to a semblance of order and gathered our books and equipment.

"We should inspect," Demetrius said.

Father Paulos, our host, looked stricken. It didn't bother Brother Iakobos, though. He stuck his nose in and helped Demetrius paw through all of our bags and books. That's the thanks I got for donating my tablet.

We said goodbye in the courtyard. Gabriel slipped his black knotted rope to me and made a gesture of blessing. I wrapped it around my left wrist as I had seen the monks do. I gave my guardian angel a forbidden hug, releasing the scent of incense and beeswax candles from black folds.

I turned away to hide my tears. "I need to make a quick trip to the ladies' room."

As I washed my hands, I heard the door swing open. I turned, expecting Sophia.

Brother Iakobos blocked the exit. "You saw yesterday how easily you could be killed. Watch what you are getting into."

He grabbed my arm as I tried to push past. His dark eyes narrowed behind his heavy glasses. "Listen to me. This is not a joke!"

Our faces were just inches apart. My skin went cold and clammy. I twisted from his hold and ran out. I wasn't laughing.

22

Born in the Purple

"The patriarch himself takes the crown and places it on the head of the master, and immediately the people cry out 'Holy, Holy, Holy. Glory to God in the highest and peace on earth.' Thrice. Then 'O such a great emperor and autocrat, many years,' and again." Constantine VII in "On the Imperial Order"

A.D. 919, Royal Palace, Constantinople

Constantine stood still, just like he had done all his life. *Stand still, be quiet and act like an emperor*, his father Leo the Wise had taught him.

But that had been seven years ago. Did the 13-year-old really remember, or was he prompted by his mother's stories?

His light silk gown revealed thin shoulders and frame, made worse by his recent bout of dysentery.

He held out arms as his eunuchs clothed him in a long robe of purple silk edged with gold embroidery and pearls. He slipped his big feet into red leather slippers. Would he ever grow into those feet?

Courtiers brought the *loros*, a jeweled stole that was a symbol of imperial power. What a joke. Constantine had been *Basilius* of the Roman Empire in name since the age of seven. Today's ceremony would be one more sign of powerlessness.

Constantine admired the room. Plum-colored granite, sparkling

with tiny white quartz crystals, covered the floor and walls. Por-
phyry, mined in Egypt, was reserved for the imperial family.

Succession preference was given not to the first-born son, but
to sons born to reigning emperors. Constantine had been born in
this room, born in the purple. It set his fate.

He braced as the weight of the jeweled stole woven with
golden threads fell on his shoulders. The *loros* clinked as cabochon
gems and pearls settled into place.

He tied a purse of dirt to his belt. From dust the emperor had
come and to dust he would return. As if Constantine needed to be
reminded of his mortality. Those who coveted his throne marveled
that he was still alive. He stood a bit taller at that minor victory.
Had he been healthier, they would have poisoned him instead of
waiting for nature to do the job.

He smiled as his mother, Zoe, entered the purple room. He held
her no ill will. Her name meant life, sustenance, and she had given
him that. But her efforts as empress and regent had been sabotaged
by power-hungry opponents.

The 13-year-old knelt as the crown was placed on his long,
dark hair. His attendants padded the crown to keep it from slipping
over his ears.

Heavy jeweled pendants hung from the crown and brushed
against his thin cheeks. It made his nose look even bigger and
longer.

He was the seventh Constantine to hold the orb of power. The
name was a burden; the first Constantine made Christianity the official religion of the empire and built a new capitol at the intersec-
tion of Europe and Asia.

With the weight of the *dalmatic*, *loros* and crown, he needed
help rising to his feet.

He took his mother's hand for the walk to *Hagia Sophia*, the
Church of the Holy Wisdom of God.

Admiral Romanos Lekapenos, his wife, and eight children
joined the procession through the gardens of the rambling Great

Palace complex.

Maybe it wouldn't be so bad having other children in the palace. The admiral's three younger sons were strong and rambunctious, trained in military arts. Would they befriend a quiet, scholarly boy? The younger daughter seemed friendly enough. They had met only yesterday, but 10-year-old Helena had smiled. Maybe she would join him in his studies.

Constantine's tutor, Theodore, had trusted Lekapenos. He opened the private harbor of the palace two days ago, welcoming the admiral's forces into the fortress, supposedly to protect the Purple-born from being pushed aside.

Guards waited at the Chalke Gate to escort them through the streets. People crowded close to see the royal bride and groom. It was only three blocks, but the weight of the imperial costume and noise of the crowd made Constantine feel faint.

Finally, they reached the church. Constantine paused. The mosaic over the imperial door showed his father bowing low before Christ.

His father, Leo the Wise, was the son of Basil the Macedonian. The untimely deaths of Leo's three wives and two children left him without an heir. He had feared the Macedonian dynasty would end after two generations.

His mistress, Zoe, had delivered their son in the purple room, giving the 40-year-old emperor a purple-born heir. But a fourth wife was prohibited. The church considered Zoe a whore.

To emphasize the child's royal blood, Constantine was nick-named "Purple-born." Better than "Constantine Bastard."

Constantine Purple-born raised his chin and squared his shoulders as Patriarch Nicholas Mystikos met them at the royal door.

It had been Mystikos who refused to recognize his parents' marriage and his legitimacy. Mystikos who locked Emperor Leo VI out of the church for the Christmas Liturgy. Mystikos who seized power and ruled in Constantine's name after his father died.

Mystikos who read a statement of Constantine's illegitimacy annually in the church. (How was that logical, Constantine wondered, to rule on behalf of someone you claim had been baptized and crowned illegally?)

Mystikos who lost support of the military. Mystikos who lied and plotted rebellions against Zoe and Constantine.

Constantine's parents had mourned the loss of Patriarch Stephen and Leo's unfortunate appointment of Mystikos.

Patriarch Mystikos led young Constantine and Helena to a side chapel for their wedding vows. Afterwards, the ladies were escorted upstairs to the women's gallery.

Constantine marched behind Mystikos as the procession entered the soaring central space of *Hagia Sophia*. May sunshine warmed the massive dome, illuminating the faces of wealthy and powerful men. They were all here today: the generals, bishops, bureaucrats, and wealthy landed families.

Normally, Constantine loved the architecture and ceremony of the court. Today, he felt sick. Sweat soaked his gown under the heavy regalia.

Constantine looked east to the Mother of God, enthroned against a gold mosaic sky. She gestured to the child on her lap, whose wise old face revealed the presence of the Wisdom of God.

He prayed, "Lord Jesus Christ, Son of God, have mercy on me, a sinner. Grant your humble servant the strength to stand with dignity."

Finally, it was his turn. He tried to lower the pitch of his high, soft voice. Speak like a man, not a child.

He placed the *loros* on Romanos. As Mystikos placed the crown, the people began to chant.

Constantine picked up the heavy crystal orb topped by a cross, representing the world under the authority of Christ. The usurper reached out eagerly. Constantine felt the weight of the world slip from his fingers.

The admiral was now *Basileopator*, father of the emperor. By

Christmas, Romanos would drop the pretense and declare himself *Basilius*.

Maybe it wasn't so bad. Constantine preferred reading and painting anyway. He had moved the classic Greek and Roman statuary in the palace complex to his quarters. Ancient manuscripts and his father's writings were gathered for his studies.

Under his father, tattered remnants of Plato's writings had been located and copied into new manuscripts. The scribes had started compiling Aristotle. There was work to be done for the imperial library.

They could banish his mother and his tutor, but they couldn't take away his books.

Perhaps Helena could persuade her father to let Constantine oversee the artists and scholars of the court. Let Lekapenos supervise the wars and bureaucrats; he would spend his time studying art, culture, history and diplomacy.

23

Plain of Thessaly

"The gods of Greece are cruel! In time, all men shall learn to live without them." Jason in the 1963 movie "Jason and the Argonauts."

We shed our jackets as we descended down the stairs to our car. Enough propriety. I shook out my hair and took off my knee socks. Who cared if some monk was issuing warnings and leering from above for a glimpse of my bare shoulders? Let him.

At the bottom of the stairs, I raised my arms and spun around. It felt good to be alive and out of the monastery. Billy whistled a hymn as he carried his books to the car.

The late sun warmed the agricultural flatlands as we sped back to Athens. The hum of the tires whispered a warning, *Watch what you are getting into. Watch what you are getting into.* How could I watch? I hadn't gotten into anything. I had no idea what had provoked someone to push me off that parapet.

"The Titans and the Olympians fought a war on the Plain of Thessaly," Carl said. "Jason and the Argonauts started their quest for the Golden Fleece here."

"Silly myths, discredited 2,000 years ago," Billy said.

"At least the Greeks knew they were stories, not like the fables you Christians sell as facts."

"You aren't going to ruin a great day. I shake you like dust out of my shoes," Billy said.

"You failed in a quest to get possession of your golden fleece. Don't take it out on me,"

No one mentioned that I had almost been killed yesterday. But then, they thought it was a clumsy accident. I didn't tell them about the threat from Brother Iakobos. They wouldn't believe me.

I found pictures of the Revelation sequence from the cloister of the monastery on my camera. Since Billy and I were uncomfortably close in the back seat, sharing images would be easy.

"This image of God enthroned is from Rev. 4. Is that the Rapture?"

"No, no. That's a total misinterpretation. This introduces the first prophecy, which predicts the war between Rome and the Jews that ended with the destruction of Jerusalem in A.D. 70."

Billy handed me his Greek New Testament. Just Greek. With no line of English printed under the wicked symbols. Cruel. Inhuman.

"You've read the first chapter of Revelation. Tell me about your previous studies of Revelation and what the first chapter said to you this time," Billy said.

"Well, the church I grew up in didn't really deal with Revelation, just little scripture passages about the ultimate triumph of God. So I didn't think about it until I started going to church with my college roommate, Kira. That church expected the Rapture and Tribulation any day. Then I made the mistake of inviting my boyfriend to Wednesday night potluck and Bible study. I mean, the food was really good."

"Read a few verses in Greek and tell me your thoughts."

I struggled through several lines. The others winced at my pronunciation, but didn't laugh. Billy actually gave some helpful prompts.

"Do you have any questions about this chapter?" Billy asked.

"My first question is the first word, apocalypse. It means unveiling, but that's a misnomer. It's shrouded in mystery."

"An apocalypse unveils the future. It's always written in the symbolic language of prophecy."

"What about τταχει? I don't understand that word here."

"It means speed."

"Speed doesn't make sense in this passage, Dr. Sullivan."

"Please stop calling me Dr. Sullivan. Just Billy is okay."

"Okay, Dr. Billy. How can John promise 'things which must occur with speed' when it's 2,000 years later and the Second Coming hasn't occurred yet?"

"Biblical interpreters have debated that question for thousands of years. What do you think?"

"Well, either John's prophecy was wrong, or 'with speed' means something other than 'soon'."

"This prophecy is God's word, so it can't be wrong. What are the other possibilities?"

I heard a cynical snort from the front seat.

"You're using the Socratic method on me," I said. "One explanation is that a day to the Lord is like a thousand years and a thousand years are like a day. So it really hasn't been that long."

Carl laughed.

Billy sighed. "That's the classic way of dodging the problem. That sort of thinking is why intelligent friends like young Carl dismiss the Bible. Another dodge is to translate the word as 'suddenly' instead of 'soon.' The Second Coming may not happen soon, but when it does eventually happen, it will be sudden, a surprise."

"I guess that's possible."

"A third dodge is that God is speaking through John to today's readers, and things will happen in our near future."

He shifted in the tight back seat. He got the honor of sticking his knees in the spot between the two front seats. That left me with knees drawn up to my chin.

"So which is correct?" I asked.

"Look at our assumptions about 'things which must take place.' Perhaps some of those things did indeed take place soon after the prophecy."

I looked to see if he was serious. "Like Hal Lindsey? The modern state of Israel and the invention of modern tools of warfare that he talks about?"

"No, Hal Lindsey is an idiot"

"Lindsey's imagery is really strong, though. He does a great job of tying Revelation to the things going on in the decades after World War II."

"Good imagery doesn't make it sound theology," Billy said.

"I'd like to focus on John's imagery in Revelation. All the End Time preachers use this really vivid imagery to paint their picture of the near future."

"My expertise is the history and interpretation of Revelation. That will help you understand the images."

Billy's insights might make Greek translation bearable.

Carl pulled off at a Greek version of a truck stop at Trilaka. We selected bread and cheeses. I added some *glikia* and *gelato* (my favorite Greek words—sweets and ice cream). We ate in the parking lot beside the car.

I turned on my phone. It immediately announced a text message from Jim Sampras.

Did you enjoy your march with the saints today? Hope your bruises are healing. Can we get together? I have more gossip about the history of the monasteries. Quite racy!

Maybe giving him my phone number had been a mistake. I tapped out a reply.

On the road back to Athens. Save your stories for another time. Surely monks didn't misbehave or gossip!

That should discourage him.

"What are you smiling about?" said Carl.

I flipped my phone into a pocket. "Oh, nothing."

"You look great in that dress, Amber. I made a nice selection."

I winced as he slid his arm around my shoulders and gave me a hug.

"Sorry, I forgot. Even with bruises you are sexy."

"Boy, are you desperate."

Still, any day that has two guys flirting with me can't be all bad. A pain pill would make it even better.

24

On the Road to Athens

The sun sank in the west as Billy helped me through the first chapter of the prophecy: Alpha and Omega, the *Pantokrator*, the Son of Man standing amidst seven golden lamp stands.

"Seven is an important number in the Bible. Seven represents the days of creation, God's complete work," Billy said. "Seven lamp stands for seven churches—the complete church."

Carl chimed in from the driver's seat. "Seven is also important in the ancient Greek world. The ancients saw seven heavenly bodies. Seven wonders of the world, seven sisters of the Pleiades, the seven who fought against Thebes."

Carl was in his element. I just wished he'd keep his eyes on the road instead of turning back to agree with Billy.

I found the passage with the seven lampstands. "So why emphasize seven when it's really an image of eight? Christ standing among the churches? That image is first in the Revelation series at Varlaam."

"No, seven is the important number. Look for seven throughout the book of Revelation," Billy said

"Seven is an ideal proportion," Carl said. "The Doric column is seven diameters high. In late Classical sculpture, a figure is seven heads tall."

"That's neat. I'll remember that."

"I doubt you'll get that question in pub quiz," Carl said.

As Billy and Carl discussed the symbolism of numbers, I thought about the Revelation interpretation I heard at Kira's church

Modern predictions of the Second Coming are inspired by the lesson of the fig tree.

Matthew 24:51 says, "Now learn this lesson from the fig tree: As soon as its twigs get tender and its leaves come out, you know that summer is near. Even so, when you see all these things, you know that it is near, right at the door. I tell you the truth, this generation will certainly not pass away until all these things have happened."

In the Bible, the fig tree is a symbol for Israel.

The modern nation of Israel declared its independence in 1948. The fig tree had leafed out! Christ would return within one generation. A standard generation in the Bible is 40 years.

But the Tribulation didn't start by 1988, forcing a recalculation. Perhaps a generation is 60 to 80 years long. That would put the Tribulation starting before 2028.

Or, maybe the fig tree didn't leaf until 1967 when the Israelis took control of Jerusalem. But the Tribulation again failed to come in 2007.

Heaven forbid if anyone suggested that people were misreading the sign of the fig tree.

I'm sick of pat answers. Too many people claim insight into this difficult book. If we ask questions or think for ourselves, we're "lukewarm," one of the most damning things you can call a Christian.

Billy seems more scholarly and open-minded about Revelation. Maybe I can ask questions and come to a comfort level with John's message.

Revelation is rich with images. That will be my focus. John saw visions. How did he describe them? How do I visualize them? How did Byzantine artists portray them?

It was dark when we left the plain and wound into the arid hills that encircle Athens. I dozed. Black vultures circled over me as I sprawled beside a road. Would I make a tasty bite of carrion?

25

Patmos

John unrolled the scroll of the prophet Ezekiel.

"Be careful when you study the *merkaba*, the chariot," the priest warned. "It is to be undertaken only by the wise."

The elder nodded, then leaned close to read.

"In the thirtieth year, in the fourth month, on the fifth day of the month, as I was among the exiles by the river Chebar, the heavens were opened and I saw visions of God." Ezekiel wrote of the living creatures, the four wheels that carried the vision of God, and of the spirit that moved among them like burning coals of fire.

"I saw something that looked like fire, and there was a splendor all around. Like the bow in a cloud on a rainy day, such was the appearance of the splendor all around. This was the appearance of the likeness of the glory of YHWH. When I saw it, I fell on my face, and I heard the voice of someone speaking."

The elder paused at Ezekiel's cautious language. The prophet never used the word *tselem*—image. He smiled at the prophet's respect for the commandments. Ezekiel would not be accused of creating an image in words, an idol.

The elder read. The light shifted to the west.

He read of the destruction YHWH would bring on Jerusalem.

"Therefore, as I live, says the Lord YHWH, surely, because you have defiled my sanctuary with all your detestable things, and with all your abominations—therefore I will cut you down. One third of you shall die of pestilence or be consumed by famine among you; one third shall fall by the sword around you; and one third I will scatter to every wind."

The sunlight faded to a soft gold.

John felt a hand on his shoulder.

"Come, my friend, the light grows dim. Let's see what our companions have caught for dinner this evening," the priest said.

"My churches will remember the words of the prophets. These images will reassure them of their place in the Kingdom of God."

26

Tuesday night

Slamming car doors woke me. My muscles ached and stitches itched after our grueling day and four hours in the back seat of the Toyota. I unwound and escaped. Why did tiny Sophia get the front seat while Billy and I were crammed in the back?

We carried our gear into the Institute. Safely home ... well, home away from home. I fished out my key and headed down the hall.

The door between the two buildings stood open, spilling light into the dark hallway. Had I left the light on and the door unlocked?

Thunk. Footsteps.

My skin went clammy.

A door slammed down that hallway. I froze. Someone was in my apartment.

Carl started to squeeze around to get up the stairs, then paused.

"Do you need help with your things, Amber?"

"Someone is in the other building," I mouthed silently.

"What?"

So much for silence. I heard footsteps coming. My fight-or-flight instincts said flight. I spun around and bumped smack into Carl. No getaway here.

"Amber, are y'all back?" Aunt Lydia bounded into the hallway and gave me a big hug, wrapping me in her exotic perfume.

"You must be Carl Helman. My husband told me so much about you. I'm glad to meet you."

Carl brushed her extended hand with his lips. "I have also heard much about you, *Frau* Jackson. Did you just arrive? We didn't know you were coming."

"When Sophia called Monday, I realized I need to be here. Besides, what's better than enjoying Greece with my favorite niece?"

Sophia *had* tattled about my fall.

"Amber, let me help with your bag," Lydia said.

"No, you'll need your apartment. I can sleep in one of the student rooms upstairs now that you're here."

"Nonsense, Amber. I want the company."

One didn't disagree with Lydia Jackson. We schlepped my stuff while Carl told Sophia and Billy about the unexpected arrival.

Oops. I had left the bed unmade and dirty clothes and towels in the bathroom when we left before dawn on Monday. Aunt Lydia had everything straightened up.

"When did you get here?"

"This afternoon. I took a nap, then grabbed dinner in the *Plaka*," Lydia said.

"I like the red hair."

Lydia shook the crazy hair. "I was feeling a bit stodgy, so I decided to try something different."

Billy charged in and gave my aunt a bear hug.

"Lydia, what a great surprise."

Lydia hugged back. "I just couldn't stay away knowing y'all were having fun without me."

Sophia watched the scene, then extended a hand. "Lydia, you finally came." She managed to look down her nose at my aunt, even though Lydia had a good eight inches on her.

"I'm glad you called. I just needed a lil' push to get me here. Can I make anyone a cup of tea?" Lydia offered. "Some brandy?"

"It's late and we are exhausted," Sophia said. "We will talk in the morning."

After pleasantries, we were alone.

"Are you really okay? Let me see your stitches."

I revealed my wounds and bruises.

"These look really painful. I'm so glad it wasn't worse," Lydia said.

"I really did think my life was over. The worst part is knowing someone tried to kill me."

Lydia took my hands and looked me straight in the eye. "Explain."

"Someone pushed me off the wall. I fell because someone shoved me."

"Sophia did *not* tell me that," Lydia said. "She told me you were lucky you weren't killed. She said you were careless. Did you tell her about being pushed?"

"I tried. She said I had a concussion. She thinks I'm not taking responsibility for my foolish actions. But I just can't shake the memory that I was shoved. It just doesn't make sense."

"Oh, poor Amber. I just couldn't lose both Robert and you in the same year."

Another hug. Ouch!

Getting ready for bed raised another issue.

"Amber, I noticed that you were sleeping on the right side," Lydia said. "That's my side, too. Can you take the left side?"

"Sure. I'm sorry I took your spot."

Robert's side had a stack of books, pens and a dock for a smart phone. He had bookmarked a history of the Macedonian dynasty with a letter from the Paris dealer. Maybe he had some notes about the chalice. I slipped the book under the others so Lydia wouldn't see anything before we had the chalice repaired.

Lydia fluffed pillows as I slid between sheets of the smoothest Egyptian cotton. Awesome. She did know fine linens.

Lydia turned off the light. "I just can't sleep on Robert's side. I'm glad you're here. I couldn't face Greece without him."

I squeezed her hand in the dark. "Uncle Robert always made

me feel smart, not like a kid with stupid questions. It's just wrong that he's gone."

DAY FOUR

"God made the two great lights—the greater light to rule the day and the lesser light to rule the night—and the stars." Genesis 1:16

In Biblical numerology, four is the number of the Earth, God's created world. We speak of four corners of the earth, four directions of the compass and four seasons.

Four also represents earthly governments. Nebuchadnezzar's dream showed four empires. Later, Daniel dreamed of four beasts from the sea, representing four kingdoms.

The Hebrews divided Earth's creatures into four categories: people, domestic animals, wild animals, and creatures of the sky and sea. In a vision of the divine, Hebrew prophet Ezekiel saw four living creatures. Later, John describes the creatures around the throne of God. Irenaeus compared John's four living creatures to the four authorized Gospels.

The church stood on four witnesses to Jesus Christ. Four meant that the gospels reached out to the entire Earth. We build tables and chairs with four legs, buildings with four walls.

The symbol of four is the square. Four is solid, earthly. The Greek numeral for four is *delta* (Δ δ).

28

Wednesday, Athens

Sunlight flooded the bedroom. I pulled silky cotton sheets over my head and nuzzled into the feather pillow. No use. I smelled coffee and food. My stomach beat all other urges.

Aunt Lydia and Billy talked over coffee. An enticing aroma rose from a bakery bag.

"Good morning, Aunt Lydia, Dr. Sullivan."

I stumbled into the tiny kitchen, made another pot of coffee and joined them at the table.

"You must call me Billy. I was just updating Lydia on the Nicene Foundation."

"You'd be terrific as their president," Lydia said.

"We'll just have to see. The director of fundraising is also a strong candidate. Let us tell you about our research at Meteora."

Billy pontificated as I selected a pastry.

"The monasteries were built between 1350 and 1550 AD, so most of the manuscripts are late Byzantine. In fact, most Greek manuscripts are from that period," Billy said

"Ummhumm." I mumbled through a mouthful.

"There are a few Middle Byzantine manuscripts. Hermit monks started living in the caves about 800 AD and brought their manuscripts. Other old books and items were brought to Meteora to keep them safe. If you remember, Crusaders sacked Constantinople in 1204, followed by a period of Latin occupation. Encroachments by the Turks led to the eventual fall of the Eastern Empire."

"What's the oldest book you saw?" Lydia asked.

Billy beamed. "That's what I'm going to spend today figuring out. I need Amber's photos to confirm my initial assessment."

"Oh, give me your gut reaction. You look as excited as a tick on a fat dog."

"Eighth or ninth century, I think. That's quite rare."

I refilled everyone's cups. "Father Gabriel showed me a totally awesome manuscript that looked really old. He said it was written by Constantine Purple-born. I have no idea who he was."

"Don't let that get you off track on your Greek studies," Billy said.

As if he could stop me.

"Let's work in the conference room so you can study my photographs on the big screen. What are you doing this morning, Aunt Lydia?"

"I'll get out personal things. The Institute sometimes uses my apartment, and I don't want a visitor walking away with an artifact thinking it's a cheap memento."

I got my laptop and camera from the guest room and added another question to the marker board. "Who is Constantine Purple-born?

Billy glanced in and frowned. "What do you mean, 'Is it a fake?'"

Oh, shit. I didn't want him to know about the chalice. "Ah, ah, well, it's just a general question when looking at old art."

"Your Greek alphabet is in the wrong order."

He didn't know about the color of letters, either.

"It makes sense to me that way."

Billy left with a snort.

I added a fourth question: "Who pushed me?"

Aunt Lydia poked her head in. "That alphabet chart looks like something Robert might do. He was a synesthete, you know.

"What's a synesthete?"

"They have extra connections in their brain, so they see letters in color, or associate sounds with tastes—that sort of stuff."

Wow. Maybe I wasn't a freak of nature. Or at least there were more freaks like me. I repeated the word several times to myself. Wikipedia time.

My phone tingled with a message. I downed my last sip of coffee. Jim again? I thought I gave him the brush-off last night.

Beautiful morning here in Meteora. Monasteries floating above the mist at dawn. We should hike the old trails and reach the monasteries the original way instead of the easy tourist bridges.

If Jim wouldn't get lost, I might as well use him for research.

Question – Is the image at Varlaam of God in heaven with 24 elders kneeling with their crowns the Rapture?

Billy waited in the conference room. Time to see what he discovered at the monastery.

29

The Fragment

I downloaded my images for Billy onto the computer that ran the AV system.

Billy hauled in books and notes "My career is riding on your images, so these better be good."

The Robert Jackson Conference Room was a visual surprise after the traditional Ivy League look of the Institute. My last time here, it was a stodgy classroom.

Lydia had redone it in the colors of the Greek islands, all bright sky blue and white. The sleek tables and chairs could be set up classroom style or pushed together in conference or boardroom style. The AV system was totally awesome.

"Focus on the fragments first," Billy ordered

I was never sure as I shot. I liked to see the pictures big on the computer. I held my breath as the first few images appeared for Billy's critical eye.

"Yes ... yes ... this will work. You did okay, Amber."

I sat up taller. "I guess my college job as an audio-visual aide was worth something."

We clicked through the fragments.

"No ... No ... That one ... Give me the whole sequence of that fragment."

He walked to the flat screen. "This is the one. This is the gem."

I couldn't see anything special about the tattered, pink-stained sheet of parchment. But then, it's Greek to me.

He paced as I advanced the images. "This is my next book," he said. "This is my legacy. They'll have to give me the Nicene presidency after this discovery."

I had fired off about ten pictures of the fragment without, I hoped, drawing suspicion from the monks. All of them went into today's study folder.

"I'll pick a few others for comparison then I can date the fragment by comparing it to known manuscripts," Billy explained. "Can you do lighter and darker versions?"

Billy paced as I played in Photoshop. I finished and turned the computer over to him.

Sophia stuck her head in. "Amber, you have a phone call from Andreus Mikos. You can take it in my office."

She watched over my shoulder as I picked up the phone.

"Hello?"

"Miss Amber, I could come now to see mystery goblet."

I squirmed. "Well, Aunt Lydia got here last night, so we're pretty busy today."

"Ah, I understand. We must keep secret from your aunt. Maybe bring it to my shop in *Monastiraki*?"

"Maybe."

"You are not free to speak. I could also meet you somewhere. Just let me know."

"Thanks."

Sophia gave me a look. I escaped to the conference room.

I set up my laptop in the other end of the room. A quick check of email showed a message from my friend Kira.

OMG! I'm sooo glad you're still alive. Stay away from high places! The devil will put obstacles in your path to keep you from achieving your goals. I wish I could visit. Carl is a cutie! I keep telling you: DON'T FEEL REJECTED. Dustin still cares about you. He asked for prayers for you on Sunday. The whole congregation is praying for you on this trip.

That's why I was so pissed—an entire congregation praying for lukewarm, confused Amber. I could never show my face there again. I fired off a warning to the offender:

You don't control me anymore. If you ever did. Finding the purpose of my life is my problem, not yours. Keep your concerns to yourself and off the church prayer list.

Jim, the guy from the cafe, already had an answer to my question.

I don't think monks believed in the Rapture at that time. It's a relatively new theological concept. And it sure isn't mentioned in Revelation. People are talking about a manuscript expert at Varlaam. The monks say the government wants to take their books. They report a miracle—you didn't tell me you fell off the parapet! They thank their Madonna Hodegitria icon for saving you. There's a dragon cave below the Varlaam monastery. If you like falling off monasteries, you'd love to visit a dragon cave!

I tapped out a quick response.

Thanks for your thoughts on the image. Yup, that was us at Varlaam. The expert is Dr. Billy Sullivan, a Greek teacher and writer for a Christian think tank. We took pictures of parchment pages. Don't know if they are significant. And the fall was NOT my fault! I think one of the monks pushed me. That monastery is spooky. By the way, what are you working on at Meteora? What's a Hodegitria? And NO, I am not hiking into a dragon cave!

I had a disk full of images to download and catalogue, plus notes to type. But first, I had a wiki-task.

Turns out synesthesia is a perceptual gift (or curse) where stimulation in one sense triggers an experience in another sense. The name comes from Greek (of course) and means "union of senses."

Some synesthetes—like me—see letters in color. Others see sounds in color. Some see numbers as points in space. Some even taste words or colors.

No wonder I couldn't learn Greek. My brain was giving me the wrong color clue for letters that mean one thing in the Latin alphabet and a different thing in the Greek alphabet.

Neurologists think synesthetes have more active interconnections in our brains. One benefit is elevated memory, probably because the extra senses provide additional memory clues. Maybe that's why I remember things I see so much better than things I hear.

Synesthesia runs in families. If I had asked Uncle Robert about colored letters, maybe I wouldn't have gone through school getting teased and knowing I was different.

I forced my curiosity to the background and started electronic filing. Some time later, Lydia peeked in the door and waved. Billy didn't notice.

My mouse hand cramped. I slipped into the hall. Voices carried through the open door to Sophia's office.

"Your niece is hopeless. She'll never learn Greek. And I'm stuck spending the summer babysitting her and that preacher instead of working for the Institute's survival."

My face burned.

"All she does is stumble around and take pictures. I bet she shoots selfies in bars with her buddies."

"She's very bright. She wants to learn," Lydia's voice floated out.

A mature adult would charge into that office and defend herself. I gave my feet a pep talk. *You can do it, feet. Move feet, move.*

"I haven't seen that. She is totally unprepared and goes off on pointless tangents," Sophia said.

"Well, this is only her fourth day here. Have you given her any help or goals?"

"She's not a scholar. She's not even safe on her own. I was appalled when she fell off the parapet. She refuses to take responsibility. Instead she comes with a stupid excuse—claiming she was pushed."

I forced back the tears. MacGyver would stand up for himself.

My feet moved.

30

Monastiraki

I stopped at the foot of the stairs to regain my composure. I needed a long, long walk.

"Amber, I have something to show you."

Drat! Carl. I faked a smile and headed into the library.

"I'm almost finished with your map of Varlaam."

I leaned over his computer. "You are an awesome map-maker. And these elevations are wonderful."

His blue eyes crinkled. "I have a mystery for you, Amber. Look at this picture. What do you see?"

I sat beside him to get a closer look. "It's a sun, or maybe a star on a shield."

"*Ja*. It is the Macedonian Sun on the shield of a Greek hoplite soldier. Sometimes, we see it on Athena's or Apollo's shield. Alexander the Great and the Macedonians adopted this symbol. Even today, the Greek province of Macedonia uses this on its flag. Usually, the sun has eight rays, or a multiple like 16 or 32."

"It's nice. So what's the mystery, Carl?"

"I took this next picture yesterday at Meteora. The Macedonian Sun is on the cloak of the Madonna."

"What? Why is a Greek soldier's symbol on Mary?"

"I ask you as a Christian art expert."

"I'm totally stumped. I'll ask Jim; he might know."

Carl draped his arm over my shoulder and spoke softly into my ear. "Forget that jerk, Amber. You and I can solve this mystery."

"I do need your notes from yesterday."

"I wrote them in German, so I will have to read them to you. Perhaps we could do that with a glass of wine after dinner?"

I slide away from him. "Perhaps we could do that after lunch."

"Lunch?"

Carl and I both jumped at Lydia's voice.

"Are y'all ready for lunch?"

Great. My aunt found me with a guy draped around my shoulder. Would she decide I was an idiot, too?

"Andreus invited us to come see icons. We can get lunch on the way," Lydia said. "Would you like to join us, Carl?"

"*Ja*, I cannot turn down lunch with two beautiful ladies."

"I bought a Father's Day gift for my dad. Does Andreus mail things from his shop?" Amber said.

"He can take care of that for you," Lydia said. "What did you get?"

"It's just a reproduction bust of Pericles, but it'll look nice in his office."

My stomach growled. I grabbed my shopping bag and beat everyone out the door.

A cab dropped us at the *Monastiraki* neighborhood just north of the ancient Greek marketplace, the *Agora*. Four hundred years of Turkish rule left a Middle Eastern feel. We weaved through flea markets and bazaars piled high with old furniture, cheap ceramics and dubious antiques.

Aroma drew us to a gyros booth. The vendor carved off slices of roasted lamb and piled them on pita bread, then layered on *tzaziki*, tomatoes, peppers and greens. The wrapped pitas overflowed the little paper sacks.

We stuffed our faces as we jostled through crowded streets.

Someone pulled my shopping bag.

I pulled back. "Let go, you jerk!"

The guy pulled harder. The handle broke, sending me tumbling on my buns.

"Stop him," I yelled as the guy in sunglasses escaped into the crowd.

Lydia knelt beside me. "Are you okay?"

"What happened?" Carl asked.

"Don't look at me. Catch the guy who stole my bag. He's getting away."

"What did he take? Did he get your passport?" Lydia asked.

"No, my bust."

Carl laughed. "Your bust doesn't seem to be missing."

"Not my bust, you numb-nut. My dad's bust. Pericles."

"You're worried about a cheap tourist bust?"

"It was *not* cheap ... I spent 25 euros. Now my dad won't get a Father's Day gift."

Lydia helped me up. "Are you sure you're okay?"

"I need to file a police report."

"Forget the cheap statue," Carl said. "Tourists get things stolen all the time. You can buy a new one on any corner."

"Not me. How dare he steal my gift?"

Lydia patted my arm. "Calm down, Amber, It can be replaced. You've broken open the wound on your elbow."

Lydia led us to a modest door on a side street. It opened to a private gallery worlds away from the unwashed tourists outside. This was the junk dealer's shop? I squirmed in my casual clothes and gave my hair a quick combing with my fingers. The clerk gave us a suspicious look.

"We're too poor to shop here," I whispered to Carl.

"Is Andreus available?" Lydia asked.

As the clerk went to the back, I spotted a cameo carved from a burgundy and white gemstone, just like the bowl of the goblet. "Oh, I've seen you before. What are you?"

Carl raised his eyebrows.

"What's this stone, Carl?"

"Sardonyx. The Greeks and Romans used it for jewelry, cameos, that sort of thing. Sardonyx has dark red and white layers.

Black onyx has black and white layers."

"Revelation says that sardonyx is used in the foundation of the New Jerusalem. Fifth from the bottom, eighth from the top. But I never knew what sardonyx was."

"Amber, Amber, you've got to stop reading *shiza*."

A graying man in a dark suit emerged from the back. Andreus Mikos' somber face broke into a huge smile as he rushed to hug Lydia.

After kissing Lydia's cheeks, he turned to me. "What happened, sweet one?"

"Someone stole my shopping bag."

His face went white.

"No, no, it was just a souvenir bust of Pericles—nothing important."

He smiled. "What relief. I fear it was something special."

Yes, *that* something special. I gave him a very slight shake of my head. "No, just a gift for Father's Day."

A clerk led me to the back for antiseptic and bandages while Andreus gathered icons and other items to show us. We were soon seated in sleek chairs.

"Icon is Greek word for 'image.' But for Orthodox faith, icon is special spiritual creation." Andreus caressed the frame of an intimate-sized icon. "We believe that God became image in Jesus Christ. Word, *logos*, is important, but image, *icon*, is equally important."

He handed me the icon.

"Look into face of God. You cannot worship Jesus Christ without image."

The sad eyes stared into mine. "To us, praying to images seems superstitious."

"No, no. We do not pray *to* image. Icon is doorway. We pray *through* image to the divine. Image brings us close to the incarnation and opens heart to God."

"Some people believe icons perform miracles?" Carl asked.

"Correct. But I believe that some images are so visually powerful that they open hearts to divine miracles."

The assistant laid out images on the table in front of us. As Andreus led us through the visual vocabulary, I couldn't write fast enough. Icons were layered with symbolism and tradition.

"Look at hands. Hands are key to understanding icon."

Andreus selected an image dimmed by years of candle smoke and wear. Christ's raised right hand was contorted in a strange gesture.

"Here, the Lord's fingers spell out his name. Index finger is straight for I, *iota*. Second finger is curved in C, *sigma*. Those are the first and last letters of *Iesous*. Third finger crosses with the thumb to form X, *chi*. Little finger is again curved in C, *sigma*. *Chi sigma* is *Christos*."

I tried to duplicate the gesture with my own fingers.

"In this image, he blesses faithful with his name," Andreus explained. "But in some icons, he seems to bless himself. His gesture invites believers, saying, 'I am Jesus, Anointed One.'"

As his assistant put the icons away, Andreus showed us his gallery. I stopped at an elegant piece of metalwork with a gold background and delicate cloisonné decoration.

"Do you have anything from the time of Constantine Purpleborn?" I asked.

"You have good eye," Andreus said. "This is from Macedonian Renaissance, middle Byzantine period."

"How do you tell the different periods apart?" I asked.

"Early Byzantine pieces very rare. Many colors, many leaves and flowers, Garden of Eden, Old Testament and Roman images. Many theophanies—appearances of God.

"Then we have gap. During Iconoclast heresy, art is not made. Officials destroy art, torture and kill artists."

He picked up the small relic case and held it closer.

"Praise God, church and emperors abandoned their madness! Art is made once more. This is middle Byzantine. Artists make pictures of right belief of church. Simple, powerful images. Bold. Much gold."

He turned the case, allowing light to play across the gold and enamel surface.

"Constantine was artist. He studied ancient Greek art and literature. Italians say they rediscovered classics and brag about Renaissance. Nonsense. Greeks did it first. We have Renaissance during Macedonian dynasty. Figures look real, drapery looks real. We inspire them."

He moved on to an icon.

"Later artists tell stories. Pictures have more people, more scenes, more complex. Images for church festivals. Then another tragedy. Those barbarian Latins attack beautiful city. They steal books and art. Renaissance is over."

He looked as if the tragedy happened just last year, instead of 800 years ago. Lydia laid a hand on his arm. Andreus smiled.

"After we drove Latins out, leaders could not afford gold backgrounds. More frescoes. Not so many mosaics. Late Byzantine pictures have details, many people. See here. In Nativity, Holy Mother gives birth. At side, precious baby gets his bath. Very sweet, pretty story."

Listening to Andreus, the difference sounded obvious. But could I recognize it?

Andreus scowled. "Crusaders stole most Middle Byzantine art. They even sold Holy Crown of Thorns to King of France."

Lydia thanked him for his time and expertise. We could not leave without more hugs and kisses all around. Andreus took my left hand and touched the prayer rope looped around my wrist.

"May I see this?"

He slid it off and examined it with his loupe.

"This is not cheap tourist rope. Very old."

"Father Gabriel gave it to me at Meteora. How can you tell it's old?"

"Beads are smooth, worn flat. Monk has rubbed these beads as he counts daily prayers. Many, many years of rubbing," Andreus said.

"Black wool is from black sheep, not dyed. Spun fine, strong and tight. Always, each of 100 knots is tied with seven knots in shape of cross. In cheap ropes for tourists, yarn is dyed synthetic, coarse."

Andreus handed it back to me.

"Beads are amber from Russia, Baltic Sea. Dark honey color, like your hair. Your parents named you well."

I smiled in acknowledgment of the compliment.

"Monk or priest receives prayer rope like this when enters monastery. Maybe handed down in family. I am surprised holy man would give this away. I could sell for you."

"Oh, I couldn't sell it. Father Gabriel is my special angel."

Andreus handed me his card. "Come again. Or call." He looked straight into my eyes. "I will help you."

I nodded.

We walked into the bright sun. How would I get the broken goblet to him now that Lydia was here? I looked at his card... and tripped on the curb as we got in the cab.

31

Four Horsemen of the Apocalypse

"I looked and there before me was a pale green horse. Its rider's name was death, and Hades followed him; they were given authority over a fourth of the earth, to kill with sword, famine, and pestilence, and by the wild animals of the earth." Revelation 6:8

First Century, Patmos

The Elder pondered. The Jews of the Diaspora and the growing group of Gentile Christians were haunted by the Roman defeat of Jerusalem. How could he explain that it was part of God's plan? There was no hiding it under honey.

But he could not write openly about the four years of war between Jerusalem and the Romans. Those words would never get off the island and to his followers. He must use the language of prophecy as those before who spoke truth in times of persecution.

He would tell the story of four horsemen.

The white horse leads the attack as Titus and Vespasian had.

The red horse speaks of the Civil War in Israel that made the Holy City vulnerable.

The black horse is the famine and food blockage of Jerusalem

The final horse is the color of death. Those who had survived talked about the dead who were tossed over the walls of the city, surrounding it with rotting flesh.

People of faith would never forget the horror.

32

The Institute

Carl and I plopped in the library while Lydia checked on Billy.

"Did you notice the icon of Christ sitting on a rainbow above a sea of glass?"

"Ja, that's in western Renaissance art also," Carl said.

"That particular image is from Revelation Chapter 4, when the voice calls John up to heaven. It's in churches everywhere. Supposedly, that's the Rapture of believers, but it seems pretty obscure for such an important event."

"All prophecy is preposterous," Carl said.

"Anyway, John—and those caught up with him—see this vision of Christ. I think the image at Hosios David in Thessalonica is Early Byzantine. It shows a young unbearded Christ sitting on the rainbow. Around him are four living creatures, a lion, an ox, a man, and an eagle. Four rivers flow out of Eden, carrying God's blessings into the world. Christ usually holds a scroll or codex in his left hand, leaving his right hand for blessing. The left hand became the hand of judgment, of casting down into hell. Sheep to the right. Goats to the left."

"Did you notice the Macedonian Sun on the icons of Mary?" Carl asked.

"Yup. I was lookin' for it. It seems like it's usually a four or eight-pointed star on Mary, so maybe it's not the same symbol."

"I will Google it." Carl muttered and cursed as he scrolled through the results. "*Shiza!* I do not care about the pop star Madonna. I want the Virgin Mary star."

As Carl struggled with the frustrations of internet research, I retrieved a Byzantine art textbook and checked the index.

"The three stars—one on her forehead and one on each shoulder—represent her perpetual virginity," I read to Carl. "The Orthodox believed she was a virgin before, during and after the birth of Christ. So the star is a symbol of virginity. I don't think it's related to your Greeks, Carl."

"It's the Macedonian Sun. Remember, Athena was the virgin goddess. Parthenon is from the Greek word for virgin. *Parthenos* means more than unmarried. It means modest, mysterious."

Carl buried his nose in some technical tome on Classical architecture as I checked my text messages.

Men. I'd read Dustin first, then scruffy Jim.

Why cut yourself off from your church family? Of course, we're all praying for you. Don't abandon your spiritual life because you're mad at me.

Why did I let him jerk my chain? And why had I thought I wanted to spend my life with this guy? He didn't deserve a reply.

What did my bearded friend have to say for himself?

You've been reading too many novels. A monk pushing you— that's funny! Are you sure you were pushed? If anyone pushed you, it must have been someone from your group. Please be careful... the academic types you are hanging around with can be cutthroat.

I am writing my dissertation on the challenges of tourism to traditional Orthodox spirituality. Watch for it on the New York Times bestseller list.

Hodegitria means she who shows the way. It's a Madonna pointing to the incarnate God in her lap. Varlaam has a nice one.

I scowled. I knew Jim wouldn't believe that I was pushed. That's why I didn't tell him before.

Why does no one believe me? Sophia treats me like a child, but she wouldn't try to kill me. I'm too pathetic to be worth her effort. It has to be someone at the monastery. Brother Iakobos was lurking around watching us. Or maybe Dr. Karmanos or Demetrius. Karmanos acts like we are a big pain in the butt.

I threw down my phone and paced. Sophia thought I was a dumb blonde. The guys thought I was clumsy and making this up. Had I blown my chance this summer?

"Aaugh!" I tousled my hair in frustration.

Carl looked up from his book. "Are you okay?"

"It's just these blasted stitches in my scalp."

I sat down and tried to smile. Didn't feel it. Felt like screaming. "I'm taking a walk."

"Do you need directions?" Carl asked. "Should you ask Sophia or your aunt?"

"Nah, I'm just gonna mosey over to Constitution Square and see if I can read Pericles' speech."

"You already know what it says. That is not a fair translation test."

I grabbed my camera and headed east, walking without seeing. Stupid, clumsy, inept. No wonder Dustin dumped me.

33

Constitution Square

The bustle of Amalias Avenue surprised me. Had I really walked that far? I crossed through traffic to the east side of the street before heading north. The sidewalk led past the National Garden. Bees buzzed amidst pink oleander blossoms. Lush gardens tempted me into their cool beauty. I could lose myself and never come out, just make my own little retreat from the world.

A smile broke through my blue funk. I was in Greece. Greece, birthplace of Western civilization! This was too good to be true.

I resisted the garden and walked on.

Harsh afternoon sun washed color out of the sky and glared off the white marble monument and yellow stone Parliament building. The blocky building would be at home in any Western European city. European powers imposed a king on the Greek people after the Greek War of Independence. This had been his palace. The architect was from Munich.

Elite *Evzones* of the Presidential Guard marched in front of the Tomb of the Unknown Soldier. Today, they wore khaki summer uniforms. I giggled at macho soldiers dressed in short kilts (called *foustanélla*). They looked silly in white tights, tasseled garters and pompom clogs. Still, they were mighty fine specimens of Greek manhood—tall, tanned and toned.

On formal occasions, the soldiers wore white kilts with 400 pleats representing 400 years of Turkish occupation and a blue vest trimmed with silver braid.

The soldiers finished their symbolic pacing and froze at attention in front of tiny guard shacks. After a few pictures of the eye candy, I refocused on the marble tribute.

Pericles' words were carved on either side of a dying hoplite soldier. The Funeral Oration saluted the dead of the Peloponnesian War between the Athenians and the Spartans.

"Ἀνδρῶν ἐπιφανῶν

πᾶσα γῆ τάφος"

"Heroes have the whole earth as their tomb" was the translation I knew.

I searched the Greek letters. γῆ. *Ge.* As in geography or geology. Earth. The Greek letters in the word earth were green and yellow. I smiled at the image.

The bottom line made sense: all earth tomb.

I examined the top line. *Andron epiphanon.* The name Andreus meant manly. Epiphany was a triumphant appearance. Triumphant men. Yup. That could be heroes.

Pericles' words were reported by the historian Thucydides. What would Pericles say about heroes now, 2,400 years later?

Would he be surprised to see his Athens, defeated and devastated by the Spartans, sprawling four million people strong and capital of a unified Hellas? How would he deal with the current financial crisis? In Pericles time, they could melt down the gold plating on the Athena statue or mine more silver at Laurinum. But those sources had been tapped out 2,000 years ago.

Noise from Constitution Square caught my attention.

Riot police formed a human wall at the top of the marble steps leading from the historic square up to Amalias Avenue and the Parliament Building. Greece's economic woes were the topic of the protest, no doubt. I dashed across the avenue and aimed my camera down into the square from behind the police.

A cluster of protestors chanted in the east end. In the rest of the square, tourists ate snacks, shopped and strolled into fancy hotels that border the square.

A nice little demonstration. Polite, controlled. During general strikes, demonstrators overflowed the square, blocked access to the hotels and broke shop windows.

The crowd swelled as commuters spilled out of the metro stop near the steps. I maneuvered so the demonstrators' faces were framed by the backs and shields of the police— dramatic pictures.

People surged behind me. I tried to hold my position, but momentum pushed me closer to the police line. Hot bodies bumped and jostled against me. Sweat trickled down my back as I bounced between protestors.

Chants echoed from behind me. Some of the officers on the steps turned to face us. The protestors on Amelias Avenue surged toward their cohorts in the square.

Bodies pressed from all sides.

Couldn't catch my breath.

Get out! But how?

Keep moving toward the riot shields and clubs? Stop and get trampled?

Couldn't see a way out.

Couldn't think.

The tide of shouting humanity carried me toward the marble steps and the police.

Finally the shoving slowed. I raised my camera and started shooting again.

Behind us, a wedge of reinforcements advanced from the Parliament Building. We were trapped between two lines of police.

Beside me, an arm hurled a Molotov cocktail toward the honor guard at the monument. I kept shooting as a yell went up from the crowd.

The bottle exploded against the guard shack. The second flank of riot police turned and ran back toward the monument. As the guard shack burst into flames, the *Evzone* stood unflinching at his post.

I zoomed the camera into the drama in front of the monument. The commander shouted an order. The soldier slowly marched away from the shack as police rushed to snuff out his smoldering kilt. I prayed the pictures would be in focus.

Suddenly, hands grabbed for my camera. I wrapped my arms around it and tucked my chin in.

Rioters kept reaching for my camera and shoving. A sea of protesters pushed from the square, forcing us into Amalias Avenue. One of the men had his hand on my camera, but the neck strap held firm. I threw a few elbows and kicks. They might have my bust, but I would not give up my new camera without a fight.

The officers by the monument ran toward us. We were encircled.

I stumbled into a riot shield as the protesters broke through the line. An officer jerked my arm and dragged me off.

Should I try to escape? Not likely. I was tugged to the side of the square along with other apprehended rioters. The benches, normally filled with resting tourists, were lined with unhappy sweaty Greeks. Add one unhappy sweaty student.

As the rioters dispersed, calm returned. I gathered my courage. Stood and walked toward one of the guards. "American. American tourist," I tried to explain.

He asked me something.

I raised my hands and shrugged my shoulders. "I don't understand."

He pointed me back to the bench. I sat down and rested my head in my hands.

A bench mate spoke up. "He think you journalist. He ask for ID and passport."

I dug in my pocket for a cell phone, ID, anything. Nothing. Just stupid me and my camera. Dirt stained my clothes. Sweat stung my eyes. I wiped my face on the hem of my shirt. I felt like road kill.

A fellow captive finished talking on his cell and handed it to me. "Do not give them pictures, please," he asked. "The police will arrest more people."

Who could get me out of this mess? "Hello, Carl? I need help."

34

Rescued

About 10 minutes later, my rescuer pulled up in a cab armed with my purse and passport. Carl reassured the police that I was not a journalist, just an unlucky student. He negotiated my release and filled out paperwork while I smiled and nodded contritely.

As we climbed into the cab, I hugged Carl. "Thank you for rescuing me."

His smile flashed. "The officer said they pulled you over to keep you from being trampled. I promised you would not participate in any more riots. You are now on the police list of potential troublemakers, so stay away from protests."

"It looked like a calm little demonstration when I started taking pictures. I do feel bad for the Greek people caught in the government's economic woes. I didn't want to give the police my pictures so they could identify rioters."

"Hah!" Carl said. "It's the thieving Greek people who cause the economic collapse. Cheating on taxes is a national virtue. Businesses don't pay sales taxes, people don't pay income taxes. If they get caught they just bribe the tax collector."

The cab driver turned and spit out a phrase in Greek. Carl spit back in the same language.

I caught the phrase "*Klepts*." That seemed to be the focus of the argument between Carl and the cabbie.

At last, we reached our destination. The Institute never looked so good. The cabbie overcharged us; Carl tossed the money into the front seat with a Greek curse.

"What was that about?"

"*Ach!* I called them all *klepts*, thieves," Carl said. "He said *klepts* were national heroes. The *klepts* were outlaws in the mountains. They burglarized and sabotaged the Ottoman Turks. I told him that Greeks forgot how to be good citizens in those 400 years of cheating the Turks."

"We're lucky we survived the cab ride."

"These lazy cheats have no responsibility or honor. We should never have allowed them into the European Union. The government lies, the people cheat. The Germans are stuck bailing them out of their problems."

"I thought you liked the Greek people."

"Oh, I do like them," Carl said. "They are fun-loving, charming cheats. They are just too irresponsible to be part of modern Europe."

Was anyone good enough for Carl? No wonder he and Sophia got along so well. Still, he had rescued me. I braced for the embarrassment facing me inside.

We heard angry voices as we opened the front door.

"I thought you were working things out with the University," Lydia said

Carl and I glanced at each other.

"They constantly threaten to cut our funding. But Robert advocated for us," Sophia said. "We were working to secure a permanent endowment and funding agreement that awful weekend. It was what he wanted. Then he died and you just ignored us."

"I should have come to Athens sooner. I'm sorry."

"You have no concern for the Institute," Sophia said.

"How dare you think that?"

"You've moped for four months while the University screwed Robert's program. If you were not so apathetic, you would be fighting for it. Instead, you seem to condone the abuse."

Carl reopened the door and slammed it hard. "We're back," he announced loudly.

Sophia emerged from the library and started up the stairs.

Lydia followed her into the entry. "Let's brainstorm how to save the Institute in the morning."

Sophia continued up the stairs without a glance back.

"Well, hi, kids!" Lydia smiled broadly. "Sounds like you had quite an adventure."

35

Adrianou Street

Lydia treated us to dinner for our first evening together. After overhearing Sophia's opinion of me, I wasn't sure if I wanted to dip my bread in the same dish with her. And how could Lydia sit down with her? Still, it was a free meal.

"How did you meet *Frau* Jackson?" Carl asked Billy.

"We both serve on the board for the metropolitan food bank. I invited Lydia to a study series I was teaching on the Book of Revelation. That's when we got to know each other better."

"Is he a good teacher?" Carl asked Lydia.

"Fascinating." Lydia said.

Billy beamed.

The waiter delivered wine and appetizers. I tore off some pita and dug into the common bowl of *tzatziki.*

"I knew Lydia was a smart business woman, but I learned that she is also a thoughtful, spiritual person," Billy said.

Did Sophia roll her eyes?

"Before I forget, Andreus asked about your trip to the monastery," Lydia said. "The abbot requested copies of the photographs you took."

"When I get time, I'll select some pictures with Amber," Billy said. "I'd rather not send the manuscript pictures until I've had more time to study them."

I noted the arrival of *tiropita* and *spanakopita,* filo pastries filled with spinach and feta.

"Billy, you started to tell us about Revelation in the car last night," I asked. "What about things that 'must soon take place?' Can you explain that?"

"First, let me give you a little background on theology."

Billy paused to bite into a *tiropita*. I grabbed one, too.

"You've heard about the Rapture? The Rapture is not in the Bible. The concept dates to John Nelson Darby about 1830. His theology was called Premillennial Dispensationalism. It was big in nineteenth and twentieth century Protestant evangelical circles. But we've moved beyond that in twenty-first century theology."

"I'm confused," Sophia said. "You don't believe that the Christians will be swept off the Earth before the rest of us are judged?"

"No, I don't," Billy replied.

"What a relief! I thought you were one of those true believers who will leave the rest of us behind," Sophia said.

"Sophia, I'm a true believer, but I'm also a scholar."

"Now you see why I found Billy's class so thought-provoking," Lydia said.

The waiter refilled our wine glasses. I squeezed in a question. "So what's the key to understanding Revelation?"

"Revelation is God's prophecy. God's prophecies *always* come true. That's the key. Look at the events predicted, then look at history." Billy ate a *spanakopita* as we waited.

I nabbed a few Kalamata olives. Olives anywhere else just aren't as good as these salty dark red beauties.

"The first two prophecies in Revelation have already taken place."

"Huh?" Not a very articulate comment. No wonder Sophia thought I was a dope.

"Revelation's first two prophecies predict God's judgment on the corrupt officials in Jerusalem and on the Roman empire as punishment for their crucifixion of Christ. That happened in the destruction of Jerusalem and the fall of Rome. We're now leading up to the fulfillment of the third prophecy, the final triumph of God."

Billy's voice gained passion and confidence. "In the first chapter of Revelation, John is told that these things must take place 'with speed' and 'after these things.' That phrase, *meta tauta*, is repeated at the beginning of Chapter 4. So we need to look for fulfillment in the first century. Nothing was more significant to Jews and Christians than the destruction of Jerusalem and the dispersal of Christians and Jews."

"It was an important victory for the Romans also," Carl said. "The Arch of Titus in Rome shows Roman soldiers carrying the spoils from the sack of the Temple."

"Don't take my word for it," Billy said. "Compare John's prophecy of the destruction following the breaking of the seven seals to the writings of the Jewish historian Josephus. John and Josephus are obviously writing about the same events."

The main course arrived and we dug in. Greeks knew how to eat.

"Why don't you give some specific examples, Billy," Lydia prodded.

Between bites, Billy obliged.

"The four horsemen of the apocalypse are a good example. The rider of the black horse holds a scale. A voice says, 'A quart of wheat for a day's pay and three quarts of barley for a day's pay, and do not harm the oil and the wine.' This predicts famine and lack of food.

"Well, there were terrible food shortages in Jerusalem during the siege. Josephus writes about people selling what they had for a quart of wheat or three quarts of barley. Then he writes about people pillaging the sacred wine and oil from the temple."

Ironic. We were stuffing ourselves while talking about Jews starving under siege.

"That theology—that Jews should be punished for deicide, for the death of God—is dangerous," Sophia said. "That led to discrimination against the Jews in the Middle Ages, the holocaust in World War II. I thought good Christians knew better than to push that old agenda."

"Oh, I don't believe today's Christians should punish today's Jews. God punished the Jews who were actually responsible in 71 AD. The debt is paid. We're in a time when Jews and Muslims will join Christians in the ultimate rule of God."

Lydia changed the subject. "I learned a lot of first century history in Billy's class. History was Robert's expertise, not mine. So it was new to me."

"What *was* your area of expertise," Sophia asked. "Didn't you major in home economics?"

Catty! I looked at Lydia to see if she took it as an insult. She just smiled.

"Yes, I studied textile design. That's where universities put it back then. My family owned a cotton ranch and textile mill, so it made sense," Lydia smiled. "And it paid off, obviously."

Touché. Remind Sophia with all her advanced degrees that Lydia was the one with the money.

The two ladies raised their glasses to each other across the table. Carl poked me with his elbow as the waiter cleared away our plates. At least he wasn't being handsy under the table.

"*Loukoumades* and coffee?" I suggested.

Carl laughed. "How is it that you can't remember important Greek words but you know the name for every food?"

"It's written on the menu in real American letters. At least I won't starve."

"So describe this dessert," Billy said.

"*Loukoumade*s are gourmet donut holes, puffy little fried balls drenched in honey and sprinkled with cinnamon."

Sophia's phone buzzed. The color drained out of her face. "What? Now?"

She looked up. "There's a break-in at the Institute. The police are on the way."

36

Break-in

Lydia and Carl jumped up and pushed their way through the tables.

"Yes, yes, we're on our way," Sophia said into the phone as she got up. "That was the security company. The alarm just went off."

I gestured for a to-go box for the *loukoumades*.

"I can't believe you're worried about dessert," Sophia said.

"Go, go. I'll take care of the check." I waved Lydia's credit card in the air as Sophia and Billy hot-footed it after Lydia and Carl.

I caught up with Sophia and Billy just before we got to the Institute.

Lydia waited on the stoop. "The police are inside checking for burglars. They won't let us in until it's clear."

Carl emerged from the alley. "They broke a window in the back to get in. The back door to the kitchen is open. I don't know if the police opened it or if the burglar left through that door after the alarm went off."

Finally, the police finished searching and allowed us in. Sophia and Lydia went through the building with the investigator, but nothing seemed to be missing.

I swept up broken glass in the kitchen while making coffee to have with our donut holes. After the police left, we gathered in the library. Sophia turned up her nose as the rest of us nibbled sticky treats.

"I can't believe someone broke in," Lydia said. "I suppose I should try to get the window fixed tonight."

"Don't worry," Carl said. "I'll sleep on one of the couches here. That way I'll hear if anyone tries to come in."

Sophia found a copy of Josephus and flipped through pages. "Scholars cannot trust the text ... later Christian scribes probably altered it."

"True of all ancient documents," Billy said. "That's one of the variables that make history so interesting."

Sophia nodded as she read. Lydia found a bottle of wine and shared it around.

"Josephus doesn't get the credit he deserves for the spread of monotheism in Western civilization," Billy said.

"Your hero was a traitor to his people. After the Jewish War, he curried favor with the Roman victors. He made it sound like the war was the fault of the Jewish people," Sophia said.

"He was a prisoner of war," Billy said. "He recorded the motivations and actions of both sides in the hostilities. And he did a lot to explain the Jewish tradition to the West."

Sophia ignored Billy as he continued his lecture.

"Western civilization is founded on the Judeo-Christian tradition. And the spiritual and intellectual power of Western thought has certainly been proved in the past centuries," Billy said. "History shows the spread of our values: justice, mercy, forgiveness, righteousness."

"I don't know," Lydia said. "Sometimes I get discouraged when I see the sad state of the world." She kicked off her high heels.

"It's in those dark times that we must focus on the light. Look at Martin Luther King or Mother Teresa," Billy said. "The Holy Spirit is powerful."

"So why are you drinking wine in air-conditioned comfort instead of healing lepers?" Sophia said.

He stretched his legs and slumped into the soft leather. "I worry that I'm not doing enough for the Lord. But my gifts are language and discernment. I've been given the ability to dig into the Word and share that insight. My calling is to educate, to change people's thoughts."

"So if we don't believe in Dispensationalism anymore, what do we believe?" I asked.

"We believe in the ultimate victory of God," Billy said. "I'm more optimistic than the Dispensational crowd. The Bible says the law of God and the authority of Jesus will take dominion over the whole world. Jesus will return to a world transformed by the Good News and the power of the Holy Spirit."

"You cannot be serious." Sophia put down Josephus and faced Billy. "You intend to impose Christianity on the world? What a farce."

Billy straightened. "This is spiritual warfare. The Bible tells us God wins in the end."

"That is insanely retrograde. Un-American." Sophia returned Josephus to the shelf.

"It most certainly is American!" Bill stood up, towering over Sophia. "Our Founding Fathers believed that Divine Providence guided our new nation. And God is still leading us."

Sophia stared right back. "Do you know how sexist and xenophobic that sounds?"

Billy raised his eyebrows. "Sexist?"

"You know 'Founding Fathers' is offensive to women."

"Hey, don't blame me. It's a fact that the patriots were men."

Lydia shot me a smile. Score one for women. I should find some female founders so I can shake up a pub quiz question.

37

A Purple-born Son

Constantinople, A.D. 938

Constantine VII set out hand-written books of Roman law, assisted by his purple-born princesses.

He smiled at little Agatha and Zoe. Girls received the same education as boys. Constantine's daughters and their tutors were welcome companions in their father's library.

Constantine was the one with royal blood, but he was relegated to junior co-emperor status. At least his father-in-law, Emperor Romanos, was finally showing respect. For years, Constantine had been relegated to entertaining foreign diplomats and attending ceremonies of the church.

Romanos had groomed his eldest son as his successor. When Christopher died in 931, he turned to Constantine as an assistant. Constantine smiled. His two brothers-in-law and their preening wives would be livid that the emperor sought his help again.

A former admiral, Romanos put the army and navy first. The Roman system guaranteed a ready group of soldiers. Those who served honorably were given land. The small farms provided a living for the families. In return the families provided loyal young men to defend the Empire.

The wealthy aristocratic families, however, liked to gobble up land and turn the independent farmers into serfs.

Romanos made his usual bold, crude entrance.

"So, my son, what have you learned?" The voice boomed

through the marble-lined room. "How can I keep those greedy bastards from gutting my army?"

"My grandfather and father started updating the laws. We have strong precedence back for almost a thousand years. We can draw the laws together, strengthen and clarify the rules restricting transfer of veteran lands."

"Good, let it so be."

"Will you take on the wealthy landed families? Laws mean nothing without enforcement."

"You write the law," Romanos said. "Leave enforcement to me. I will take care of it, even if we have to hack the balls off a few of those lazy leeches."

Constantine's daughters played around his knees as he instructed the scribes.

His chamberlain entered and bowed. "Excuse the interruption, most excellent one."

"Speak."

"The time has come. The midwives have been called and Empress Helena has been moved to the Purple Room."

He loved his daughters, but an emperor—even a powerless junior co-emperor—needed a son as a legacy. Would the day bring another daughter or the prayed-for son?

"Call my guards to escort me to *Hagia Sophia*. I will light candles for the Empress and my child. We will dedicate the Divine Liturgy to them."

Constantine recalled the frightened 13-year-old who had made this journey with his 10-year-old bride. He and Helena had become a good team during the past 19 years. He had knowledge and royal blood; she brought boldness and tenacity that he lacked.

He paused under the royal door to acknowledge his father, then proceeded to the nave. The patriarch had been informed of the special dedication for today's service.

Constantine enjoyed the liturgy's formality and chanting. He squared his shoulders with pride when he saw the chalice. The cup, crafted to Constantine's design, was used when Constantine was present for the Divine Liturgy.

The silver octagon base symbolized baptism and resurrection. The bowl was carved from a huge sardonyx gemstone. The morning sun struck the chalice, casting a tint of the red wine through the white swirls of onyx. Light sparkled off the embossed silver rim of the cup, revealing the palm leaves of the Tree of Life in Paradise.

Finally, the liturgy was finished. His chamberlain met Constantine in the narthex.

"Most high emperor, you have a son."

"And Helena? How is she?"

"The Empress is also well."

Constantine paused. Tonight, he would celebrate the birth of his son with friends. There would be wine, music and feasting. But first, he must thank God. He turned and reentered the church.

This son would be named after Helena's father. Would the usurper be pleased that his daughter had given him a legitimate purple-born grandson?

Constantine would compile a book of advice for his son. *His* Romanos would not be an uncouth commoner like the current emperor. Constantine would teach him the wisdom and grace of a true Roman emperor.

38

Memories

"A certain woman named Lydia, a worshiper of God, was listening to us; she was from the city of Thyatira and a dealer in purple cloth." Acts 16:14

After the break-in and squabbling, I couldn't focus on my studies. I stared at my questions on the marker board.

On the left I had written:

"Uncle Robert"

"Is it a fake?"

"Who pushed me?"

I added "Theft?" and "Be Careful Bees."

The questions on the right were more academic:

"What does Revelation mean?

"Who is Constantine Purple-born?"

I checked that off. At least I had answered one question.

"Theft?"

The question drew me back. I jerked open the desk drawer. Uncle Robert's box was still there. I quickly checked the contents. The burglars had not gotten this far.

I took my Greek New Testament to bed. Lydia and I fluffed up the feather pillows to read. Lots of pillows, because the back of my head hurt more than yesterday. My bruises were turning green and stitches made it hard to comb my hair.

I turned a page. More Greek. Yuck! The letters were becoming orderly colored symbols instead of chaos, but it was still Revelation in Greek. I couldn't stand another minute.

"What do you know about purple dye? Carl says it was very rare, but I see purple cloth all the time," I asked Lydia.

"Now, we use chemical dyes. A chemist invented a purple dye in the mid-1800s and purple exploded as a color. Queen Victoria loved the new purple. Impressionist painters filled their images with lavenders. Before that, it was the dark, wine-colored purple that they milked from snails."

That made sense. Did I dare ask about synesthesia?

"Tell me about Uncle Robert's synesthesia."

"It bugged him at first, but once he knew what it was, he considered it almost an extra sense—a secret extra tool. Why do you ask?"

I pointed to my head. "I see letters in color. If I would have talked to him... when I got in trouble at school, Mom and Dad said I was crazy and should keep my mouth shut."

"Robert kept it quiet, too. People just don't understand." Lydia grabbed a tissue and blotted her eyes.

I hadn't wanted to make her cry. Time to change the subject.

"Why did you and Uncle Robert open a textile import business in Greece? I've always wondered why you traveled so much."

Lydia set aside her book. "Actually, we wanted an excuse to spend time in Greece and the Middle East."

She smiled at the memory. "Robert majored in history, so my parents gave us a trip to Italy, Greece and Turkey for our honeymoon. We vowed to come back."

"I thought you had to travel for business."

"Not at first. Our next trip was Egypt. We wanted to write off the trip. So, I collected textile samples and visited Egyptian cotton mills and wholesalers. Before we knew it, we were importing textiles and exporting cotton to justify our trips."

Lydia hopped out of bed, unlocked the closet and started rummaging. Behind the locked door was a trove of artifacts and expensive items.

"Here's the photo album from our honeymoon trip."

"Oh, you look so young! Uncle Robert looks like pictures of my dad when he was younger and my brothers now. I see the family resemblance."

"Robert didn't think of himself as handsome, but I always thought he was the best-looking man in any room, certainly the smartest. Y'all get your brains and good looks from Robert and your dad. The Jacksons have genius genes."

"I love this one of you in front of the Parthenon. And eating in the Plaka."

We giggled over the faded color snapshots.

"In the 60s and 70s, the economy in Greece was really bad. We saw this run-down building in the Plaka and immediately bought it. It was convenient to have an office in Europe, plus it gave us a tax-deductible home overseas. I've got a picture of it somewhere."

Lydia flipped through the pages to find the snapshot.

"It was a dump! Weren't you worried about owning a building overseas?"

"Robert was good at finding local people and negotiating deals. Once our building was livable, we found ourselves with a constant stream of guests, even when we weren't here," Lydia smiled.

"Then, the alumni office found out we had a home in Athens. We couldn't hold all the graduate students and professors on sabbatical. Robert solved that problem by buying the building next door."

"Oh. I thought the Institute was here first, then you located next to it."

"Oh, no, no. Robert and the dean dreamed up the Institute. It gave the University an overseas program, plus Robert could support his alma mater and indulge his passion for history. And the dean had an excuse to travel to Europe."

Lydia dug out albums of trips to Egypt, Istanbul and the Greek

Islands. They were laughing in all the snapshots.

"What's your favorite place?"

"At first, we were awed by the historic sites. Then, as we developed business relationships and friendships, we became drawn to the people."

"Hah! Uncle Robert is dancing like Zorba, the Greek."

"We loved the Plaka in the old days, before it became a tourist trap. Back then, the family-owned *tavernas* were filled with local people. The shops had Greek handcrafted items, not junk imported from China to sell to tourists. Real people danced, not paid performers for tourists."

Tears glistened in Lydia's eyes.

I wrapped my arms around her. "I'm sorry I made you sad."

"These are happy sad tears. It's good to cry because I have wonderful memories instead of crying because I feel empty and alone."

"I'm so sorry your time with Uncle Robert was cut short."

"We were so careful about bee stings. We don't even grow flowers in the yard. And Robert kept EpiPens everywhere."

"You took really good care of him."

"I suppose we got careless—it was such a warm weekend. Sophia was there to work on plans for the Institute, and we had a charity dinner for the food bank. I thought it was okay to set up tables on the patio. Someone must have left the doors open. Or maybe the florist brought bees in with the arrangements. Who would expect a swarm of bees in the house in February?"

"Don't blame yourself."

"But I do. I should have noticed bees in his den. I should have been there to hear him fall. When he dropped the EpiPen I could have reached it for him. He was suffocating and I wasn't there to save him."

I passed her a handful of tissues.

"Did the police come? Did they check the EpiPen for fingerprints?"

"I called 911 when I came home and found his body. The medics wouldn't even try to save him—they said he was already dead. The police filed a report since it was an unattended death. Then we had to wait for the medical examiner's office and the mortuary."

I hugged her as she cried on my shoulder.

"Enough tears," Lydia said. "I allow myself ten minutes a day."

We put away the photo albums and turned out the light.

Robert's death kept replaying in my mind. For the life of me, I could not see how his EpiPen managed to fall from his desk drawer and roll all the way across the room under the bookcase. And why would his final message be, "Be Careful Bees"? Lydia wasn't allergic to them. What was his dying message to us?

I always hoped I would find my soul-mate like Lydia and Robert did. So far, love had eluded me. Instead of an engagement ring, I got a lecture about my commitment to the Lord. My parents said someone who loves you doesn't ask you to change. Those words of comfort just reinforced my bad judgment.

Maybe love was overrated. Lydia was devastated by love. A summer fling with Carl might not be a bad idea—no commitment, no tears. And Carl *had* rescued me from the riot.

I rolled over for much-needed rest.

Rumbling intruded on the silence. Flashes of fire exploded, sticking to trees and grass. Hail and blood rained down with the fire. The earth began to shake.

I struggled awake. Why was the riot so awful in my dream? Fire and blood raining down from heaven? Oh, Hell—more images from Revelation. The seven angels with trumpets raining destruction on the earth.

Makes my life seem downright pleasant.

DAY FIVE

"Let the waters bring forth swarms of living creatures, and let birds fly above the earth across the dome of the sky." Genesis 1:20

Five is the number of Moses, the number of authority. The Teachings—Torah—contain the five books of Moses. In Greek, these books are known as the Pentateuch (five containers).

The five foundational books for Christians are the four gospels plus the Acts of the Apostles.

Five refers to a handful, five fingers.

In medieval Western Europe, the pentagram or five-pointed star represented the five wounds of Christ, used to ward off witches. In modern times, the pentagram has been twisted into a symbol of witchcraft.

The Greek numeral for five is *epsilon* (E ε).

40

Thursday

Lydia looked around the unhappy circle gathered in her apartment. The sound of workmen replacing the broken window drifted in from the alley.

So much for my anticipation of working on a team of committed scholars.

I poured coffee and offered pastries. Sophia turned everything down. Carl, seated on the sofa beside her, took a cup of coffee. Lydia settled for coffee, too. Billy sprawled in Uncle Robert's chair. He wasn't shy about breakfast. I put the pastries on the end table beside him and pulled up a chair so we could share.

"Should we fight to save the Institute as it is, change it in some way, or just let the University shut it down?" Lydia asked. "That's why we're together this morning."

"What's the problem?" Billy asked.

Sophia answered. "The University is pulling funding. The dean claims he doesn't have the budget to support my salary here. I am back on campus teaching a full load in the fall. He's just making excuses."

Lydia nodded. "Sophia is right. I'm not sure why they pulled this stunt."

"Do you need university funding?" It was a stupid, simple question, but I asked anyway.

"We need affiliation to offer academic credit," Sophia said. "Plus benefits, tenure, retirement, those sorts of things. It's more than just salary."

"We already endow the chair to supplement the salary for the extra expenses abroad," Lydia said. "The University's costs are really quite small."

"What did the University tell you, Lydia?" Billy asked.

"I've had several meetings with the president, the dean and the endowment chair. They change the subject and talk about building plans. They have architect's drawings for the Robert Jackson Humanities Center, his so-called legacy."

"Ahhh," I said. "They know you sold the company and want a big chunk of change, not just annual support for the Institute."

"But why punish the Institute? Are they trying to make me mad?" Lydia asked.

"If the Institute is not a priority for you, why should it be for the University?" Sophia said.

Lydia looked at Sophia. Sophia stared back.

"This is getting nowhere," Lydia stood and paced.

"What should the Institute be? And what will it take to save it?" Carl asked. "We should talk about that."

Lydia sat back down. "Thank you. Those are the questions. Any thoughts?"

We looked at each other. Who would go first?

"Sophia, tell us your plan," Carl prompted.

"Before this fiasco, I wrote a proposal for a more rigorous academic program. We waste resources on students who treat their time here as a vacation in Greece. We could be on the cutting edge of Classic scholarship by focusing on upper level and graduate programs. We don't need to babysit undergraduates."

Was Sophia talking about me? I focused on my coffee.

Carl joined in. "We implemented some of Sophia's plans last school year. In the fall semester, graduate students and professors worked on independent research. Twice a week the group met to share results and advice. But my favorite was the spring semester. We offered a curriculum for upper level and graduate credit."

Carl paused. "Officially, I taught art history and architecture while Sophia taught history, political science and research. But we took a team-teaching approach. It was an interdisciplinary immersion that was transformational for the students."

"Robert was excited about Sophia's ideas," Lydia said. "His one worry was that the Institute wouldn't have room for serendipity. Robert believed in throwing people together from different areas. He liked being exposed to different ideas and places, thinking in new ways."

"But we can not be everything to everybody," Sophia protested. "We are fighting for survival. A small institution like ours must specialize."

Lydia turned to Billy for his ideas.

"The Institute limits its approach to history. You only look at classical Greece and the Mediterranean. It's over-studied. Then you miss whole eras. You completely ignore Biblical studies."

"So you would change the focus," Lydia said. "Any ideas on how we save this?"

"Cut costs and raise revenues," Billy said. "I'm sure real estate is pricey here in the Plaka. The University could sell this and buy in a different neighborhood. That would ease the financial strain."

Carl and I both stiffened. Sophia scorched Billy with her stare.

"That would ruin the experience," Carl protested. "We are crowded with 12 students, but that's part of the success. We study together with intense passion in this wonderful place."

"Plus the University doesn't own the building," Sophia said. "Robert and I were working on plans that weekend he died. He told me he would donate both buildings and set up a permanent endowment. I thought he had put it in writing. Instead, the building went to Lydia's new foundation. No wonder University is pulling funding."

It felt downright icy. I refilled cups with hot coffee. Lydia looked at me. I gulped.

"I've just been here a few days, but I like the location and the close experience. Maybe you could add a guest professor to expand the curriculum."

"Stop talking about 'what if' and focus on saving this place," Sophia said.

"Okay," Lydia said. "What plan do we take to the University and to the Jackson Foundation?"

"But aren't you the foundation?" Sophia asked.

"Yes and no. It will have a board and guidelines for grant requests." Lydia took a sip of coffee and pondered her answer. "After we sold the company, Robert and I got hit up for donations at every cocktail party. The new foundation gives me a layer of protection.

"In a way, this summer is my experiment in serendipity. Amber's interest is outside our normal scope." Lydia turned to me. "When you asked for help with Greek, I saw the potential for something special. By putting you and Billy together with Sophia and Carl, everyone sees new things."

Sophia stood and picked up her notes. "I do not believe in serendipity. Scholarship is discipline, not chance."

"I'm trying to help. Isn't that what you've been asking for?" Lydia asked.

"Help? First you ignore me then you send a charlatan to sit in Robert's chair and an idiot as your surrogate. Can't you make a decision by yourself?"

Sophia marched out. Carl gave a shrug of his shoulders and followed her.

"What have I done to tick her off?" Billy bitched. "I know we disagreed last night, but I hoped it was a discussion among colleagues."

"You got off lucky," I said. "You're just a charlatan. I'm the idiot."

"She's mad at me, not you two." Lydia put her head in her hands. "That went as well as a tornado in a trailer park."

I picked up coffee cups and breakfast remnants. I could clean up this mess. The mess facing Lydia would not be as easy to clear away.

Billy and I stared at each other. Lydia retreated to her bedroom. I grabbed my interlinear so Billy could help me with today's Revelation assignment, Rev. 6 and 7.

I laid out the photographs of the Revelation cycle at the monastery.

"It's hard to believe God sent all this violence and suffering on Jerusalem. The seven seals and the seven trumpets are grim."

Billly pointed. "Here, this one of the sixth seal. This prophecy came true during the destruction of Jerusalem. Josephus wrote about how the last survivors—the tyrants—hid in the caves and caverns under Jerusalem. He writes, 'they were not able to hide either from God or from the Romans.' His descriptions match very closely with the prophecy John had written."

"It's hard to see this as good news."

Billy picked out the pictures of Rev. 6:9-11 and Rev. 7:1.

"Here, in this one right before the sixth seal, we see the martyrs crying for justice and receiving white robes. And right after the sixth seal the angels put a protective mark on the believers' foreheads. If you recall history, the Jewish believers escaped to Pella before the siege, fulfilling this prophecy. You have to look for images of salvation placed between the seven seals, the seven trumpets and the seven cups."

I made a mental note to look for this symbolism.

Lydia suddenly entered. "Aren't we going to the museum this morning?"

We went.

As we stepped out the front door, I tripped over some debris on the front stoop. I picked up the pieces.

It was Pericles. My stolen bust. A word was scrawled across his helmet: *"Klept."*

I shivered despite the heat. The shopping bag thief had found me.

41

Byzantine and Christian Museum

Morning sun shimmered on the gray-white walls of Villa Ilissia as the cab dropped us off at the Byzantine and Christian Museum. Two stories of arched colonnade porches gave grace to the facade. The palace was built for an American heiress in 1837, shortly after Athens became capital of the new Greek nation.

We stepped from summer glare into cool air and soft light, a warp of time and season. The Neoclassical exterior gave way to a modern, crisp interior. Thick marble walls hushed the noise of the city. The rich patina of the Byzantine-era relics and icons invited us in.

The musty aroma of old books lingered in the manuscript rooms in spite of preservation and glass cases.

"I need late uncial manuscript samples to date my fragment. Start in the ninth and tenth centuries and work back. Copy the IDs for me so I can request images by the acquisition number," he instructed.

My work wasn't hard, because there were few manuscripts that old. Billy examined the ancient documents with an old-fashioned magnifying glass.

"Now I need to use the library. I hope they have space. They only let three scholars in at a time," Billy said.

As Billy signed in at the desk, I checked messages. Mr. Scruffy from Meteora had sent a text.

Re: Macedonian Sun and Mary's star. Classics are not my area—I don't know much about the Macedonian Sun. Mary's star has four or eight points. It represents virginity. You also see it in Nativity scenes—the star in the East, the Christ star. Also stars in the sky. Sometimes even mosaics in the floor. So maybe it's a symbol of the incarnation.

You're worried about the monks, and they're worried about your group. What is your boss looking at?

We need to get together! If I can't tempt you with a dragon cave in Meteora, I could give you a tour of church icons in Athens. Or we could go to Hosios Loukas. It's awesome

I tapped a quick reply:

We are at the Byzantine Museum looking at 9th and 10th century uncial manuscript samples. Something to do with dating fragments. I have no idea what Dr. Sullivan is studying. Athens is a long way from Meteora. That sounds like a lot of effort just to answer questions about Christian iconography. What's so special about Hosios Loukas?

The next message was from my least favorite man. I decided to share some of Billy's insights with a certain person who was on fire for Revelation.

You can stop worrying about me. My studies are great and I'm getting a good feel for Greek. In fact, I might even put a joy in the prayer list. My Greek teacher is an amazing Biblical scholar. We're studying Revelation. There's quite a history of failed predictions of the End Times. Even in Paul's time Christians worried about the delay of the Second Coming. End Time predictors don't have a good track record.

Billy finished at the desk. "They can take me in a few minutes. My research may take an hour or so."

"Don't worry, we can entertain ourselves," Lydia said. "I haven't seen the textile exhibit since the museum was redone."

We went in search of old fabrics.

"My favorites are the Coptic textiles from Egypt," Lydia said. "I have some Coptic pieces that we got in Cairo before it became illegal to export them. I'll get them out tonight and put them up."

She paused before a child's tunic with two bands of woven decoration.

"I like the rich, bold colors of the wool against the flax or linen. The themes are natural, everyday images ... people, flowers, animals," Lydia said. "After the Christians lost Egypt to the Arabs, images of people disappear, but you still find flowers and animals."

An embroidered angel called to me. "This is amazing for being almost 2,000 years old. I love the greens, blues, brick red and tans."

Lydia nodded. "Yes, those colors inspired one of our textile collections in the 80s. It's always been one of my favorite design efforts."

I noticed an eight-pointed star. "Carl says the Byzantines stole the Virgin Star from the ancient Greeks, from the Macedonian Star."

"It certainly wouldn't be the first time a culture borrowed a symbol from the past and gave it a new meaning," Lydia said. "So how are you coming with your Greek? Is Billy helping at all?"

"Yes, definitely. He taught me to write the Greek letters, not just read them. I've done a color-coded chart matching the Greek to the Latin alphabet. So now I can see the letters in the right color."

The next gallery featured more elaborate Byzantine pieces. The affluent must have loved patterned fabrics with brilliant colors and sensual textures. The scraps spoke of quality craftsmanship and prosperity.

"This doesn't look like the Dark Ages."

"The concept of the Dark Ages comes from Western Europe," Lydia said. "The western half of the Roman Empire fell to the `barbarians' in the fifth century. History ignores the Eastern Roman Empire, which lasted another thousand years. The Greeks didn't forget about books, math, or engineering. And they certainly kept their taste for fine living."

We browsed along displays of woven silk fabrics alive with lions, birds, vines and flowers arranged in geometric patterns and roundels. The opulence of the priestly garments stunned me. A brilliant red silk robe was embroidered with real gold thread and embellished with appliqués and pearls. I tried to picture Father Gabriel in such garb. Somehow, his simple black robes seemed to fit his faith better.

We checked the library to see if Billy was finished, then I steered us to an exhibit of metalwork. Frankly, Uncle Robert's broken chalice was nicer than most of the museum's collection. The materials and motifs seemed similar, though. I tried not to act too curious.

Billy found us in the gift shop.

"How did your research go? Find anything interesting?"

"Lydia, I'll tell you about it later." His voice dropped to a whisper: "They're too interested in what I'm doing."

An inexpensive brass goblet with embossed Byzantine motifs and Greek letters caught my eye. I made a quick purchase before following Billy and Lydia out of the museum.

42

We couldn't miss the note on the message board in the entry hall at the Institute. "Dr. Sullivan—See me! Dr. Wright"

"What have I done to offend that snob now?" Billy muttered.

We traipsed up the stairs to Sophia's office and apartment on the second floor.

The director's rooms echoed the Neoclassical exterior of the Institute's building. Persian rugs (the real thing) softened hardwood floors. The furniture was an eclectic combination of styles and ages, too well made to be new. An ancient amphora balanced in a brass stand atop the bookcase.

Sophia worked at her computer.

Billy interrupted. "You wanted to see me? What's up?"

"Dr. Karmanos called. He's coming to interview you about your research."

"That was fast. The librarian was nosy, but I expected it would be a day or two before anyone followed up."

"Sit down. What are you working on?"

Lydia and Billy took the arm chairs. I pulled in a chair from the conference room and tried to blend into the background.

"They know what I checked today at the library. Dr. Karmanos probably briefed them about our visit to the monastery," Billy said.

"Their interest could be good for your research and for the reputation of the Institute," Lydia said.

"We need to be cautious," Sophia said. "We already have an excellent reputation. Dr. Sullivan, you need to be solid in your scholarship or it will reflect badly on us."

"I assume we cooperate with the Ministry of Culture," Lydia said. "Any downside to telling them what you're working on?"

"Well, as Sophia said, I need to be sure of my conclusions before announcing anything. And scholars always need to protect their interests. I called my publisher and some friends. One of my colleagues is coming tomorrow to help me."

"If you're already talking to your publisher, this must be big," Lydia said. "So just between friends, what do you have?"

We waited.

"Obviously, it's too early to be sure. ..." Billy stood and paced.

We watched.

"It's an early church writing. Translators have worked from a damaged Old Latin version. This fragment is Greek. It could be closer to the original."

"That seems safe," Lydia said. "Not like scripture."

"Not so, Lydia. Early witnesses who comment and quote from early scripture are a key to dating and verifying the Christian Bible.

"This early witness tells about writing the New Testament. It could push back the dates of some of the books. It could change Christian theology."

"Holy shit!" It just slipped out.

I got kicked out.

43

Number of the Beast

"It causes all, both small and great, both rich and poor, both free and slave, to be marked on the right hand or forehead so that no one can buy or sell who doe not have the mark, that is, the name of the beast or the number of its name. This calls for wisdom: let anyone with understanding calculate the number of the beast, for it is the number of a person. Its number is six hundred sixty-six." Revelation 13:16-18

Patmos, First Century

Why had God allowed the Romans to punish Jerusalem? John had done his best to explain that horrible time. Now, the punishment of the Jews who crucified the Son of God was finished.

Justice will come, he must reassure his churches. God will punish those who persecuted the followers of The Way.

The seven-headed beast had filled his head since the vision. John used a Hebrew code to so believers could read the name, but not Greek or Latin speakers.

He wrote *N R W N Q S R (Neron Kaiser)* and converted the letters to their corresponding numbers in Hebrew. 50 + 200 + 6 + 50 + 100 + 60 + 200.

He calculated the total: 666.

44

Since I had been kicked out of the adults' meeting, I found Carl.

The name still seemed wrong for him. "Carl" was all red and yellow, intense and passionate. Carl the person, for all his flirting, was cooler. He hid his real thoughts behind the banter.

"What do you know about studying manuscript fragments?" I asked. "And don't give me the usual shit about not being your area of expertise."

He laughed.

"There are four things. First, is it real or a forgery? Second, what is its date and source? Third, can you translate it? Fourth, what does it mean? Each is a different expertise," Carl explained. "Why do you ask?"

"Billy's found something significant."

Carl got up from his laptop and stretched. He made even that motion sensual.

"It could take weeks or months to make a thorough study and verification," he said. "Dr. Sullivan does not have the credentials or facilities to do it on his own."

"Oh. That makes sense. Have you had lunch?"

Carl smiled. "Let's pack a picnic and hike through the Acropolis and Ancient Agora. I'll raid the refrigerator."

We loaded a backpack with cheese, bread, fruit and Carl's wine.

The doorbell rang. We looked at each other. The doorbell never rang. No one came here except the people who studied and lived here. And we all had keys.

Carl opened the door to a middle-aged man in a business suit. "Dr. Karmanos, what a surprise."

"I am here to see Dr. Sullivan. I spoke to Dr. Wright earlier. They are expecting me."

Not quite so soon, I suspected. Carl escorted Karmanos to the library, then ran upstairs to report our visitor. That left me to be friendly but uninformative.

Karmanos moved closer to a framed collection of old coins and raised his glasses to see the details.

"Interesting."

"My uncle Robert collected a coin portrait of each Roman emperor. He said it made history come alive."

He moved to a cabinet with architectural fragments and pieces of pottery. They looked old to me, but what do I know? I bet he did.

Thankfully, Sophia came downstairs. "How can we help you, Dr. Karmanos?"

"As I told you, I would speak with Dr. Sullivan about research. Before this week, I had not worked with your institute, so I also hope for a tour. You have very fine artifacts here."

"Perhaps we can work something out that will respect the privacy of Dr. Sullivan's scholarship and meet your needs," Sophia said. "Carl and Amber, we don't need you. I'm sure you have plans."

"*Ja*, I am taking Amber on a hike through the Acropolis and Agora this afternoon."

We headed to the kitchen to finish packing our lunch. Lydia came to get beverages for the guest.

She slipped me a key and spoke softly. "Before you leave, could you lock my closet? And lock my apartment and the doors between the two buildings. He seems too interested in the artifacts in the library. I don't want him in my personal things."

We cut through the back hall and slipped into the Jackson Textile Imports building to secure Aunt Lydia's apartment.

I locked her trove of artifacts and antiquities. A few pottery and fabric samples had worked their way out onto the tables and walls of the apartment.

While Carl locked the other doors, I grabbed Uncle Robert's goblet and put it in a backpack.

We cut up the stairs. Carl's room at the front of the Jackson building had a balcony overlooking the street. He had artfully arranged photographs, maps and architectural drawings of classic temples on the walls. His bookcase was meticulously ordered. A life-size Greek helmet rested on the desk.

"That's a sweet replica."

Carl shook his head "Not a replica. Your uncle loaned it to me when I took the job here."

"Oh. I see why Lydia wants to keep Karmanos out."

We locked more doors as we crossed back into the Institute building.

As we walked down the main stairs Billy's voice carried up. "Will your experts sign confidentiality agreements? I must protect first publication rights."

"That is totally unacceptable. You seem to forget that these fragments belong to us, not you," Karmanos protested.

"Actually, they belong to the monastery," Sophia said.

Karmanos' assistants lounged against their double-parked car in front of the Institute. Carl greeted them in Greek as we set off to walk the path of the ancients.

45

Acropolis and Agora

"Those old Greeks, our celebrated ancestors, are a nuisance and I'll tell you why. They haunt us. We can never be as great as they were, nobody can. They make us feel guilty." Patrick Leigh Fermor in "Roumeli"

Tourists crowded Plaka shops buying leather goods and tee-shirts. Merchants stood on the sidewalk, coaxing potential customers into their shops. "Come in and see. I will make you a good deal."

Carl pointed. The tee featured a drawing of the famous statue of David and the word "Athens." We actually laughed out loud.

"Do you suppose we can buy tee-shirts in Florence picturing the Parthenon?" I said.

Carl just shook his head. It was impossible to underestimate the taste of tourists.

We headed south toward the new Acropolis Museum at the foot of the Acropolis. I looked back over my shoulder. Had I seen that black ball cap before? And that profile looked familiar.

"Carl, someone is following us."

"Of course, people are following us. This is the main street to the museum and the south entrance to the Acropolis."

I picked up the pace.

"Slow down, you'll wear us out," he complained.

I ignored him.

The sidewalk to the museum crossed above an archeological excavation under the building itself. The modern city was built on top of ancient Athens.

Carl paused at the excavation. "We'll skip the museum today. I think it helps to see the sites first, then the sculptures."

"I'll just use the bathroom." I glanced behind.

The cloakroom had lockers for backpacks and packages. I secured Uncle Robert's goblet in a locker and hid the key in my bra.

Tour buses belched their hordes on the south slope of the Acropolis. Carl and I joined the river of people. Guides herded groups, shouting instructions and history in a polyglot of languages.

The tiny Temple of Athena Nike perched on the edge of the hilltop, outside the walled high city. We resisted the flow of humanity and paused at the jewel.

"This temple has been assembled three times," Carl said. "Restoration scholars take it apart and put it back together as they learn more and develop new theories."

I laughed. "Don't tell me that restoring temples is like putting together a jigsaw puzzle."

"*Doch*, very much so. That is why it is not a dead area of study as Billy thinks. We now use computer modeling and GPS data to learn more and make virtual reconstructions."

Carl lingered.

"It is so small and elegant," I said.

"It is one of my favorites. Inside is just five meters square. This temple breaks the rules. It has Ionic columns, but they are a 7:1 ratio like Doric columns. Normally, an Ionic column is 9:1 or even 10:1. Ionic columns look tall and delicate. But these columns look solid. This temple was built to ask for Athena's help in the war against the Spartans. *Nike* means victory."

We entered the Acropolis through the ruins of the *Propylaea*, the massive gateway.

"The Brandenburg Gate in Berlin is modeled after this," Carl said. "The gates kept out the undesirables. Criminals and slaves could not come and claim protection of the gods."

We walked through the remains of white marble columns and walls as craftsmen worked on restoration.

Maybe I could break through Carl's cool veneer. "Why do you study ancient architecture?"

"It's innately beautiful. It has balanced proportion. The repetition of elements—like the columns—sets up a rhythm. It is the foundation for everything we think is beautiful today. I study mathematical relationships in classic architecture. Proportion and number are important. I seek pattern and order in the world. This is my quest for truth, my search for the divine."

We emerged into sun glaring off the limestone hill beneath our feet and the marble structures that surrounded us.

To our right was the Parthenon; to the left was the *Erechtheum*.

The massive columns of the Parthenon were built by stacking huge drums of carved marble. The builders joined the drums with wooden pegs, then wet the wood so it would swell to a tight connection that stabilized the stacked column.

The original marble had weathered to a soft, warm gold as minerals in the stone rusted over the past 2,500 years. Some missing drums had been replaced by concrete tinted to a similar golden tone, the work of early reconstruction projects. Workmen had just finished making brilliant white drums that shimmered and sparkled in the sun.

"Today, workers use new marble from the ancient quarry to replace broken and missing pieces. The quarry is set aside for restoration work," Carl explained.

The gaping center of the Parthenon struck me once again.

Photographers show the nearly complete ends of the temple. The center, blown out during a war between the Turks and Venetians, was rarely photographed. The Turks stored ammunition in the Parthenon. The Venetians struck it with cannon fire. Boom!

Humanity is so stupid.

I turned slowly to savor the panorama.

Are we stupid to destroy such beauty in petty battles for power and prestige? Or are we stupid to pour the resources of a community into a structure destined to be worn by wind and rain, toppled by earthquakes and destroyed by jealous neighbors?

Our American culture is so young. How would it feel to be part of a culture so old, that left such a legacy?

"How did the Athenians haul all these blocks of marble up the hill?" I asked.

"Oh, Athenian citizens did not haul marble. They had slaves captured during their conquests, workers, laborers. Military success gave them the brute force to haul marble to the top of a mountain. Besides, they were quite skilled at engineering and mechanics."

We walked around the east end of the Parthenon to admire the front of the temple with its solidly-proportioned fluted columns and triangular pediment.

"The Parthenon is the perfect Doric temple," Carl said.

Carl and I rested on a rock and shared a bottle of water. The sun was hot here above the city. Athens' dry air left me continually thirsty.

"Your aunt and uncle have done an important thing here. I could not be in Athens this year without them." Carl took both my hands. "I hope you can persuade Lydia to save the Institute."

"I don't have much influence. My aunt hasn't asked my opinion other than at our brainstorming this morning."

"Sophia was very upset when Herr Jackson died. She admired him very much. They were supposed to meet for lunch that day, but he never came. She tried calling, texting, nothing. She learned he had died in a blast email."

"Oh, that's terrible. I hadn't realized they were so close. I'm sure Lydia didn't mean to snub her. It was just so crazy," I said. "So that's why Sophia is angry at Lydia and me."

"Frau Jackson is not as interested in the Institute as her husband was. And now that crazy preacher is stealing her money and attention," Carl said. "I shouldn't ask for help. I just have such a passion for this place. Sophia's explosion this morning may have doomed us, I told her to forget her feelings and remember that Lydia is our crucial patron."

"So what's the secret to earning Sophia's respect?"

"Hard work. Confidence. A questioning mind."

"And not falling off the sides of monasteries."

He laughed. "That would be good."

"I still don't understand how I fell. It just doesn't make sense."

"Let it go," Carl said.

"And all these other strange things—robbery and burglary, Karmanos butting in. This is just my fourth day here. Something went wrong at that monastery Monday morning. Things just don't add up."

Carl just shook his head. "Let's get back to art history. That I do understand."

We turned to the Parthenon's less famous neighbor.

"The *Erechtheum* is more complex and challenging than the Parthenon. Teachers tend to gloss over it because of that," Carl said.

"It seems like a hodge-podge."

Carl smiled at my slang. "The architect had a sloped site and several existing sacred spots. To the ancient Athenians, the *Erechtheum* was more revered, more important. The sacred procession ended here, not at the Parthenon."

On the side of the building facing the Parthenon was the famous Porch of Maidens. Strong yet graceful women carried the weight of the cornice and roof on their heads.

"The design was cut back during construction to save money for the war. They stuck this porch on the south side to cover a structural support. So the most famous feature of this temple was a patch to hide budget cuts," Carl said.

I had seen one of the maidens at the British Museum. Lord Elgin kidnapped her and spirited her back to his castle in Scotland. He destroyed another maiden trying to remove her. The six maidens serving as columns today were all replicas. Four original ladies were safe inside the museum at the foot of the hill, minus their captive sister in London.

We climbed over uneven ground around the shell of the *Erechtheum*. The temple had burned at some point in its 2,500-year history, leaving the marble block walls blackened, cracked and misshapen.

"The temple has four areas on different levels, divided to house sacred relics."

The tall slim Ionic columns on the east side seemed airy after the solid mass of the Parthenon.

"This is the entrance to the main temple room," Carl explained. "See the delicate carving."

He was right. An elegant basket weave was carved around the base of the columns. The graceful scrolls on the Ionic capitals rested atop egg-and-dart edging and stylized leaves.

"Each of the four porches is a different variation on the Ionic order. The ancients who visited this temple knew the complex relationship of deities and the subtle changes of architecture intended to honor each."

I glanced toward the rock where we had left our backpacks. Someone was bent over, rifling through them.

"Hey, those are ours!" I yelled.

Carl and I ran toward him.

A man in a black ball cap stood up and raised his hands. "I thought someone lost them."

He backed off as we got closer, then turned and high-tailed it away.

"See. I told you something was going on."

Carl checked inside his pack. "Our lunch is still here. Are you missing anything?"

"No, I just have a couple of bottles of water and a hat."

"So let's find a shady place to eat."

We left the realm of super-human achievement and followed the path down the northern slope to the world of the mundane.

Carl breathed deeply. "We are walking on the Panathenaic Way. This is the road ancient Athenians followed in their sacred processions up to the Acropolis before their games."

An informal procession of tourists stirred the dust of the ancient gravel.

"This other hill is the Areiopagos, where the first judicial court was built," Carl explained.

"The Areiopagos is in the Bible," I said. "Paul gave a speech introducing the Athenians to Christianity there."

Carl found a rare spot of shade under a scruffy tree and unpacked lunch. He retrieved insulated water bottles that had kept our wine chilled.

"To beauty," he toasted.

"To beauty."

We sipped the pale golden liquid. Had the Athenians paused here to enjoy their wine? Did they realize we would follow their footsteps 2,500 years later?

A man in sunglasses plopped down on the other side of the path and pulled out a guidebook. That profile looked familiar. I felt the key pressing into my breast. Let him follow us.

"Did the Greeks make white wine or red wine?"

"In the pottery paintings, we see a game where they flick the dregs out of their wine glasses. Red wine is more likely to have sediment, so I suppose it was red. That's not my area of expertise." Carl laughed at his scholar's excuse. "This is a German wine, much better than Greek."

Hiking had built our appetites. We ate every bite and searched the backpack for more. Carl licked my fingers then brushed his lips against mine.

"You think I put the moves on every woman, but I am very selective about romance. I promised Sophia that I would not sleep with undergrads. But you are a visitor, not a student."

He kissed my neck and nibbled my ear.

"Carl, be careful of my bruises. Besides, those people are watching us."

"They are just jealous that I am with a beautiful young lady," he whispered as he moved his kisses around to the nape of my neck.

"Carl, a casual summer diversion is not a good idea."

He continued soft kisses as he slid a hand around my back.

Things were getting dangerous. In another minute, he would find the key. I hopped up and packed away our things. Was the guy in sunglasses peeking over the top of his guide book?

"Amber, stop acting like a Catholic school girl. You are a passionate woman. Let yourself feel that, let me show you," Carl urged.

"No, thanks. Passion leads to pain."

"Ah, you have been hurt. Good sex with no demands is what you need."

I handed him a backpack. "Let's hike."

"You are stubborn, but I am right." Carl shouldered his backpack.

We entered the ancient Greek Agora.

"This marketplace area dates to the height of Athens' classical era, the fifth century B.C.."

Rows of stone blocks outlined the foundations and roads of the ancient city. Stone fragments revealed architectural details. How could archeologists tell so much from these broken foundations?

Carl pointed to a church on the edge of the Agora. "That church is from the 10th century. Tell me, why do you study churches and religious art?"

"I guess this is *my* quest for truth. Christianity is so divided. Each faction claims that it has a lock on the truth and everyone else is wrong."

We continued down the sacred path.

"Carl, do you think I'm lukewarm?"

Carl laughed.

"No, I'm serious. Am I lukewarm?"

"Maybe a cock-tease, but not lukewarm. You just lack confidence in your ideas. You over-study and over-think."

"I've been told that I am lukewarm in my commitment to the Lord."

"Don't worry about cults—you're too smart to fall for that crap."

We walked in silence. Fewer tourists came to the Agora. It had a feeling of abandoned serenity.

"Socrates and Pericles walked here," Carl said. "Now, my feet walk the same street as the great architects. I join Mnesicles, Ictinus and Callicrates. For you, it is the Apostle Paul who walked this path. We all seek truth and beauty, the way of the divine. Some people see the world in black and white. They find their truth easily. You don't. You see all the shades of gray. You will always be a seeker."

He paused. "You asked me how to earn Sophia's respect. You need to stop worrying about what other people think of you. Be your own thinker. Stand for something. Respect comes when you stop seeking it."

I tripped over an irregularity in the path. Carl helped me up.

"Sorry, I was listening and not watching. I guess I can't talk and walk at the same time."

I tried to explain my quest. "Images speak louder to me than words. I get tired of arguments about words. Maybe the key to the truth is captured in images from the past. I want to learn for myself instead of having someone's agenda preached to me on Sunday morning."

I looked back up the path. Could we find our truth by looking at the path taken by those who came before?

The man with the guide book was about 50 feet behind us. He quickly looked away, seemingly studying the ruins beside the path.

I ran toward him. "I'm tired of you stalking me."

He looked around as I approached.

"You. I'm talking to you. Leave me alone."

I punched his chest with my finger. "Stop it."

As he drew back, I recognized that profile.

"Demetrius! Why are you following me?"

He raised his hands in surrender and smiled. "Dr. Karmanos worries about you. He heard about your arrest in riot and break-in last night at Institute. When you left on hike I thought to keep an eye on you."

"Well, well..." It was hard to stay outraged. "I don't need a keeper. So leave me alone."

Carl had joined us. He crossed his arms over his chest and tried to smother a laugh.

I set a brisk pace back to the Institute. Carl caught up.

"I *was* right. We were being followed."

He shook his head. "Amber, Amber. You do keep life interesting."

As we circled back to the Plaka, Carl paused beside the remains of the Forum and Hadrian's Library.

He rested his arm across my shoulder. "You can tell this is Roman-era rather than Greek because the columns are smooth instead of fluted. Julius Caesar and Augustus Caesar funded the Forum as a marketplace. The walled courtyard had an inner colonnade where business was conducted. That building over there was the public toilet. Even the toilets were beautiful. *That's* why I study Classical Architecture."

He held my hand as we wove through loud streets filled with shoppers and gawkers.

46

Byzantine Renaissance

January, A.D. 945, Constantinople

The din of the rioters in the streets below was even louder today. The crowds around the palace complex had grown each day.

Constantine and Helena proceeded to the purple room to don the full regalia of their offices.

"Don't walk too fast," Helena coached. "My brothers may be panicked, but we are not. We will speak to the people as emperors, not prisoners."

"I always walk like an emperor, my dear," Constantine said.

Helena smiled in approval.

Stephen and Constantine Lekapenos had sent the imperial guards into the streets to control the mobs, but there was an unwritten rule that the military was not to be used against the people of the capitol. Were the rioters daring the guards to attack?

The fading 74-year-old Emperor Romanos Lekapenos had refused to turn over power to his sons. Instead, he had elevated Constantine VII over his own blood in the succession.

His sons kidnapped the emperor during a nap, put him on a boat, and shipped him out from the palace's private port. Now, he napped all he wanted at an island monastery. The initial purges had gone peacefully.

The brothers had confined Constantine to the palace complex. When the purple-born co-emperor failed to appear for the liturgy, people feared the usurpers had killed him. That's when the riots had begun.

The eunuchs brought the heavy embroidered robes and *loros* to Constantine and Helena.

"We will not allow my brothers on the balcony with us. That only gives them equal status," Helena instructed. "You are the legitimate emperor. The conspirators in the imperial guard will be forced to turn on my brothers when the people demand the real emperor."

"We have waited a long time."

"You were born to be emperor, and to pass the throne to your son."

Constantine and Helena knelt as the crowns were placed on their heads. Always before, it had felt like a golden mockery. Today, the crown seemed to fit comfortably over Constantine's long dark hair.

As they stepped onto the balcony, sunlight exploded against the gold and jewels that covered their bodies. People below knelt on the rough streets. The gesture moved like a wave through the throng and along the crowded streets of Constantinople.

The shouts turned into a chant.

"O such a great emperor and autocrat, many years."

Helena smiled. The people loved Constantine VII. The military and church would follow. Constantine would remember the people.

As the chants echoed through the streets, Helena gestured for their children to join them. In a few weeks, the Lekapeni usurpers would at last be gone from their palace.

Over the next 15 years, Constantine restored lands to the peasants, improving the economic base of the empire. He was respected by the people as a just, legitimate ruler. He was good at picking subordinates and delegating responsibility—important qualities for one wishing to continue his pursuit of scholarship and the arts.

47

The Institute

We laughed as we escaped the afternoon heat and glare into the air conditioning of the Institute.

A letter was propped on the front entry table. I saw my name and the logo of my future graduate school. I turned it over in my hands. It felt too light to be forms and instructions for the fall semester. My stomach knotted.

"Want to see my collection of ancient erotica?" Carl teased. "You like images. These are very eloquent."

"What?" I looked up. "It's five in the afternoon, for Pete's sake. Do you think about sex all the time?"

"What's wrong with a little flirting?"

"I'll pass on the pornography. And on the afternoon delights. I'm not in the mood."

Carl tilted his head and looked at me. Then he shrugged and headed upstairs.

The library was peacefully empty. I hid in a corner chair and examined the envelope. I stuffed it into a pocket and checked my email. Guess who.

Hosios Loukas monastery is older than the monasteries in Meteora. It's about the same age as the monastery at Daphni and has beautiful mosaics. I would love to show it to you.

I have a puzzle here in Meteora and I could use your help. Can you come tomorrow? There are tourist buses from Athens.

Just FYI, I know Billy Sullivan. He was a professor when I was an undergrad. He is controversial. He tried to get all the religion professors to affirm the Apostles' Creed. He left when he didn't get tenure. Be careful around him.

The grad school letter poked me. I eased the flap open and scanned the letter. "On hold" was the polite term. My acceptance into grad school had been pulled. I tried to read the appeal process through a veil of tears. I needed a shoulder to cry on.

I found Aunt Lydia in her apartment, but Sophia was there, too.

I slipped into my study room to pull myself together. The conversation penetrated the door.

"I apologize for my outburst this morning. I was unprofessional."

"I haven't given the Institute the attention it deserves," Lydia answered. "I guess I trusted you to handle things."

"And I have. But you need to get up to speed and make some decisions."

"I'm just surprised that you're so negative about Billy."

"I do not trust people who substitute religion for intelligence. But he is your guest. I will treat him politely."

Darn. With all Lydia had on her shoulders I couldn't burden her with my disappointment. I hid out until the conversation calmed.

I tried to act cheerful and casual. "What happened after we left?" Too perky?

"Dr. Karmanos is inquiring about Lydia's artifacts," Sophia said. "He requested an inventory and documentation to prove we have them legally."

"It's harassment!" Lydia said. "That snake is pressuring Billy into revealing his discovery. But we don't have a choice. We're compiling a list of items displayed in the public areas of the Institute. I don't want them digging through my private things."

"We will give them what they asked for; nothing else," Sophia said.

Lydia got up from her computer. "I can't think ... Amber, you do this. You know the software from doing my inventory at home."

I grabbed a handful of cookies.

As Sophia and I sorted the data for the inventory, Lydia slipped into the bedroom to call Andreus for advice and sympathy. She stuck her head back into the room.

"Andreus asked what gratuity you gave Dr. Karmanos for his time on Monday and Tuesday at Meteora."

Sophia looked at me. I looked at her and grimaced.

"We didn't," Sophia confessed.

Lydia gave the bad news to Andreus.

"I didn't know we should tip government officials," Sophia whispered. "We always tip our guides, drivers and waitresses."

Lydia rejoined us. "He says the financial crisis has made budgets really tight. A nice gratuity moves things along with bureaucrats."

"That is bribery." Sophia said.

"Gratuity is a nicer word," Lydia said.

"Andreus was there," I protested. "Why didn't he do it?"

"I sent a donation for the monastery and for the bishop here. But I didn't think about anyone else. Oh, well. It probably wouldn't have made any difference. We'll offer a gratuity when Karmanos comes back tomorrow to check our list."

I printed an inventory sheet.

"Lydia, do you trust the dealers you purchased from?" Sophia asked.

"Well, we bought some things on street corners, especially at first. And Robert didn't always give me the receipt if it was a gift. Andreus was our agent for some of the artifacts. So I have good documentation on those," Lydia said.

"Oh." Sophia's tone let us know what she thought of Greek men who hug women and bribe officials.

Lydia and Sophia left to check the inventory sheet against the artifacts displayed in the various rooms.

I retreated to my hideaway and read the letter again. No graduate school in the fall.

The Greek alphabet poster on the wall seemed pointless. The broken Pericles bust on my desk captured my week perfectly.

Crying on Kira's shoulder via email seemed like the best option. I took a quick look at my messages. Mr. Scruffy-Beard had sent me a reply.

Dr. Sullivan's theory makes no sense. John wrote Revelation during the reign of Domitian (81-96 CE). Domitian was the son of Vespasian and the brother of Titus. So it was written AFTER the fall of Jerusalem in 70 CE. Some early church fathers even believed a different John, John the Elder, wrote the Revelation. Irenaeus, a second century church leader, wrote that John saw the vision "towards the end of Domitian's reign." We're not BFF yet, but I can tell you the truth.

When you come to Meteora tomorrow, we can talk about this. There is definitely something going on at the Varlaam monastery

Why do I keep reading emails from this guy?

Just when I'm starting to understand things, someone points out a hole! I will ask Billy about when Revelation was written. Of course, something is going on at the monastery. That's what I've been trying to tell everyone since Monday.

Life was going to Hell anyway. Revelation couldn't be any more depressing.

I laid out the photos of the frescoes and tried to match them with the scriptures.

The beast and the birth of the child was in Rev. 12. The image of people kneeling before the dragon and the second beast, a ram, on the mountain from Rev. 13 impressed me. Time for help from Billy.

I knocked as I entered the conference room.

"Do you have a few minutes to talk about Revelation?"

He saved his files as I spread out my dilemma.

"Pictures are fun, but are you actually reading the text in Greek?"

"As best I can. It motivates me to try to find these images in the scriptures and read the original Greek."

Billy picked up the photo of the woman giving birth, the dragon attacking her and the angels protecting her.

"This is John's prophecy of the persecution of the Christians by the Romans. With the help of the angels, a new world religion is born. This transitions from the first prophecy against Jerusalem and the second prophecy against Rome," Billy said.

"This second image is John's condemnation of earthly governments. The beast with many heads has been cast out of heaven and takes the role of the Roman empire, Nero Caesar and the other emperors. The ram is other earthly leaders who collaborate with Rome. And all these fawning people follow the cult of emperor worship.

"John declares guilt against the Romans, the reason for the judgment coming in the seven plagues. This prophecy against Rome, was fulfilled over the next two, three hundred years."

48

Thursday evening

Lydia found us in the conference room and suggested pizza. Who ate pizza in Greece? Billy and I were skeptics, but Lydia was right. The aroma of baking bread enfolded us as we walked in. My mouth watered and my stomach growled.

The waitress handed us a menu in English. We selected our pizza toppings and wine.

"Can I have some water, please?"

The waitress gave me a puzzled look. How does one order just plain old tap water, not fancy bottled water? Because of the dry air in Athens, I was always thirsty, and buying bottled water got expensive.

Billy and Lydia laughed at my struggles, then explained in Greek to the poor waitress. I guess she knew just enough of each language to know which menu to hand to foreigners.

When the bread and salad came, we joined hands in prayer. After grace, Billy took the loaf of bread.

"Every time we gather in table fellowship, I think of Jesus. He broke bread with his disciples on a daily basis. That's why it was such a powerful memory when he broke bread on that crucial night. By breaking bread together, we join in fellowship with Jesus Christ and all believers."

Billy broke the loaf and handed Lydia and me each a piece. We both waited. He dipped the bread in olive oil and took a bite.

"Don't be so solemn," Billy said. "Let's eat and toast to good friends."

"To good friends."

As we attacked the salad, Billy and Lydia talked about how to get the research verification he needed without turning his work over to others. His colleague would arrive from the United States in the morning.

The pizza was totally awesome—the crust was crisp on the outside, thick and tender and tasty on the inside. Probably the best pizza I'd ever eaten.

"Billy, I have a question. One of my friends says Revelation was written during Domitian's reign, after the destruction of Jerusalem."

"That was the common theory in the 20th century. I don't share it." Billy took another piece of pizza.

"Why not?" I waited as he chewed.

"Revelation was written during a time of persecution. During John's lifetime, two emperors persecuted Christians, Nero and Domitian."

He paused for more pizza.

"I like the time of Nero, the earlier date. First, in Chapter 11 John is told to measure the temple. After 70 AD, the temple was gone. Second, in Chapter 17, it says there are seven kings. 'Five have fallen, one is, and the other has not yet come.' The sixth Roman emperor was Nero."

"But what about Irenaeus?" I asked. "Didn't he say that John wrote Revelation during the reign of Domitian?

I reached for the last piece of pizza. "Anyone want to split this?"

Billy and Lydia both shook their heads. The whole slice landed on my plate.

"Irenaeus is mistranslated," Billy explained. "Irenaeus writes about 'ancient copies' of Revelation. Then he writes about those who have seen John. He ends with a phrase '*that* was seen no very long time since, but almost in our day, towards the end of Domitian's reign.' So what does '*that*' refer to? Is '*that*' the vision of

Revelation, or is '*that*' John?"

"So how do you decide?" Lydia asked.

Billy smiled at her.

"Irenaeus describes the copies as 'ancient' but he describes '*that*' as 'almost in our day.' Obviously, '*that*' can't be the vision recorded in the ancient copies. It must be when the brothers saw John."

We decided cheesecake was in order.

"That ambiguity is exactly what I want to study in the fragment I found. The original Greek may be clearer."

Lydia raised her eyebrows.

"Critics have used Irenaeus to discredit Revelation. They say the apostle John didn't write Revelation. Then they say it was written long after the time of Jesus." Billy's face flushed. "They want to discredit the inspired Word of God. This fragment will end that."

"Amen, brother!" I used my best church affirmation voice.

Billy and Lydia both laughed.

Billy shook his head. "I guess I was sounding a little preachy."

The waitress arrived with our dessert. We dug in.

"Lydia, you're struggling with decisions about the Institute and your new foundation," Billy said. "I'm willing to be a sounding board."

"The reaction at the University is strange. The dean and Robert were buddies. They ran the program together. But the dean retired. Since Robert died, I get lots of attention from the president but he doesn't give two hoots in Hell about the Classics Institute."

Lydia took another bite of cheesecake. "This is good. This is my favorite pizza place in Athens, but I never had dessert here. You are expanding my tastes, Amber."

I mumbled thanks through a mouth full of cheesecake.

"You're right to be skeptical," Billy said. "It sounds like the University has a building project and wants a donor. I've seen you in action on the food bank board. You don't just write a check, you want to shape the projects you support."

"I agree with Billy," I said. "I've always admired the way you and Robert gave guidance to your charities. If you were starting today, what are you passionate about? What would you choose to do?"

"Obviously, I'm fascinated by the things you two are studying. Biblical manuscripts and early Christian art are new areas for me, and I see your passion for them."

"But now that you're retired, what do *you* want to do?" I pushed.

"I have a special place in my heart for the workers we've known. We're squeezing out the traditional crafts. Textiles have become a big international business with a horrible safety record in some countries. I'd like to support Fair Trade co-ops or maybe make micro-loans to help Third World women."

"That's a wonderful thought."

"And I like helping people explore their ideas and dreams. That's why I would hate to kill the Institute."

"Sounds like you have three interests," Billy said. "First, Christian studies. Second, traditional crafts in the textile industry. Third, the Institute or individual scholars in some other way."

"Now why couldn't I figure that out?" Lydia asked.

"Because you've been overwhelmed, first selling the company then Robert's death," I said. "You haven't had a minute to breathe."

"Have you thought about your foundation board?" Billy asked.

"I have some ideas," Lydia answered. "I have an investment manager and a law firm. I may call on you to serve on the board."

Billy laughed. "I'd like to put in a formal funding request for the Christian roots research project that I talked to you and Robert about. That may eliminate me as a board member."

"Oh, I bet we could work around that." Lydia turned to me. "Do you think you could handle being executive director?"

I was stunned. "That's a big job."

"Part time. You could still do grad school. Think about it."

I sat back as my mind raced. How could I break the news that I might not be going to graduate school?

"My other challenge is my antiquities. Attitudes have changed since we started collecting. It's no longer accepted—or legal—to take items out of the country where they were found. I might have trouble getting some items out of Greece. But Greek museums have no money to make acquisitions. I suppose I could loan or donate the best pieces." Lydia shook her head. "Enough problems. We can't solve that one tonight."

"I feel bad that my research is causing you trouble," Billy said.

"I may be worrying for nothing. Hopefully the documents we faxed this afternoon will satisfy them. Or I'll try a bribe."

"Remember, it's a gratuity," I teased.

The restaurant had filled with late-dining Greeks. Billy picked up the check and got off cheap. We gave up our table and headed back to the Plaka.

We settled in for coffee at Lydia's apartment. I noticed a funny smile on her lips.

"I think I'll give the University president a little call," she said.

We watched as she dialed and waited for an answer.

"Hello, Suzie. This is Lydia Jackson. Y'all will never believe where I'm callin' from. I'm in Athens, Greece."

Aunt Lydia could turn the Southern accent on or off at will. It was full force.

"Is the boss in this afternoon?"

She nodded as she listened.

"Have him give me a jingle on my cell. I just wanna confirm that the University isn't having classes here at the Institute in the fall. Now remember, it's eight hours later here."

Lydia took a sip of coffee.

"Good talking to you, Suzie. Oh, could you do one more little thing for me? I need the phone number for the athletic director."

She listened to the number without writing it down.

"Oh, I just need to release my sky box on the 50-yard line. If I'm not going to be associated with the University any more, he could sell it to a new donor. Bye now!"

She laughed as she hit the off button. "How did I do?"

Billy shook his head. "I know someone who's going to shit his pants."

As the adults visited, I checked my email.

Meet me at noon tomorrow at Varlaam. There's an alcove tucked behind the katholikon where it's quiet and shady. You can help me with this mystery. Besides, at least 10,000 saints have invaded the monasteries. We could plot a strategy for fighting back the invasion!

Why should I go to Meteora to spend time with a stranger with baggy clothes and a scruffy beard? He did have beautiful brown eyes, though. And a lavender caramel name.

I'll think about it. Text you IF I get on the bus.

I could pack a bag and catch the bus early. Or I could slip up to Carl's room to see his ancient erotica. I got a vision of Carl wearing the Athenian helmet and nothing else. Naughty and nice!

But what would Lydia think? She and Billy had settled in for a long conversation. My absence would be pretty obvious. Better stick to my computer. Kira sent me a message.

Can't believe you got arrested in a riot, assaulted by a street thief, had a break-in at the Institute AND got that unfair letter from the grad school. The devil is working hard to put roadblocks in your way, so you must be doing something right. Be careful! I don't want to lose my BFF!! Is Carl still flirting? Dustin asked about you at Wednesday night Bible Study. He thinks you're being led astray by the devil.

Revenge is more fun than romance anyway. Dustin needed another dose of humble pie. This would requite an email.

Here are five more failed prophecies of the end times:

* 1326 CE, precisely 1,000 years after Constantine declared Christianity as the official religion of the empire.

1202 CE, during the lifetime of Joachim.

1324 CE. The Beguines said the Antichrist had already appeared on the papal throne. I can understand why; the pope was not nice to the virgin women of this mystical order.

8 a.m. on Oct. 19, 1533.

1683 CE.

Saturday, May 21, 2011.

You have been worried about my lukewarm faith. That is a misinterpretation. I have a lukewarm acceptance of your favorite doctrine of the imminent end of the world. Throughout history, believers have mislabeled disagreements about doctrine as failures of faith. Don't fall into that trap.

It felt good to get that off my chest, but also a little mean-spirited. Maybe revenge isn't sweet. Maybe it's bitter. I shut down my computer.

"I may go back to Meteora tomorrow," I told Lydia.

Billy shook his head. "No, that won't work. I need Carl to pick up my publisher and his assistant at the airport. Besides, you need to organize my images."

"Already done. You'll be working. Lydia and Sophia will be dealing with the artifact police. No one needs me. Carl can stay here to help you. I'll take the bus."

"Are you safe by yourself?" Lydia asked. "You fell last time. If someone did try to kill you, you shouldn't be there."

"Lydia's right," Billy said. "You went through a terrible trauma Monday. It's affected your memory. You've got this crazy feeling of being pushed. I don't think you should travel alone yet."

"I have a friend at Meteora. He'll meet me. I haven't decided for sure if I'm even going."

I escaped to the bedroom for a hot shower, a pain pill and a soft pillow.

As I wrestled the covers, I debated plans for the morning.

In the darkness, a vulture soared on a current of air. It screeched to me. *You saw how easily you could be killed. Watch what you are getting into.*

It circled lower and lower, perhaps over a bit of road kill. It closed in on a broken body lying beside the road. Amber-colored hair had spread over the body's face, but I knew who it was.

A dark cave opened. A gray-scaled reptilian dragon peered out —the beast.

What a choice—pecked to death by a vulture, or swallowed whole by the beast.

Day Six

"So God created humankind in his image. In the image of God he created them: male and female he created them. God blessed them, and God said to them, 'Be fruitful and multiply, and fill the earth and subdue it.'" Genesis 1:27-28

Six is the number of man. God created humankind on the sixth day. Humans fall just short of perfection (represented by the number seven). Six is the number of incompleteness. God's creation wasn't complete until day seven. Man without God is incomplete.

The sixth day is the day of the crucifixion, the sacrifice made necessary by man's sinful nature. The sixth day is the day of Christ's descent into Hades.

Ironically, the sixth day is also the day of sex, when men and women are told to be fruitful and multiply.

The Greek numeral for six is *digamma*, an obsolete letter (F ϝ). It is also written with a final *sigma* symbol (ς).

50

Friday

My eyes popped open. These crazy dreams were not good for my beauty sleep. One of my friends said dreams were a subconscious message, something our rational mind blocked. Did my subconscious know who tried to kill me? If so, I wasn't getting the message. I certainly didn't know any vultures personally—unless their black feathers suggested a monk's robe.

I slipped to the bathroom and opened the blinds. The eastern sky was washed with dark indigo, edged with a rose-pink glow just along the horizon.

My legs ached from hiking up the Acropolis. I should go back to bed and rest my weary body. I tiptoed back to the luxury sheets and fluffy feather pillows. Any sensible person would slide back in between those smooth, silky sheets.

My hands searched in the dark for my things on the bedside table. I blindly located clothes and crept out of the bedroom. I stretched out my arm to locate a light switch.

Thump.

"Oh, shit."

I sprawled over a footstool. I would never make it as a cat burglar. I rolled over to catch my breath; surely Lydia couldn't sleep through that. With all my other bruises, though, no one would notice one more.

After a few minutes, my eyes adapted to the dark. I crawled to the light switch.

I slipped into hiking shorts and a tank top, topped with a camp shirt with lots of pockets. A change of underwear, wrap skirt and toothbrush found places in my backpack. A raid of Lydia's kitchen yielded some granola bars and other snacks; I never traveled without emergency sustenance.

I wrote a quick note.

Aunt Lydia,

I woke up early and decided to go to Meteora. I'll be back Saturday. I'm meeting my friend Jim Sampras. I'll call this evening. Good luck with Billy's research and the artifact police.

Love, Amber.

As I let myself out, I ran through a checklist. Camera, credit cards, cash, book, map, phone, water. I stuck my left hand in my pocket—no prayer rope. I rescued it from under the wayward footstool.

Indigo spread across the dark sky as the rose glow widened. The streets were quiet; no footsteps followed behind me. Good.

I caught a whiff of the ocean. The historic port of Pireaus was just a few miles away. In another hour, the car exhaust and Greek cooking aromas would overpower the ocean air.

Lights popped on in the square windows of blocky concrete apartment buildings as Athens awakened. Early-morning workers shuffled into the subway. I joined the quiet line. Greeks were not cheerful in the morning.

Miraculously, I got off the subway at the right stop for the bus station. I bought a ticket and found coffee and pastries.

I filled the seat next to me with my backpack. An old guy stopped and gestured. I shrugged my shoulders, pretending not to understand. No luck. He picked up my pack and handed it to me.

Great. My seatmate was a sweaty old man with bad breath. He'd probably stare down my shirt the entire trip.

The bus moved against the mass of four million people as we headed out of the city sprawl. Streams of commuters flooded the highway flowing into the metropolis.

The road led back to the home of the beast.

Why would anyone choose this road?

Someone who was tired of being a failure. Someone who was tired of nightmares. Someone who needed to know the truth.

Me.

I am on a bus to Meteora. I must be CRAZY! I'd better get a nice dinner out of this. You are buying me dinner, aren't you? You definitely won't be my BFF if I don't get fed.

We passed a ragged camp along a river on the outskirts of the city. Gypsies. Many had settled into urban life, but Europe still had nomadic Gypsies, or travelers. Sophia said these nomads suffered from discrimination and lived in poverty. Carl said what did you expect, they're gypsies.

We traveled north on E75, winding along the coast and up and down through the mountains that isolate Athens.

Greek drivers accelerate to the bumper of the car ahead, then slam on the brakes. Traveling through the Greek countryside felt like a carnival ride, especially in a lurching bus.

I retrieved a couple more text messages. I clicked on Dustin first to get the unpleasant task out of the way

You can't stop me from praying for you. You can be all intellectual and make fun of believers. But you can't sit on the fence and be an observer in the battle between good and evil. Make a choice and a commitment. I will stop putting you on the prayer list, but that means we won't be there to stand in the gap for you. I hate for anyone I care about to be left behind.

Awe, that old threat again.

Thank you for coming. I need your help. Meet me at the alcove behind the katholikon. Put on a hat or sunglasses so the monks don't recognize you.

At least Jim still thought I was okay..I dug the Greek New Testament out of my backpack. Today's topics were the Great Whore of Babylon and angels pouring out seven plagues.

The view down my shirt must not be too exciting. Snoring started gently beside me, then grew in strength and volume. The old coot's sweaty head drooped onto my shoulder.

I found the proper place in my interlinear and the photos I had filed between the pages. The seven plagues had fewer images. Artists seemed to skip forward to the Great Whore of Babylon.

I did some quick research on my phone to see what happened to Rome before the empire's eventual fall.

The first bowl of plague brings sores. Alaric led the Visigoths in a siege of Rome in A.D. 408.

The second plague kills all living creatures in the sea. Alaric captured Rome's seaport, destroyed the grain supplies and cut off the wheat ships coming from Africa.

The third plague turns water into blood. The Rhine River froze in 406 CE, opening the border to the Vandals, who spread blood and destruction over what is now France.

The fourth bowl is poured on the sun. The Vandals invaded Rome in A.D. 455, burning buildings. They shipped residents of the city to Africa to be sold as slaves.

The fifth bowl is poured on the throne of the beast, plunging the kingdom into darkness. Romulus Augustus surrendered to Odoacer in A.D. 476, ushering in the dark ages in Western European.

The sixth bowl is poured out on the River Euphrates, opening the way for the kings from the east. Attila and his Huns poured into Europe from Asia in A.D. 441, displacing the Vandals, Goths and Germans. It forced those groups into Roman territory.

The seventh bowl brings the end to the great city. I suppose this could refer to the Goth attacks in A.D. 546-549.

Given the numerous wars through history, it's really hard to assign the bowls of destruction to a specific fulfillment. Besides, Rome was a Christian city by this point. Why would God punish fifth century Christians for the acts of the Romans in the first century?

I think Billy's explanation here is much more tenuous than the first prophecy against Jerusalem.

The Great Whore of Babylon is obviously a summary of the prophecy that Rome will fall. She certainly makes an impression on artists riding on a scarlet beast robed in expensive purple and jewels.

The bus made a pit stop at Lamia. A local woman pointed out an untidy pile of sticks atop the old stone church across the street.

Factoid: Stork nests are a sign of good luck and God's blessings. Storks are considered to be great mothers and a symbol of the annunciation to Mary. Storks are also natural enemies to snakes, and we all know how the snake tricked Eve.

The miles rolled gently through the Plain of Thessaly. My phone twitched with a text message from Carl.

You left Athens without telling me. Just when I thought we were becoming closer friends! I am stuck being an errand boy for Billy and his friends. They think they are too good to stay at the Institute. Billy treats me like shiza. Sophia and Lydia are upset. The Ministry wants an inventory of Lydia's personal collection. Last night, I thought about our hike. How about a moonlight hike up Lycabettus Hill?

Why did guys always invite me for hikes? I like nice dinners and dancing.

Back tomorrow afternoon. I enjoyed our hike, but I also like dancing. Be nice to Billy. Aunt Lydia is putting him on her foundation board. She wants me to be executive director. Not sure if I can do it. Nice to have a pay check during grad school. If I go to grad school.

The bus dropped us in the center of Kalambaka.

51

Varlaam

I snagged a cab to negotiate the narrow curves and switchbacks to Varlaam. The monasteries perched on the edge of a mountain range. Snow-capped peaks rose to the north. Just the vision sucked the breath out of me. This really could be heaven on earth.

Tour buses and vending trailers filled the parking lot. Yuck. Talk about killing the mood.

I shook out my wrap skirt and covered my bare legs.

The monasteries had wrap skirts and shawls available for tourists (both male and female) who left too little to the imagination. Their sacky cover-ups were made from disgusting cotton print fabrics that looked like rejected men's pajama prints from the 1950s. They must special-order fabric that ugly. I wouldn't be caught dead in it! Maybe that's the point of having something soooo ugly—no one would steal it as a memento of their visit to the monastery.

At least I would look acceptable if I died here today.

I secured my hair in a scrunchie and bought a cheap pair of sunglasses and a gaudy hat at the tourist trailer. Cancel that thought of looking acceptable. I'd better watch my back, because I wouldn't want to be found dead in these accessories.

Tour leaders held up small flags or paddles to keep their groups together. Some tourists sped ahead and others lagged behind as they struggled up the long stone stairway that wrapped up the side of the pinnacle. English tourists were a pain—they always walked on the wrong side instead of staying right.

I stood in line to buy a ticket then went through the turnstile. The broad paved courtyard was lined with stone buildings on all sides. The katholikon stood in the middle with its holy water fountain in front.

Clumps of people filled the courtyard. No pictures inside the buildings, the guides announced. It would back up the flow of people. Heaven forbid if someone actually had time to study the artwork and be moved by its spirituality. There were euros to be made.

I found Jim's alcove behind the *katholikon,* an island of serenity in an ocean of pushing and crowding. The stone buildings with red tile roofs seemed timeless. The tower of the *katholikon* had eight sides, each pierced by a window to allow light up into the dome where the *Pantokrator* sat in judgment. The sense of reverence returned.

The door opened behind me.

I turned and collided nose-to-nose with a monk.

Brother Iakobos!

I sucked in air. Forgot to breathe out.

Jim had betrayed me.

50

I tried to scream, but it came out as a pathetic croak.

Iakobos jerked me through the doorway with one arm and covered my mouth with the other. He kicked the door shut.

"Quiet. People will hear you."

Duh. That was the point. I stomped his foot and kneed him in the groin. He doubled over.

"Stop!" he grunted. "It's me ... Jim ... I'm not ... going to hurt ... you."

I stared. Come to think of it, that scruffy beard did look sort of familiar. He took off his hat and heavy glasses. His bangs were secured in a man bun.

"You tricked me, you lying turd!"

"Let me ... catch my breath ... you'll have me ... chanting soprano ... for a week."

I didn't feel one bit of sympathy for the snake. I grabbed for the door to make my escape.

"Wait. Don't you ... want to know ... the truth?"

I paused. Thought about it. Turned slowly.

"This had better be good. Start by telling who you are. Really."

"I really am Jim Sampras. I'm living here ... while I work on my dissertation."

He still wasn't breathing right.

"A likely story. You could have been honest with me."

Iakobos started to straighten up as he leaned against the stone wall in the narrow corridor. I leaned against the opposite wall and crossed my arms. I would not be so gullible again.

"You liar! I can't believe you sneaked into Kalambaka to spy on me and stole my phone number."

"No, no, you've got it all wrong," Jim said. "I came to Kalambaka to see that you were okay."

"You could have asked."

"I thought I would do better as a fellow student than as a representative of the monastery. Besides, a pretty girl wouldn't give her phone number to a monk."

I looked down my nose at him. "Compliments won't get you out of this."

"We really hit it off. So then I couldn't tell you."

"We hit it off? Hah. What a stupid excuse for lying."

"Would you have flirted with a monk who thought you were sexy?"

"Of course not. I've had my fill of sanctimonious men who first want to have sex and then decide I'm not holy enough for them."

"I'm definitely not going there." Jim did his best big brown beagle-eyes look. "I was starting to explain when you screamed and attacked me. Will you forgive me?"

I tried to stay mad. I really tried. But I couldn't keep a straight face. His goofy look made me giggle.

Jim/Iakobos put his hat and glasses back on.

"Come. I have a quiet place we can sit down. I need your help."

I crossed my arms again. "I'm not going anywhere with you."

"You've come this far. At least hear me out."

I relented.

"Turn off your cell phone."

I can't believe I complied. He led me through a long hallway. Light from a few high windows reflecting off the white plaster walls, breaking the darkness.

He opened a door and looked into the courtyard. "It's clear, but let's move quickly."

We made it to an enclosed cloister. One wall was pierced by windows. The opposite wall was frescoed with the images from Revelation I had photographed on Tuesday. Jim tried to hurry me along.

When we reached the cells, Jim led me upstairs to the second level.

"There are about 60 cells. We only need a few now, so the second and third floors are empty. The floors creak, though, so we have to step carefully. The monks are right beneath us. My cell is at the other end, so we'll cross down this hall, then cut down the back stairs."

The cells were simple white-washed cubes with small windows and wooden floors. Each had a heavy wooden door. Jim/Iakobos walked carefully, hugging the wall. I followed. He seemed awfully comfortable with this cloak and dagger stuff.

We reached the back stairs with no major stumbles or creaking boards. At the bottom, Jim peeked around to see if the hall was clear. We slipped into his tiny cell and closed the door.

The seven-foot square had a cot on one side, a row of hooks on the wall and a simple table and chair. Haphazard stacks of books teetered against one wall. The table held a laptop and a desk lamp.

He started soft music on his computer.

"The monks put me on the opposite end because they don't listen to music. I can do without television, but I can't live without my computer and music."

I squared my shoulders. "Give it up. What's going on here?"

He pulled out the chair for me, then plopped on the cot. I leaned forward to hear his soft voice over the music.

"So, the monks are worried about what Dr. Sullivan is working on. Since he won't tell, they're afraid he's going to embarrass the monastery. Or maybe conspire with the ministry to take away our manuscripts."

"That's not why I came. I want to know who pushed me. You said something was going on."

"No one pushed you. Dr. Sullivan's mystery fragment is the only thing that's going on."

"So you lied again to get me here."

I stared.

He blinked. Took a deep breath. "Please, just tell me if Dr. Sullivan is working on anything that would damage the monastery."

How much should I share? Could I betray my colleague and my aunt's friend? He might even become my next uncle.

"It's nothing sinister. Billy wants to make a big discovery and get famous."

Iakobos/Jim shook his head. "I hope you're right. I don't trust him. One of my friends at college had a run-in with Dr. Sullivan."

"I can't tell you any more." I crossed my arms over my chest.

He tried the puppy dog eyes again. "We won't stop Dr. Sullivan's research. We just need to know what he's interested in."

Jim poured on the innocent student charm, but I remembered how Brother Iakobos acted before. Who was the real man in black?

"What do you want me to do?"

"We've pulled the uncial fragments you photographed. Just look at them and tell me which ones Dr. Sullivan is studying."

"That's it?"

"Yup."

I thought about it. It was a simple request. Almost too simple.

"Why all this cloak and dagger crap?"

"You think I should tell the abbot that a girl I'm flirting with might know something? I'll just point out fragments that might be interesting. No one has to know it came from you."

A flimsy excuse. Was this the real Jim, the love-sick student trying to do the right thing? Or was this the act, turning on the charm to put me off guard? Maybe Iakobos was the real person, willing to lie and even push me off a wall to protect whatever he was up to.

"Wait a minute. How do you know that uncial fragments are the important ones?"

"You told me. You said Sullivan was looking at uncial manuscripts to verify dating."

Tricked again! I was tired of being on defense.

I rose and turned to the window. Across the valley was the Great Meteoron, the Monastery of the Metamorphosis. The image was one of serenity and holiness. But we humans have a way of turning everything into competition, lies, and complications.

Was he a monk or a student? What did he really want? How could I get Iakobos/Jim to show his true colors?

The wicked idea just popped into my head. It might work. I shouldn't. But it would serve him right.

I wiped the smile off my face as I casually pulled the scrunchie from my hair. I shook out my hair around my shoulders and unbuttoned my shirt. Was my tank top tight enough for the job? Could I keep a straight face?

I turned to face Iakobos.

"I'm so torn. I like you, but I just can't betray my mentor. I don't know what to do."

I lowered my eyes, then looked up and batted my eyelashes tearfully. Was this working?

Jim got up and took my hand. "I'm so sorry to put you in this position, but I can't see any other way."

I squeezed out a few tears and leaned my head on his shoulder. He stood stiffly for a moment, then awkwardly put an arm around my shoulder. He was acting rather Iakobosly. Maybe the bit about being a student was a lie.

"I'm just so confused. I don't know who to trust."

"You can trust me, Amber. We really need your help."

I looked into his eyes; I couldn't read them. Was he buying this weepy female bit? I slipped my arm around his waist and snuggled into his chest.

His body was muscular. I had figured those baggy clothes hid a wimpy computer geek body. Those were great abs I felt through the black cassock. I stroked his back.

Iakobos stepped back and loosened my arms. He gritted his teeth.

Very monkly. One more attack just to make sure.

I slipped off his hat and glasses and laid them on the desk. I stepped closer, nuzzled into the soft part of his neck and gave a gentle kiss. He tried to pull away again. If he was into me, I wouldn't be doing all the work.

"We shouldn't be acting this way," Jim whispered. "I promised to live like a monk for six months."

"You shouldn't be lying to the abbot or sneaking women into your cell either."

"That's true," he mumbled as he buried his face in my hair.

I brushed over the nasty beard and found his lips with mine. A few soft invitations with my tongue, and he opened to me.

Hum. Iakobos could French kiss with the best of them. They sure didn't teach this in monasteries. Finally, we came up for air.

"It killed me to pretend not to notice you on Monday and Tuesday," Iakobos whispered. "The chemistry hit me like a lightning flash the moment you walked in."

I had my answer. I could stop now.

Except he was kissing me again. Even with the scratchy beard it felt pretty good.

I *could* stop now.

My fingers fumbled with the buttons on his cassock as he nibbled my ear. Under the long black robe he wore a tee-shirt and light cotton pants. I slid my arms under his shirt and felt him gasp. I was right—he had great abs and muscles.

I explored with my fingers as he kissed my forehead.

"Amber, Amber, what are we doing?"

My question exactly. What was I doing? I could stop this. I should stop this.

I silenced him by covering his lips with mine.

Suddenly, he stopped hanging back.

He pushed me against the rough stone wall. It pressed against the stitches on the back of my head, but I didn't care. He explored my neck with his lips, then started down the front of my tank top. I was going to have beard-burn in quite unseemly places.

He found a nipple and sucked it in, fabric and all. I gasped.

He stopped. "Quiet, my love."

"Only if you promise not to stop."

He pulled aside the fabric and returned to his task.

My back arched, pushing my hips against his. I slid my hands down and cupped them around his butt. It was hard and smooth. It wasn't the only thing that was hard.

Our hands explored, touching forbidden areas. We stumbled toward the narrow cot. It gave a loud creak as our combined weight fell on it. Who cared? Just get these clothes off.

"Do you have a condom?" I asked.

"You're the one who staged this seduction. It's your job to bring the condom." He continued unfastening my shorts.

"I'm serious. You invited me. You should have condoms."

He didn't seem to hear my whispers. He had my shorts undone and was heading for the panties.

I rolled off the top of him and fell onto the hard floor. My mind whispered stop. My body shouted go, go, go.

Jim threw his head back and clutched his hair. "Oh, shit. Crap."

He pounded his hand against his forehead.

"Why would I have condoms in a monastery? I'm supposed to be celibate for six months."

Eventually, my breathing slowed. I sat up and pulled my top back into place. It was hard to miss the aroused nipples poking against the knit fabric. My face and body burned.

Jim rolled into a sitting position and cradled his head in his arms. At last, he started putting his clothes back in order.

"What do you need? I'll help you."

Jim looked up. "My failure to deliver didn't ruin my chances?"

"Hey, don't push your luck. Just tell me what you want."

"When we go to prayers at one o'clock, go down the hall.

There's a workroom in the center. We're studying the fragments to figure out what caught Dr. Sullivan's eye. Just make a note of which ones are important."

"I can do that."

"Friday is a fasting day, so we have about 45 minutes of prayer instead of lunch. Then, we come back here for a nap before the monastery opens to tourists again at 3. You can either come back here or go back to the alcove and wait. By 3:30 the crowd should be thick enough so that you can slip out."

I pondered my choices.

"I'll meet you back here so I can tell you which one it is."

He pulled back his shaggy hair and buttoned up his cassock. With glasses and hat, he was Brother Iakobos again.

I sat at the desk while he looked out the window. It was difficult to stay physically separate in such a small space.

I heard a rich, deep gong calling the brothers to prayer.

A long hollowed timber was suspended by ropes in the courtyard, creating a drum or gong-sort of sound when struck by a mallet. The *semantron* was the only musical instrument in an orthodox monastery. The liturgy was chanted a cappella.

Through the window, I heard the tone of the *semantron* at Metamorphosis. It sounded like tympani echoing from peak to peak. Each monastery's wooden gong produced a slightly different tone.

Iakobos straightened his shoulders. "It's a good thing I wear a cassock. I'd hate to go to prayers with a hard-on. Explain *that* to Father Paulos."

He picked up his prayer rope. "Give us about 10 minutes—the elders can be slow."

The door closed. I was by myself.

51

I dug a granola bar and bottle of water out of my backpack. The monks might be fasting, but I wasn't. I put on my long skirt and shirt and opened the door a crack. No noise. I listened for a minute, then stuck my head out.

The hall was clear. I stepped out and took a few steps down the hall.

A sound behind me. I froze.

Something touched my leg.

A soft pressure brushed against me.

Skia rubbed against my legs and let out a demanding "Yeaow."

"Go away," I whispered. "Scram."

No use. The sleek gray tomcat followed me to the workroom.

About a dozen fragments were spread on a heavy table. Beside each fragment was a legal tablet, with notes written in Greek. They had already narrowed their study to uncial manuscripts—those written in all caps. So the writing looked the same to me.

Could I even recognize Billy's treasure? A few were too small. Others were too big. I closed my eyes and tried to visualize details from the photographs. I remembered a purplish pink stain in the upper right corner. I opened my eyes.

There it was, in the center of the top row. How had I missed it? I stared. What was so important about this tattered scrap of animal skin marked with lamp soot?

I tried to read the Greek writing, one letter at a time. The calligraphy was so neat and regular. How did they do it? The ink was still strong and black on this fragment—not like some of the others, where most of the ink had flaked off through the centuries.

Voices outside the door. I dived behind the table.

My heart drummed in my chest. How could they not hear me?

And Skia. He sat there, twitching his tail like he had cornered a mouse and was ready to pounce. I glowered back, willing him to be quiet and go away.

How could they miss the cat stalking me?

The brothers visited for a few minutes, then split to go to their individual cells. Four pairs of traditional shoes moved to the left. A pair of athletic shoes lingered in front of the table, then split to the right. Skia stayed.

When the footsteps fell quiet, I crawled around and peeked to the left. Coast clear.

I high-tailed it down to Iakobos' cell and burst through the door.

"Thank God. I didn't know where you were. I knew you hadn't left because your backpack was still here."

"I spent too long looking at the fragments. I was hiding behind the table."

I sat down and took a long gulp of water.

"So could you tell which one it is?"

"Of course."

"So which one is it?"

"What's it worth to you?" I smiled and cocked my head.

"Amber, don't play games. Just tell me."

Spoil sport. "It's the one with the pink stain in the top row. Center."

Jim thought a minute as he slipped off his cassock and draped it on a hook.

"A commentary quoting the Apostolic Fathers?"

"That's the one. Billy said it was by an early church leader, one that was hard for translators because the known manuscripts were bad."

"I never would have picked that one." Jim sat on the cot and yawned. "Ok. I'll focus on it this afternoon. Do you want to slip out of this building now? I could lead you back to the alcove. You can wait there until the afternoon tourists arrive."

I sat down beside him. "I'd rather stay here with you for the next hour. I don't know when I'll see you again. Besides, we're both exhausted."

"We get up at 4 a.m. to pray. I'm always tired here. Just a nap?"

"*Just* a nap."

"Darn. You owe me a rain check on the seduction."

We spooned together on the narrow cot. Within minutes, I felt Jim's rhythmic breathing as he relaxed against me. Had I done the right thing by sharing Billy's secret?

Too soon, Jim's timer buzzed. He rolled over. Thud onto the floor.

He was quiet as he got ready to go back to work.

"Be careful when you leave. You can probably slip out in about 20 minutes. There should be plenty of people by then."

"Okay. Meet me tonight in Kalambaka? You owe me dinner."

"No, I really shouldn't. We work till six when the tourists are kicked out. We have evening prayers while the crew cleans up after the barbarian hordes. After that, we have an hour for study and prayer. I'll talk to Father Paulos then, before we go to bed."

"Do I call a cab when I get out, or what?"

"Usually there are tour buses with empty seats. You can offer the driver 20 euros to fill an empty seat back to Athens. You might have to visit another monastery, but it's faster than taking public transportation."

Jim put his arms around me. "When will I see you again?"

"I'm supposed to go back to Texas in three weeks."

Jim crushed me in a big black hug. Ouch.

"So we all gather for Divine Liturgy on Sunday morning at the Great Meteoron, then I'm free until Monday afternoon. I'll come to

Athens and take you to see *Hosios Loukas* on Sunday afternoon. It's totally awesome, better than the Church of the Angry Jesus."

I couldn't answer; my lips were otherwise occupied.

"Who knows? I could even collect on my rain check," Jim whispered as he tried to slip out the door.

"Skia, let me out. Get away from the door."

Skia complained loudly. Darn cat.

Alone with 20 minutes to kill. I stretched out on the cot with the cat. The afternoon sun warmed the stone room. Skia's purrs sent low vibrations through the pillow.

In my dream, I was climbing a ladder. On one side was Carl, tall, blond and magnificent in a white Greek *chiton* and the Athenian helmet. On the other side was Jim, dressed in a black cassock with a monk's soft black *skoufos* on his head.

Each of them reached out for me, inviting me to walk his path. I looked up. Should I keep climbing toward my goal, or travel a different path with one of them? Deep chimes began to ring, announcing the time of decision.

I jerked awake. The wooden *semantron* sounded again, calling the brothers to Vespers.

Hellfire and damnation! The chime wasn't in my dream. I had slept the afternoon away.

52

Romanos II

A.D. 959, Constantinople

Romanos II paced. "How long can the old man linger?"

Emperor Constantine VII had suffered for months, growing weaker with each day of fever. Today, the 54-year-old ruler struggled for each breath. The priests and generals stood vigil in the emperor's chamber.

"I hate waiting," the 21-year-old heir complained to his wife.

"Your mother doesn't show you proper respect," Theophano said. "She should have turned things over to you when your father fell ill."

The dark-haired Spartan beauty was dressed like an empress-to-be. But it had not always been so. She had been a tavern-keeper's daughter when she caught the eye of young Romanos.

"I'm ready to be emperor," Romanos said. "There's no reason I should not be in charge."

"Your mother's always controlled things. First she controlled your father. Now she's trying to keep you out of power."

"Well, she can't do it much longer."

"When your father dies, don't let her and your five sisters remain here. They will try to manipulate you. Helena will keep running things, just like she did for your father."

Theophano didn't intend to share the royal palace with her husband's over-educated sisters. The eldest, Agatha, served as her father's secretary and acted like she knew everything. And young Theodora had been her father's pet. Everyone said Theodora was so pretty. Well, there was room for only one beauty in the palace.

Theophano had already produced a purple-born heir, Basil. She rubbed her belly. She had not yet told Romanos that another heir was on the way.

"They should go to a monastery to deal with their grief," Romanos said. "And my father's friends and advisers will be gone. They think they know so much."

"You will be a great emperor. You will recapture Crete and be forever remembered by your people."

A miracle-working monk, Loukas, had predicted in 941 that Emperor Romanos would regain Crete. But Romanos I Lekapenos was deposed by his own sons without that achievement.

"I remember when my father's forces made the assault on Crete ten years ago. He said we would fulfill the prophecy and take back Crete in my name. He promised me a victory."

"He was too timid. A hundred ships were not enough. You will be bolder."

Their conversation was interrupted.

"You must come at once, Most High," the eunuch requested.

Theophano smiled secretly at her husband as she took his hand. His sisters had spread rumors that Theophano had poisoned the old man. Let them gossip; no one could prove anything.

As they walked into the emperor's chambers, the tears flowed down her cheeks. Young Romanos ran to his father's bedside and knelt beside it.

He clutched his father's cold hand and buried his face against it. Let them think he was crying. His father had been stodgy and moralizing. The empire needed a bold young emperor.

The young emperor was too fun-loving to read or go to war. His father's general, Nikephoros, retook Crete in A.D. 961, fulfilling the prophecy for Romanos.

Romanos and Theophano had three children: Basil II, Constantine VIII and Anna, the Purple-born. Romanos II was only 26 years old when he died following a hunting trip. Gossip was thick following his death. Was it an infection from a hunting accident? His drinking and womanizing? Or a bit of poison from an angry wife?

53

Varlaam

Friday evening, Brother Iakobos' cell

Trapped. Should I stay and admit my mistake to Jim, or find someplace to hide overnight?

First things first. I was desperate to find a bathroom. I crossed my legs as I plotted strategy.

Surely the monks went to the bathroom at night. There had to be something in this building. An extra cassock hung on the wall. The robe was a little long, but it might fool someone on the cleaning crew for a few seconds.

I worked my way down the hall, pausing at each door and listening before opening. Finally, next to the central room, I hit pay dirt. What a relief! The facilities were simple but adequate.

In the central room, the legal pads remained but the fragments were gone—probably locked away in the treasury overnight.

How long were Vespers? Maybe 45 minutes remained to find a place to hole up for the night. I visualized Carl's map. The library was nearby.

I edged up to a window. Shadows spread across the courtyard. The red-tile peaks of the buildings and towers reflected the orange rays from the setting sun. A worker swept the paving stones. Another gathered trash. A hose was rolled out, ready to wash away the dregs of worldly visitors.

Maybe there was an inside passage. I backtracked to the stairway. No luck up or down. I noticed a small door tucked under the stairs. Outside was a small private patio where the outer wall of the complex jutted away from the block of cells. A small gap was left between the buildings. I followed it around the side of the building.

I flattened into a deep purple shadow as I looked into the courtyard. Workmen loaded trash bags into a cart. They disappeared as they pushed the cart toward the front gate. Coast clear.

A dash brought me to the door of the library. The door swung open when I tested the knob.

Constantine's book was in its place on the back row. I opened the glass case and lifted the silver-covered boards. Inside, the pages spoke of grace and elegance. I could see the classical influence of the Macedonian Renaissance.

What time was it? I buttoned the book inside my shirt and pulled the cassock back over it.

I eased the door open a crack; the workmen had returned. One hosed the courtyard while the other worked the push broom. They disappeared around the side of the *katholikon*. I was living right.

Quick strides carried me to the walkway. The shadows offered refuge as I retreated back to Iakobos' cell.

The cassock and my long skirt served as window shades to contain the flash as I took pictures. Should I just shoot the illustrations, or every page? I opted for the latter.

I noticed the gap under the door—bright flashes bursting into the hall would be bad. Jim's blanket filled the gap nicely.

The thick board covers on the codex kept the pages flat when closed, but the parchment pages naturally curled when the book was open. I discovered that my scrunchie did passable duty holding the open edge down while I shot photographs.

"What the h!" Iakobos stumbled over the blanket, then clamped his lips and slammed the door.

"What are you doing? Stop that." He whispered, but the meaning was clear.

I had shoved aside his laptop to make work space for my task. He retrieved it and turned on music to cover our conversation.

"What's going on here? You're supposed to be gone."

His face was red as a vulture's head as he circled in his black robe.

"I fell asleep when you left. I didn't wake up until I heard the *semantron* for evening prayers."

"So you decided to sneak around and steal manuscripts? I thought I could trust you."

What could I say? He was right. Yet another blown relationship.

I turned away to regain my composure. Salty tears rolled onto my lips. Big girls don't cry; I counted to ten, rubbed my hands over my face, squared my shoulders and turned back to take my ass-chewing like an adult.

"You're right. I screwed up by falling asleep, and screwed up again by wanting one more look at this manuscript. I let you down."

"Oh, Hell. You're crying."

He tried to hug me as I turned away.

"I'm not crying to get your sympathy. I'm crying because I'm mad at myself."

He kissed the back of my neck and rested his head against the back of mine.

"Please don't cry. I'm sorry I yelled at you."

"Don't be nice to me ... it will just make me cry more."

He plopped down on the cot. I did my breathing routine and had a few sips of water.

"Do you need a chocolate candy bar?"

Chocolate? Did I hear the word chocolate? I slowly turned around.

"I thought you were fasting."

"I am, but that doesn't mean you are. I picked up a few treats at the gift shop yesterday. I got distracted by your special treat earlier and forgot to give these to you."

He retrieved a couple of chocolate bars from a drawer. "Which one do you want?"

"Just one?"

"One now, one later."

Jim went down the hall to refill his water pitcher while I slowly savored the candy bar. Dinner looked meager.

He returned with water and a big basket of pistachios. "On fasting days, we don't cook. We can eat leftover bread from the day before, and dried fruits and nuts. We never eat red meat—Orthodox monks are usually vegetarians. On fast days, we give up olive oil and all dairy products. We can have water, but no coffee or wine."

We made a silent toast with our glasses of water and dug into the nuts.

"How many days do you fast?"

"Mondays, Wednesdays and Fridays, plus the day before high holy days and Lent. Serious monasteries fast almost two-thirds of the year."

"Lots of not eating."

"Why do you think my clothes are falling off me? I've lost almost 20 pounds between fasting and climbing those cursed stairs."

"You have great abs—do those come from climbing stairs?"

Jim laughed. "We do 100 prostrations with our private prayers each morning. That's like 100 push-ups a day. Being a monk does have some benefits."

"Yeah, but there are no women to appreciate those great abs."

Did I see a blush? He dug around and came up with a box of raisins. "Dessert?"

"I hope you know this doesn't count for the dinner you owe me."

"And this doesn't count for the dessert you owe me."

After dessert, we light-proofed the room again. Jim turned the pages while I snapped pictures.

"How did you get this book back here?"

"I went out the back door onto the patio, slipped through the walkway between the buildings and into the front door of the library. It was open."

Jim laughed.

"What's funny?"

"The patio. Monasteries don't have patios. That's our back door fire escape. If we can't get out the front into the courtyard, we're supposed to go over the wall and climb down the folding ladders and nets to the path below."

"Have you ever done that?"

"No, but I'm told it's possible. It's maybe a hundred feet down."

"No, thanks."

We returned to the manuscript.

"What's this book about?" I asked.

Jim studied a few pages. "Handwriting styles vary, so I'm slow reading manuscripts. It seems to be a commentary on the Psalms and passages in the Old Testament about being a good king. It talks about Joshua, David and Solomon."

"That makes sense. Gabriel said it was written by Constantine Purple-born, who was an emperor during the Macedonian Renaissance."

We bent over the pages together.

"This one is Psalm *Eta*. I guess that would be Eight," Jim said. "The commentary is a homily by a Patriarch Stephen. He writes about God's creation and our new creation in the Resurrection of Jesus on the eighth day."

"That church illustration looks a little like Daphni. Who's Patriarch Stephen?" I asked.

"No idea. There's another of his homilies commenting on Psalm *Pi Eta*."

"I've seen the chalice in that illustration."

Jim kept reading. 'This Psalm—Eighty-eight—is a plea for God's help. The patriarch writes about God answering mankind's plea for salvation by raising Christ from Hades. Now what were you asking me?"

"Oh, nothing." Constantine Purple-born had drawn my chalice, probably his own design. No wonder someone was trying to steal it.

Jim smoothed the pages to put the book away. "Here in the front, it is dedicated to Romanos."

"Romanos II was the son of Constantine VII."

Jim growled and gave his already-messy hair a vigorous shaking.

"I'm trying to decipher the date. The calligraphy is very ornate. Once I figure out the letters, I then have to remember what letter stands for what number. Then, we convert it from either the Byzantine Creation Era or the Alexandrian Era."

"What?"

"Years were numbered from creation based on the Septuagint version of the Bible, which is the Greek translation of the Hebrew Scriptures. The older Alexandrian Era set creation as 5493 years before the birth of Christ. The Byzantine Era of the World set creation 5508 years before the birth of Christ. That's a 15-year difference. The empire officially changed the dating system in 988."

Jim finally gave up on the date. We wrapped the manuscript in a pillowcase for protection and put it on the desk. We sat side by side on the cot holding hands. I rested my head on his shoulder.

"So how are we going to get you out of here?" Jim asked.

"I assume I can slip out in the morning with the tourists. What time does the gate open?"

"Nine o'clock. It's a Saturday, so we should have more individual tourists and fewer tour buses. This time, I'll make sure you get out."

Jim got up and stirred around in his stuff.

"I have an extra tee-shirt and pants that you can sleep in. I'm going to take a shower. Do you want to come?"

"Aren't you worried the monks might walk in on us?"

"They generally use the bathroom on their end of the building.

This one is for guests and me. I think you'll be safe."

"I don't know. It sounds pretty risky to shower together in a monastery bathroom."

Jim shook his head. "You have a dirty mind. I didn't mean together. I meant one at a time."

"Oh. That would be safer."

Jim gathered towels and soap while I found my toothbrush.

The hall was dark. I slipped his extra cassock over my head and shoulders and walked right behind him. Jim stopped; I plowed into him.

"May you live," Jim said.

I heard a Greek response echo down the hall in a rich voice—Abbot Paulos.

A door clicked closed somewhere down the hall. Jim quickly finished the last few steps to our destination.

He locked the door and chivalrously turned his head while I showered and did my things.

"If someone knocks while I'm showering, just ignore it. They'll hear the shower and go away," he instructed.

While he showered, I kept my eyes averted—mostly.

Skia greeted us with a lively "yeow" as we emerged. The cat wove between our legs as we tried to sneak quietly back to Iakobos' cell. Thanks, cat. He slipped in with us, then complained when Jim tossed him out.

"There's not room in here for three of us. Besides, I hate sleeping with a cat. I don't know why you made friends with that beast."

He pulled one of the mattresses and pillows from the cot and set it up in the narrow gap between the cot and the table.

"You get the cot, I'll take the floor."

"So you have an extra mattress and pillow for sleepovers?"

"No, comfort. All the elders have two mattresses and pillows on their cots. I tried doing with just one for a week, but one thin mattress is just too stoic."

We settled into the silence and darkness. Bed slats pressed through the mattress.

"I'm sorry I pulled the seduction routine earlier," I whispered.

Jim's heap rustled. His words floated to me. "I thought you were into me. I didn't realize it was a routine."

"I said that wrong. 'I'm sorry' is the important part. Forget the rest."

Silence. I reached down and felt for his hand. He pulled away.

"I'm sorry that I didn't believe you at first. I just didn't know which was the real you. The seduction was the only way for me to test your story."

"So it wasn't a routine, it was a test. That makes me feel a whole lot better."

"No, no, no, I didn't mean that."

"Amber, my alarm goes off at four o'clock in the morning. As the novice, I ring the morning *semantron* for personal prayers. So I think we need to go to sleep."

"But I don't want to go to sleep with you mad at me."

Silence.

"Are you mad at me?"

No answer. I had bruised his male ego. He was definitely mad at me. Testosterone again.

DAY SEVEN

"So God blessed the seventh day and hallowed it, because on it
God rested from all the work he had done in creation."
Genesis 2:3

Seven is the number of completeness.

Creation took seven days—six days of work and one day of rest. Rest was a crucial part of creation.

In Exodus, God instructs Moses to make a gold lamp stand with seven lamps.

Seven is the sum of three (the divine number) and four (the number of the earth). So seven includes both the divine and the human.

In Revelation, John sees seven lamp stands and records letters to seven churches. He sees seven torches for the seven spirits of God. Both the dragon and the second beast have seven heads. Seven is also the number of seals on God's scroll of judgment. God created the world in seven days, and judges it in three series of seven disasters.

The Greek letter for seven is zeta (Z ζ).

55

Saturday

Varlaam, 4 a.m.

Jim dressed in the dark and disappeared into the night. In a few minutes, the mellow tone of the wooden drum rolled across the peaks, echoed by the deeper tone from the *semantron* at the Great Meteoron.

He tiptoed back into the cell. That sneaky cat slipped in with him.

"Good morning"

"Shhhh. Go back to sleep."

"Can I watch you pray?"

"It's a pretty small place—I can't stop you. Besides, we pray out loud, so you'll hear me."

He placed an icon on the window sill and lit a small candle.

"What do you do?"

Jim retrieved his prayer rope from his left pocket and showed it to me.

"Each rope has 100 knots. We use our right hand to make the sign of the cross and our left to move through the knots to count our prayers," Jim explained.

"I'll do the Jesus prayer three times around, then three rounds of prayer to the *Theotokos*. The next time around I do the saints honored on today's calendar, then another round for all the saints. Then, each monk does a round to the saint who shares his name. Finally, we end with three more rounds of the Jesus prayer."

"That's a lot of praying."

"Actually, it's twelve hundred prayers. We are supposed to do a hundred prostrations as well. I don't like to do them all together, so I do a prostration with the first 10 prayers of each cycle."

"Were there any saints named Iakobos?"

"The leading one is James, the Just, brother of the Lord."

"I thought your monk name was Iakobos."

"Iakobos is Greek for Jacob. Jacob and James are the same name, just like Joshua and Jesus are the same name."

Jim stopped whispering and breathed deeply. When he was in the zone, he leaned forward, stretched out and touched his forehead to the floor.

"Kyrie Iesou Christe, Yie tou Theou, eleison me ton hamartolon."

I recognized the prayer Father Gabriel chanted for me. *Lord Jesus Christ, son of God, have mercy on me, a sinner.*

He stood and repeated the process again. The pace picked up once Jim got through the ten prostrations. Other voices floated down the hall and in through the window, giving strength and support to Jim's voice. Each prayer chant had its own tones and rhythm.

Skia draped himself around my head. I fell back asleep to saintly chanting and purring.

Rough beard brushed my cheek and warm breath pushed against my ear. Not the cat.

"Amber, wake up for a minute."

I mumbled.

"I'm going to Orthros and liturgy. We finish about seven, then we have breakfast together. I'll be back by eight and help you get out. There's a candy bar here for your breakfast."

His hug was firm, filled with longing—or lust. Jim forced his way out of my arms and was gone.

Through the window, the full moon dipped toward the horizon, shimmering through mist and fog. The candle sputtered against the darkness.

Five o'clock in the morning. I got myself in trouble by over-sleeping yesterday afternoon. No way would I be caught napping again. I turned on my cell phone and set it to vibrate. The symbols for voice mail and text messages lit up.

Lydia wanted to know about my outing. When would I be home? The artifact police were inspecting both buildings on Saturday.

Carl didn't like Billy's friends; he threatened to do rather graphic things to them. Another message from Carl inviting me to go dancing Saturday night. Great minds think alike.

Billy with a question about the AV system. Lydia wishing me a good night. And worrying about the inspectors going through her personal things.

My colleagues needed me. Time to return to Athens.

Iakobos' cell looked like a tornado had moved through. I couldn't leave a mess like this.

After a furtive visit to the facilities, I attacked the tasks. Get dressed. Pack my backpack. Hang Jim's clothes neatly. Stack the mattresses and pillows on the cot, straighten the sheets and covers.

Eat chocolate bar as a reward. Write message on the wrapper. Slip it under Jim's pillow.

Everything was back in its place, for Jim's return.

The Constantine manuscript rested on the desk, protected in a pillowcase. It and my backpack were the only evidence of my presence here last night.

Orthros and liturgy would end in about 20 minutes. Surely that was enough time to return the manuscript to its rightful place. No need to make Jim sneak it back later.

I hefted the book and my backpack and slid out of the cell. Coast clear.

The cool night air raised goose bumps on my arms. The eastern sky glowed with the approaching birth of the sun. The monastery floated above pink and salmon-colored clouds. The monastery on the next peak emerged from mounds of pink cotton candy.

I did feel closer to heaven here.

Prayers would end shortly after sunrise. Better hurry.

I left my backpack on the patio and edged through the gap between the buildings, clutching the book to my heart. Skia glided beside me, a silent gray shadow.

No one disturbed the serenity of the quadrangle as I peered around the edge.

I ventured into the open. It seemed like a mile as I silently paced to the library door. My warm hand wrapped around the cold metal handle and gently squeezed the latch.

It resisted. The door was locked.

BZZZZ! BZZZZ! BZZZZ!

A security light on the side of the building began to flash.

Crap. My feet carried me back to my hole between the buildings. I was halfway down the passage before I stopped.

Had I been seen? Was I being followed? I listened for running footsteps, but all I could hear was my pounding chest and the blaring alarm.

BZZZZ! BZZZZ! BZZZZ!

I'd better keep moving. But where? I couldn't think with that racket.

I paused behind the cell building. Should I retreat to Iakobos' cell or cut across and try to reach the place where I met Jim the day before?

BZZZZ! BZZZZ! BZZZZ!

I looked around. I should to go back to the courtyard and confess. Would Sophia send me home? She had already threatened twice.

BZZZZ! BZZZZ! BZZZZ!

My back was to the wall.

The wall.

The leading edge of the sun loomed huge on the horizon. Over the edge was fog. How far down was it?

BZZZZ! BZZZZ! BZZZZ!

An ancient folding ladder led down into the fog.

Instead of a continuous vertical support, the sides were made of rough-hewn timbers cut about four feet long. The vertical supports were assembled like a series of nesting letter "V"s. Round branches mounted through holes in the sides of the timber worked double duty as rungs and as rods to hinge the side supports together.

A crazy excuse for a ladder. Didn't look like it could hold a skinny monk, let alone a well-fed girl like me.

Finally, blessed silence. The alarm had been turned off.

Voices echoed from the courtyard. They would be here soon.

Confess and be sent home.

Go over the wall.

I hadn't been afraid of heights until Monday.

I stuffed the manuscript in my pack, strapped it on my back and wrapped the prayer rope around my left wrist. I needed the power of Gabriel's prayers.

Courtyard or wall?

I unfastened my long skirt and tossed it into the mist, freeing my legs for action.

I clambered onto the wall and tested my weight on the rungs.

56

Meteora

*"And there shall be another place, very high ...
The men and women whose feet slip shall go rolling
down to a place where is fear. And again they mount
up and fall down again and continue to roll down.
Thus shall they be tormented for ever."*
Apocalypse of Peter 11

Dawn, The rocky spires

My hands gripped rough side boards as my feet searched for the way down. I stretched down with my right toe and pushed on the rung. It sagged a little, but held my weight. I shifted my weight to the lower foot, then moved my left foot down beside it.

The rungs were about a foot apart. I could do this a hundred times.

I felt like an inch worm as I moved first my hands, then my feet down the weathered timbers. The fog isolated me; fog above, fog below, fog to my back. The gray stone wall and the ladder were my only links with reality.

Mist coated the ladder and wall. After ten rungs down, I paused to wipe my hands on my shirt. It didn't help; my clothes were as damp as the cold stone.

Right foot down, left foot down, hands down, rest. The descent became a slow rhythm.

Right foot down, left foot down, hands down.

A splintering sound. The rung gave way under my feet.

My legs swung free into the fog.

I tried to hold on. My weight pulled my hands off the wet timbers.

My left arm jerked; burning pain shot through my bruised shoulder as it bore the entire weight of my body.

I found the side rail with my right hand and stretched my feet down, down for the next rail.

Finally, something solid beneath my feet.

I sucked air into my desperate lungs as I looked up to see what had caught my arm. The rope on my left wrist had snagged the end of a rung. Gabriel's prayers had saved me once again.

My arm was being torn from its socket. Climbing back up a few steps to relieve the tension was the only way to get loose.

I avoided the broken rung and managed to get my feet up two steps. To untangle the prayer rope, I would have to let go with my right hand. Did I dare let go and trust my feet?

I snaked my right arm through the ladder and worked the rope off the end of the rung as I said a few Jesus prayers. I didn't deserve another chance. But I got it anyway.

What had the count been? In the slip, I lost track. My arms trembled—fear or fatigue?

A foot at a time, I inched down again.

Rough stone sanded the skin off my knuckles as the timbers deposited splinters in my palms and fingers. Backpack straps dug into my shoulders. Broken rungs led to breathless moments.

My cell phone kept vibrating in my pocket. Like I'm going to take a call while dangling above the abyss.

St. John Climacus's ladder to heaven had only 30 steps. This ladder seemed to stretch down forever. How many steps were on Iakobos' ladder?

A cracking sound. The ladder split apart on the left side, leaving me dangling precariously. Another crack. The lower part of the ladder broke away.

Taking me with it.

We landed with a clatter on a ledge. Angels must surely be on my side. I caught my breath and checked to make sure my arms and legs still worked.

A rolled up net beside me was secured to the ledge. This must be the climbing net that Jim mentioned. I secured my load and started down again.

The cut stones of the walls transitioned into boulders of the foundation. I could see patches where the ancient crumbling mortar had been repaired. Too few patches, if you ask me.

The boulders changed to the sandstone pinnacle that supported the foundation. Wind and weather had pitted and stained the soft sandstone through millennia of exposure.

Sunlight filtered through thin, patchy fog.

How far down? This net was pretty beat up.

My toes couldn't find the next row. I stretched my right toe down as far as possible, said a few more prayers, then looked down.

57

Below Varlaam

Flat rock at last.

The path was about six feet below the bottom of the net. I worked my arms down as low as possible, then let my feet swing clear. It would be about a four-foot drop. Piece of baklava.

My feet hit and I rolled onto the path. I shed the backpack and leaned back against the mountain. Sitting on hard rock had never felt so good.

Why did I try to clean the room and return the manuscript to the library? Instead of impressing Jim, I proved I couldn't be trusted alone. I banged my head against the rocks.

Fog clung in the caves and trees below, but was gone above. I looked up ... way up. If I had been able to see, I wouldn't have started down. Unfortunately, anyone looking down could now see me.

I snapped a few pictures to record my descent, hefted the pack and followed the path snaking around the peak. It better lead somewhere. I wouldn't make a good hermit in a wind-swept cave.

The path wove down the slope and under an overhanging ledge. The view from above was blocked; I sprawled in the shade and retrieved my link to the outside world.

A dozen missed calls and messages. It was a few minutes before eight o'clock in the morning, for Pete's sake. If things had gone according to plan, I would have been sleeping at a nice hotel in Kalambaka. Why were people calling me so early?

A certain pseudo-monk had sent ten messages.

Did you set off the burglar alarm? I told you to stay put and I would get you out. Now you've got things all stirred up. Where are you?

Where are you? And where did you put the Constantine manuscript?

This is not funny. Did you think you could slip out of here and take the Constantine manuscript without me knowing?

I'm not angry. I just need to find you and get you out of here safely. Let me know where you are.

The gatekeeper decided that Skia must have set off the alarm. They found the cat sitting by the library door. They haven't figured out yet that the manuscript is missing. So we can still get out of this OK. Please answer.

I've checked the alcove where we met. I've checked the upstairs of the cell building. I confess, you've tricked us all. Now just tell me where you are.

I see your skirt caught on the rocks below. Are you OK?

My love, are you hurt? I have a horrible image of your broken body on the rocks. I'll never forgive myself!

Please, answer. I'm seriously considering confessing to Abbot Paulos and calling for help.

If I don't hear from you in 15 minutes, I'm calling a search and rescue crew.

I'd better answer if I didn't want all hell crashing in on me.

I'm OK. I climbed down the ladder from the patio. I'm on the path below. Do you know where this leads? I need a map.

I waited. Sure enough, the phone started dancing in my hand.

Thank God you're OK. You actually made it down that wreck of a ladder and the nets? Stay put and I'll come rescue you.

Who did he think I was, some weakling who had to be rescued by a man?

I can hike back to town or to the road. Just tell me where the path goes. Your manuscript is with me. I tried to return it to the library. I should have left it on the patio, but I panicked.

That cursed manuscript. This backpack would be a lot lighter if I had just left it behind. I really am stupid.

Path was too good a name for the course I followed. I worked my way around and across sandstone outcroppings and crevices to what seemed to be a dead end.

The only way forward was a narrow ledge around a tall spindle of weathered sandstone. Initials and Greek letters were carved in the stone. Medieval Christian pilgrims had tagged the sandstone. Sweet.

I recognized *NIKE*, the Greek word for victory.

Omega Pi Eta. Alpha and *Omega. Omega* and *Alpha.* Beginning and End, End and Beginning? What was the message of switching the order?

Ancient graffiti is like Scrabble. Later pilgrims built a new word coming off a letter from a previous word. *Omega Pi Eta (Ω Π H)* was built off the *Alpha Omega.* That new one had me stumped.

Chi and *Rho—XP,* the first two letters of Christ—were written on top of each other to form a six-pointed star. Constantine saw this symbol in the sky at the Mulvane Bridge. Byzantine soldiers fought with *Chi Rho* on their shields.

Folks who complain about Xmas always annoy me. X is the original abbreviation for Christ, dating back two millennia.

No time for studying graffiti now. I gritted my teeth, pressed my back to the stone and slid my body around the narrow ledge. Wind whipped my hair and gave me an unsteady feeling. The sandstone felt like an emery board against my back. Great vista, though, if you could stand to look.

The ledge finally widened into a clearing. I looked up the mountain to the monastery. High overhead was the ledge with the herb garden. Farther along the wall was the winch tower. A rope net still hung from the rusted hardware.

I was near the monastery's historic front door. Before the modern bridge and stairway, this was the way in. A shout would summon the monks. The net would be lowered to haul visitors and supplies up to the tower.

After that dreadful ladder, the hoist net looked safe.

Narrow steps and footholds were carved in the sandstone leading down. Darn. More climbing.

I tripped and sprawled on the rough path. I brushed rocks and debris from my hair and face. Something was digging into my knee. I rolled over and checked for scrapes. I had tripped over my lost camera...what was left of it.

The digital screen was cracked and the lens was scratched and jammed. I gathered up pieces of metal and plastic. I tried powering it up. Hopeless cause. The memory card was dirty, but seemed intact. Maybe my luck was turning.

My phone twitched in my pocket. "Hello?"

"Amber, thank God. Are you alright?" Jim whispered.

"I'm fine. I'm right below the winch tower."

"Wait. I'm coming to the wall."

I lied about being fine. I was muddy, scraped and bruised. I used a corner of my shirt to clean up. With a little combing and lip gloss, I might just be able to pass myself off as someone who was fine.

When the black-robed figure appeared at the wall above, I waved cheerfully. Jim's voice answered softly on the phone.

"I am so glad to see you. I was afraid you were dead."

I struck a model's pose and tossed my hair. It caught in the wind.

"I couldn't climb in that long skirt. I didn't think about leaving a clue behind. Now how do I get back to Athens?"

"Follow the old steps down. When you reach the split in the path, take the branch to the left. It's a new path that leads back up to the parking lot and highway. The old path leads past the dragon cave to Kastraki, a little village at the foot of the mountain."

"I can do that. Once I get to the parking lot, I bet I can catch a cab to Kalambaka or hitch a ride on a tour bus."

"No, I'll meet you in the parking lot. I need to see you."

A hug did sound good. I visualized a girl scantily clad in shorts and tank top kissing a man in the cassock and black cylinder hat of a monk. Not good.

"Won't that blow your cover?"

"To hell with my cover and my dissertation."

"Wait. You see me now. Don't do anything rash. We'll talk later."

I blew the love-sick monk an exaggerated kiss and hit the path.

58

The Road to Athens

I grabbed a local cab to Kalambaka and found a private tour guide. I settled into the back seat with sweets and coffee for the trip to Athens. The aroma of warm honey filled the cab. Baklava or halva cake first? Baklava won. I licked honey and walnuts off my fingers as I dialed Aunt Lydia.

"Hello."

"Hi, it's your long-lost niece. I'm on my way back to Athens. How ya' doing?"

"It's as much fun as giving the cat a bath. Billy presents initial findings to some manuscript experts at 4 o'clock tomorrow. Carl is sulking. The snoops are inspecting my collection while I try to bribe them. Sophia is being ever so sweet."

"I'm sorry I abandoned you. I'll be back by 2 o'clock."

"I shouldn't complain. I'm just sick of these demanding men. Did y'all have fun?"

"It was interesting—manuscripts, monastery art and hiking."

"How about your friend Jim?"

"Yeah. I got to know him a lot better."

"Would you call Carl and find out what that sweet boy is upset about?"

"Will do. See you soon."

I fortified myself with a halva cake, then dialed.

"Amber, you must return at once or I will kill someone."

"Thanks for asking about me. I had a nice trip, thank you."

"I've endured absolute hell. Billy is a polite, educated religious bigot. But his friend Herr Smoot is a lump of *shiza*. He says Germany has lost its soul to secular humanism. His group will return us to Christian rule, just like Calvin's Geneva. He would have us burning witches. And his assistant is like a dog following his master around."

"Why don't you tell them you have other commitments and work on your own research?"

"I told Sophia to suck up to Lydia if she wanted to keep the Institute going. So I can't insult Lydia's guests."

I thought for a minute.

"My aunt might understand more than you expect. She doesn't like pompous jerks either."

"I won't burden her with my crap. Besides, if Billy will make decisions on our funding I need to tolerate that *shiza*-head Smoot. Will you be here soon?"

"I'm on the road to Athens right now. We're between towns, so I'll probably lose cell service."

"It's more fun when you are here. Maybe dancing tonight?"

"Sounds good. Maybe dinner?"

"*Ja*, if you would like. And *dessert*, of course."

He gave it just the right inflection. He was not suggesting baklava.

I shook my head at the thought of the chaos back at the Institute. I didn't have the heart to tell them I would arrive with a stolen manuscript.

This day couldn't get any worse. Might as well read about the horrible punishment planned for sinners who steal manuscripts. I opened my second latte and my Greek Bible.

Billy says John's third prophecy, the one now underway, starts in Rev. 19. The present age of the church leads to the triumph of Christianity throughout the world and the coming of Christ.

The fresco shows a crowned rider on a white horse, followed by an army dressed in white. The red beast tumbles off the edge as birds attack Satan's army to eat their flesh. I thought this was the second coming of Christ.

No, Billy says. This is the church charging forth to defeat the evil in the world.

I was struck by the phrase "The sea gave up the dead who were in it" in Rev. 20:13.

I've seen heads sticking out of jaws in pictures of the Last Judgment. I just figured it out. These images show the sea giving up its dead. The dead rise, head first, out of the wicked jaws of dastardly sea creatures. Death has been defeated.

It's resurrection. The dead are reconstituted and rise from a watery grave.

I had totally missed that before.

The text message icon flashed on my cell phone.

Are you OK? Did you find a ride back to Athens? Things are calming down here. They haven't discovered that the manuscript is missing. I will come to Athens tomorrow and bring it back with some other books as cover.

We are working on translating the fragment. It seems to be something from Irenaeus' "Against Heresies." He may be quoting Papias.

Irenaeus was a second century Christian leader and author. He was a Greek who became bishop at Lyons. His writings were more popular in the west than the east, so most of his surviving manuscripts are in Latin. A fragment in original Greek rather than a Latin translation could be significant. Abbot Paulos is intrigued.

I'll let you know what we find. Thanks for your help.

Maybe Billy really had discovered his next book. Lydia would be pleased. I texted Jim back.

Things are not calm back at the ranch. The artifact cops are hassling the Institute, atheist Carl is threatening to kill the true believers, and Billy needs me to finish the AV stuff for his presentation to manuscript experts at 4 p.m. tomorrow.

I am in a taxi sipping coffee and eating baklava. I'm sure this is better than your breakfast. Or did you even get to eat with the chaos I caused? I really screwed this up. I'm sorry.

What next? I retrieved the card from my original camera, cleaned it with spit and a napkin, then blew it dry.

I slid the memory card into my new camera, said a prayer, and powered it on.

59

Images

Hallelujah! Images! The tiny pictures flipped through as I advanced the digital display. I had duplicated many of them the next morning, but some were different.

An image from the parapet came up. I shut my eyes and shuddered.

Had I been pushed, or was I a clumsy oaf as Sophia believed?

At the time, I had been sure I felt a pressure against my back. But there was no reason for anyone to attack me. Besides, who would do such a thing? I had suspected Brother Iakobos—Jim was guilty of lying, but could he try to kill me then kiss me like he did?

The camera whirred as it turned itself off.

Good. I wouldn't have to look at those pictures. I opened my eyes and stared out the window. The fields roll past, but I didn't see them. I saw the fall, the beast.

I saw Hell.

It won't scare me any more. I hit the power switch and studied the pictures. Miniature green fields far below. Sandstone weathered smooth by wind and rain. The good thoughts struggled back. A gray cat stretching in the sun. Solid stone walls. Clear thin blue sky.

I forced myself to advance to the last few pictures. The camera had captured my shadow cast against the courtyard wall.

The next picture showed two shadows. My stomach churned as I stared.

Whir. The image went dark.

I put my finger on the power switch. Push it. Push it.

No. No.

YES, darn it.

The screen lit up. I clicked the forward arrow.

The second shadow grew an arm.

I threw up in the baklava sack.

The cab driver took pity and made a stop so I could recover from my "motion sickness." The fresh air and cold water helped clear my head.

The image was irrefutable. Someone *had* tried to kill me.

I ran through the events Monday morning. We had taken pictures as we toured the monastery, made a brief visit to the library, then taken a break. I mentally retraced the steps across the courtyard to the restroom. We posed group pictures. I talked to Andreus Mikos about the chalice, went to the bathroom, and then walked to the railing to shoot pictures of the valley below.

The chalice.

I thought it was a message from beyond the grave from Uncle Robert. But it must be cursed. Things started going badly when I opened it.

I shook my head. Worrying about curses was almost as ridiculous as worrying about being left behind at the Rapture.

Andreus Mikos was interested in the chalice. Did he push me to get his hands on it?

Ridiculous. He was a nice, grandfatherly sort of man. Besides, he wouldn't try to steal it on the street or break into the Institute. He would need an employee, a thug, for that.

Did he trade in stolen artifacts? Sophia distrusted him.

At least the chalice was safe now, locked away in the coat room of the Acropolis Museum.

I looked around for snacks. Darn. Just a bottle of water. How could I plan a trap for an antiquities thief and murderer without chocolate?

I started a shopping list.

The private tour guide dropped me at *Syntagma* Square, near the main shopping district. Which store would carry a GPS tracker?

60

Nikephoros II

Dec. 10, A.D. 969, The Royal Palace, Constantinople

Running footsteps violated the stillness of night. The metallic ring of swords and battle axes echoed in the marble halls.

Emperor Nikephoros shouted to the palace guard.

"Check every room. Assassins are in the palace."

"They could not have slipped past us," the commander protested.

"My spies tell me that my life will be taken tonight. The traitors are here, now." the emperor insisted.

Nikephoros II's six-year reign had been stormy.

The great general had commanded the armies in the east under Constantine VII, then defeated the Saracens in Crete for Romanos II. He returned to the eastern front, winning victories all the way to Syria for the Eastern Roman Empire.

Then Romanos II died suddenly. The young regent empress turned to Nikephoros for help. He agreed to save the dynasty for her children by marrying her and fighting the challengers.

Even as emperor, he was a military commander at heart. He waged wars on three fronts: Mesopotamia, Bulgaria and Italy. The people should have been grateful to the "Pale Death of the Saracens." Instead they resented heavy taxes to fund the campaigns.

The bureaucrats were angry at the frugality he imposed. The empress was bored with a husband in name only. He should have been hailed as a hero. Instead, he had eunuchs who tasted his food each meal. There were whispers that the empress had poisoned the previous two emperors.

As Nikephoros shouted orders, the guards worked their way from room to room, looking for assassins.

Young Basil and Constantine watched quietly as the imperial guards searched their rooms. Axe-swinging Vikings, tall pale fighting men from the north, had earned a place in the honored guard.

Basil, age 11, was stocky with sandy hair. He loved everything military. Basil savored his stepfather's book on military strategy and his grandfather's books on diplomacy and the triumphs of the empire. Constantine, the younger brother, looked more like his grandfather and namesake: tall, lean, dark-haired.

The guards demanded entrance to the *gynaikonitis*, the private chambers of the empress and the other women of the palace. The axe-wielding Vikings grew restless in the hall.

Basil heard the high voices of the eunuchs who guarded the empress and her attendants. "You are not allowed inside with the royal ladies," the eunuch said. "We are the only guards allowed."

After extracting a promise from the eunuchs that they would search among the ladies, the guards moved on.

The frantic search turned up nothing. Nikephoros retired to his chambers. The 57-year-old emperor had spent his life fighting for the empire. Soon, the borders would be secure and Basil would be old enough to take the throne on his own.

He placed a row of icons on the floor, lit candles in front of them, and stretched out prostrate in prayer. He spent many nights like this. As the candles sputtered, he fell into a restless sleep.

The young Basil, too, had a hard time sleeping. He liked the ugly old emperor. His own father had ignored him. His stepfather let Basil train with the palace guard. He enjoyed tales of strategy and victory shared by Nikephoros and his nephew John. Basil didn't know what had caused a split between the two.

Rustling in the dark hall woke him. Peering out, he saw figures emerge from his mother's quarters. The men clutched women's cloaks over their uniforms. His mother stood in the door and kissed one of the men.

"Good luck, my future emperor and husband," he heard her say.

The man turned; a flickering candle caught his profile. The emperor's 43-year-old nephew was leading the team of assassins.

Basil ducked behind a column as the men crept past. He heard the brush of leather slippers on the marble floors and followed.

The assassins silently slit the throats of the guards sleeping outside the emperor's door, then entered the darkened chamber.

Basil heard the sword strike, then shouts.

"There he is, on the floor."

Swords clanked on stone. Wood splintered. The sickening thud of fists on flesh.

Basil heard a shout from the emperor. It turned into a scream. He crept closer.

He saw the young general standing on the bed as the guards dragged the wounded emperor to John's feet.

"Tell me, you stupid tyrant!" John roared. "I was the one who raised you to the heights of the Roman Empire. Did you think you could push me aside and ignore me?"

He pulled back his sword, then swung it in a great arc. The emperor's head tumbled off.

The blood-splattered assassins cheered for the new emperor. John waved his bloody sword in triumph.

The assassins mounted the emperor's head on a pike. Blood dripped onto the marble floors as assassins paraded it in the hall. Others dragged the headless body to the royal balcony and tossed the remains into the street.

"Now we are free of that ungrateful madman," John shouted.

Nikephoros II's tomb read: "You conquered all but a woman." He deserved better.

Seven years later, Emperor John was murdered.

61

Athens

Saturday, 1 p.m., the Classics Institute in Athens

The Plaka swarmed with tourists, perfuming the air with sweat, dust, and Greek cooking. I squeezed past a government car double-parked in front of the Institute.

In the library, Lydia and Sophia faced a couple of men across a table stacked high with folders and paperwork. The artifact police were here.

As the men asked questions, Lydia sorted through receipts and records. They didn't seem to believe that she brought some antiquities into the country. Or that Greek dealers provided honest documentation. I was beginning to have my doubts about that, too.

I raided Aunt Lydia's apartment for a few items, escaped to my study room and locked the door to rig my trap.

Nail polish remover stripped clear lacquer off the brass goblet from Byzantine Museum. I slathered it generously with lemon juice and raw egg to tarnish and pit the metal. After stepping on it a few times I rubbed it with a nail file. I washed off the juice and egg, then glued on a few faux pearls and colored glass rhinestones. I held it over a candle to get it nice and sooty.

Not bad. My shiny new goblet now looked like a battered old piece of junk.

I switched on my newly-purchased GPS tracking device and synched it with my phone. I wrapped it in tissue and planted it in the hollow stem. Melted candle wax filled the stem and base nicely. Anyone glancing at it would think the wax was there to give weight to the base so the goblet didn't tip over.

I laughed at my butt-ugly fake as I packed it into a box and put it in a bright pink shopping bag.

Next task: hide the Constantine manuscript. I visualized my options. Where does one stash a priceless national treasure?

After a small detour, I joined the men in the conference center.

Billy smiled. "Amber! You're my angel. We need you." I winced as he hugged my bruises.

"This is my colleague, Walter Smoot. I work with him at the Nicene Foundation."

Walter's big hands almost crushed mine. Before we could finish pleasantries, Billy gave me his legal pad with notes and lists of images.

Lydia would introduce Billy as the AV showed his credentials, a few pictures of his published books, shots of him in academic settings. Billy would explain the project as I clicked through some overall shots of the monastery, the library and the group at work. He'd give a brief overview of the types of manuscripts he had examined.

The main presentation would close in on the manuscript fragments. We would start with a picture of the cache, then run through a few examples before showing Billy's discovery.

"Don't show the whole fragment too long," Billy instructed. "No more than 30 seconds or so. Keep it moving so they can't do an independent translation and steal my scholarship."

Billy would first establish the date by comparing letter forms.

For translation, Billy had marked specific phrases and comparison documents. I suggested scattering in Byzantine images relating to the translation.

To identify the author and passage, Billy had marked other manuscripts for comparison. He suggested an image of Irenaeus. Ah, hah! So he and Jim agreed on the meaning of the fragment.

We'd wrap up with Q&A.

"Do you understand what I need, Amber?"

"Yeah. How long should it be?"

"Less than an hour. Enough time for questions, but not too much. I'll establish my credentials and my claim, but not reveal the results."

Walter's voice boomed. "This manuscript will change scholarship about the origins of the New Testament. You should stress the theological and policy implications of this discovery."

"No, these are just officials to get past. We stick to the factual part and save the powerful stuff for the media. Remember, Walter, *National Geographic* spent more than $2 million to unveil 'The Gospel of Judas.' We have to hold back details if we want big media play."

"Our mission is to advance the Law of God, not make money," Walter said.

"Why do you think I want media coverage? It's to change the thinking of policy makers. We can get major grants that will advance God's Kingdom, not just publicize this discovery."

Carl rolled his eyes throughout the exchange. He and I slipped out of the room.

"Amber, I turn these assholes over to you."

"Thanks a whole lot, Carl. I'll remember this."

We laughed as we slipped down to the kitchen. I brewed some tea.

"You Southerners and your iced tea—it must be the official beverage of Texas."

"Yup. Chicken-fried steak, mashed taters and cream gravy, fried okra and peach cobbler, all washed down by sweet tea. You'll have to visit some time and I'll show you a truly decadent way to eat. You think Greeks know how to roast meat, but you haven't seen what a Texan can do to a slab of ribs or a brisket."

"I know you and your aunt like Billy, but I do not trust him and his friends. They want to find proof for their ideas, not expand the scholarship."

"You aren't an objective observer. You're turned off by their religion."

"*Doch*, they are the ones blinded by their religion."

Lydia and Sophia gratefully accepted glasses of tea. The Greek guys looked down their noses at my tea and requested bottled water instead.

I returned upstairs armed with iced tea and *finikia*. Orange spice cookies taste great with iced tea.

Lydia and Sophia joined us in the conference room as I put the final touches on the introduction. The fragment would be harder, with crops, zooms and side-by-side comparisons.

Lydia collapsed into a white leather chair.

"Thank God that's done. If I have to pull one more receipt, I'll scream. I just hope my generous tip is enough."

"Have they signed off on the inventory?" Carl asked.

"Yes and no," Sophia said. "They will examine the documentation. Lydia told them to call our attorney if they need another inspection."

Lydia attacked my cookies.

"Let's run through this intro," Billy said. "Lydia, you're first up."

"I feel like I'm hogging the credit. Sophia, don't you want to welcome people to the Institute?"

"No, Lydia. This is our first outside event in the Robert Jackson conference center. This renovation was his idea. You should be the one to welcome our guests."

We looked around the crisp blue and white classroom with its high-tech features and vivid paintings of Greek islands. Lydia had done an awesome job.

"I hadn't seen it finished until Tuesday," Lydia said. "I'd be honored to make introductions."

"Who's coming?" I asked.

Sophia checked off the guest list.

"Georgios Karmanos from the ministry of culture. He is bringing two experts from the Byzantine museum, an expert in paleography—that's handwriting—and an expert in tenth century Greek translation. Andreus Mikos is coming on our side of the table. And we have Mr. Smoot representing the Nicene Foundation. All of them will sign non-disclosure agreements giving Dr. Sullivan first publication rights."

We ran though the introduction. I had worked in some nice shots of the Institute and Uncle Robert along with the pictures of Billy looking important. Everyone loved it.

The section introducing the monastery and library had a picture from my recovered memory card. A shaft of light spotlighted Billy in the stacks as he looked at a silver-bound manuscript. It had a great mood, with old bookshelves and a fresco of the prophet David on the wall above.

"I don't like that picture," Billy protested. "Don't you have something showing Dr. Karmanos and me looking at fragments?"

Darn. That was one of my best shots.

As we finalized the introduction, the Institute's phone rang. Sophia returned shaking her head.

"I do not know who is talking, but that was Father Paulos at Meteora. He and his assistant Iakobos invited themselves to our presentation. They know you are looking at Irenaeus."

"I thought the people from the Byzantine museum were going to get the fragment from the monastery after we made our case tomorrow," Lydia said. "We're negotiating a rather nice contribution to the conservation lab. I'm surprised they told Father Paulos."

I sunk into my chair. I knew the source of the leak: Jim had used me again. That was why I swore off men. I couldn't believe I actually kissed that furry face. Gag!

I gulped some tea to rinse the memory from my mouth, then stuffed in a few more *finikia*.

Billy and I finished the visuals for the manuscript comparisons.

Billy gave me another hug. "You've done a very professional

job."

"I hope it goes well tomorrow. Helping is the least I could do for Aunt Lydia."

Now, I needed to do something for myself. But I needed a co-hort.

I thought about Carl's invitation to go dancing. Maybe he would enjoy some subterfuge as well. My tired legs protested as I walked to his room. Voices carried into the hall.

"What's the strategy for tomorrow?" Carl's voice.

"We keep a low profile. You welcome people and show them to the conference center—like the butler. I will serve coffee and be the maid." Sophia's voice.

"That's too funny, Sophia. You've never been the maid type. You're too much of a feminist."

"Oh, I will be *so* helpful and supportive for Lydia. And keep my academic reputation as far as possible from this fiasco."

"*Ja.* So that's why you are reluctant to share the spotlight."

I heard Carl's light, slightly mocking laugh. But Sophia wasn't laughing.

"I am giving that charlatan preacher enough rope to hang himself. I do not like him sweet-talking Lydia and stealing our funding. I can not believe she would put that ideologue on her foundation board."

Sophia was blunt. But I hadn't seen her devious side before. Was she vicious enough to push someone off a wall?

Somehow, Carl didn't seem like the right person to help me set a trap.

I sent a certain black-robed traitor a text message as I pondered my next move.

62

The Trap

There was no getting around it. I needed law enforcement. I dialed Georgios Karmanos.

"Hello, Dr. Karmanos. This is Amber Jackson."

"Yes, Miss Jackson. How may I help you?"

"I've come upon an artifact that might be important, but someone is trying to steal it. Can we get together and talk in person? The Acropolis Museum in 45 minutes?"

"Yes, I can do that."

"I'll be in the coffee shop on the main floor."

How long would it take to explain to Karmanos and set the trap for my suspect? Security officers were already posted and surveillance tapes would be running. I just needed Karmanos to persuade them to cooperate. Surely I could do that in 45 minutes.

I found Andreus Mikos' card and dialed.

"Mr. Mikos, this is Amber Jackson."

"Yes, my dear. And how are you today?"

"I'd like to give you this Crusader goblet so you can see if it's worth restoring. Could you meet me at the Acropolis Museum in an hour and a half?"

"Of course, my golden-haired child."

"I'll see you in the coffee shop on the main floor."

The cab dropped me at the front entrance to the museum. I walked over the bridge, swinging my pink shopping bag. I paused to marvel at the layers of history beneath this river of tourists.

The shopping bag ripped out of my hands.

I spun around.

The sidewalk was crowded. Where was the thief?

I scanned for the bright pink bag. I thought it would be easy to follow, but the thief had a head start.

Andreus shouldn't expect me for almost an hour. The grab wasn't supposed to happen yet.

I sprinted through the entrance and accosted the first security guard.

"Someone stole my package. I need to speak to the head of security."

He looked around for someone who spoke English.

"Never mind." I dashed to the coffee shop. Karmanos was waiting for me.

"Someone just stole my package. I need the head of security."

"What is going on?" Karmanos asked. "What package?"

"My uncle had an artifact. I told Andreus Mikos about it. Ever since then someone has been trying to find it. Someone just stole the chalice. Security needs to track the thief and catch him."

Karmanos shook his head in confusion. The head of security had joined us.

I turned to him. "Do you have security video?"

"Yes, but thieves steal shopping bags from tourists all the time," the security chief said.

"But they're trying to steal an antique Byzantine chalice. For the divine liturgy. In church."

Karmanos laughed.

I got out my phone. "I planted a GPS tracking device. Here— we can track the thief on my phone."

The security chief grabbed his radio and spoke in Greek. Other guards descended on us. The security chief and Karmanos spoke rapidly in Greek.

"English, please."

Karmanos made a quick phone call, then turned to me.

"If this is hoax, it will waste many hours of police work. Are you sure this is valuable?"

"My uncle bought a medieval Byzantine chalice. You've seen the quality of antiques my aunt and uncle have. And you were there when someone tried to kill me on Monday. And the break-in at the Institute. It's theft and attempted murder."

"We would know about any Byzantine chalice on the antiquities market," Karmanos said.

"Do you want to lose it? You're letting a thief escape."

Karmanos shrugged at the security chief. The chief left with my phone and the GPS code book.

"Let me explain," I told Karmanos. "Sunday, I found the chalice in my uncle's apartment. It had been shipped to him just a few weeks before he died. I told Andreus Mikos about it at Meteora on Monday. Then I guess Mikos shoved me off the wall and has been trying to steal it ever since."

"Did anyone else know?"

"Well, the original dealer. But he thought it was a Crusader goblet and sold it for 4.000 euros. Then I told Andreus. He could have told someone else. And I told my friend in America about it."

"So you are not certain Mikos is behind this?"

"I don't have proof. That's why I planted the GPS device. I was going to ask for your help before Andreus came at six o'clock. I figured he would have one of his thugs grab it as I came into the museum. But somehow, they were in place early."

"We will see what police can do. I do not have great hope." Karmanos walked away.

It had been such a good plan. I got some chocolate *gelato* to comfort myself as I waited.

"Miss Amber, why do you look so sad?"

I looked up from my empty ice cream dish. "Andreus. I forgot you were coming."

"I am wounded. I was so pleased when a lovely young lady invited me to meet her."

I smiled. "Please sit down. My mind had just wandered."

He sure seemed cool. But I guess a criminal mastermind and black market antiquities dealer would be cool. Andreus ordered coffee for himself and another ice cream for me.

"Did you bring the chalice?" he asked.

"I was wrong about it." I watched for his reaction.

"You must be disappointed. I know you want something special for aunt. I thought the stone might be sardonyx."

"Oh, would that be valuable?"

"Venetians have sardonyx chalice of Emperor Romanos II. It was stolen by Crusaders. Imperial chalice from Middle Byzantine period is very rare. But there were many emperors and many churches. Emperors worshiped at both *Hagia Sophia* and Church of Holy Apostles. I have watched my entire career for another such chalice."

I smiled. He would be disappointed when his thugs opened the package and found my dented brass goblet. I saw Karmanos enter the coffee shop and head for our table.

"Have you recovered my package?"

"Yes. I am most embarrassed." Karmanos paused.

I gestured to a chair.

Karmanos sat down. He looked at his hands as he spoke. "We caught the thief. It was Demetrius, my assistant."

"What?"

The people seated around us looked up at my sharp response.

"Demetrius heard you and Mr. Mikos speaking in the courtyard. He claims he tries to recover a stolen piece of our heritage."

Andreus couldn't keep quiet any longer. "Chalice was stolen?"

Karmanos laughed nervously. "Yes, but it was a bad fake. Miss Jackson, you and your uncle were cheated out of 4.000 euros. And then Demetrius was fooled."

He stood up. "The police will question him. They may need your statement. And perhaps your aunt, since the fake belongs to her."

He returned my phone, then rejoined the security chief.

Andreus patted my hand. "Amber, do not blame yourself."

Oh, I blamed myself all right—for suspecting the wrong man.

I couldn't hold back the smile as I looked up. "Want to see the real chalice?"

Andreus' smile was bigger than mine.

"I knew someone was trying to steal the chalice. And you were the only one I told about it, so I suspected you. I'm sorry."

Andreus made a brief wave. "Understandable. No problem."

The coat room was blessedly empty. I discreetly pulled the locker key out of my bra, double-checked the number.

I pulled the box from the locker. "Shall we look now, or go someplace private?"

"Please. Now."

Andreus and I sat on a bench with the box between us. His fingers twitched as I opened the shipping box. I pulled back the bubble wrap.

The first piece out was the octagon base. Andreus accepted it eagerly, reading the Greek inscription around the bottom. He stroked the pearls and pulled a loupe out of his pocket to inspect the enamel portraits.

He set it down as I produced a chunk of the stone bowl. He lifted it to the light, setting the translucent stone aglow with white and dark red swirls. "Sardonyx. Definitely Sardonyx. Do you know how rare and valuable ancient sardonyx is?"

I showed him how the chunks came together to form the carved bowl.

The final piece was the silver rim.

"It's almost all here. This is magnificent." He looked up through tears. "You have made a Greek very happy."

63

The Institute

I checked my messages as I headed back to the Institute. Jim again.

Don't call me a Judas after all we've been through together. You never said the presentation on Sunday was confidential. Of course, I passed it along to Father Paulos. He called Dr. Wright. You're not being fair by calling me a rat.

I haven't been able to think of anything but you since you arrived here on Monday morning. When you walk into a room, you fill it with energy. Has it only been six days? I couldn't stand it when I thought you had died this morning. Please don't be angry.

The rat didn't deserve a reply.

I found Lydia in her apartment, contemplating heaps of artifacts dragged out for inspection.

"Shall we start putting it back in order?" I offered.

"That will take weeks. I just can't face it tonight. "Let's get dressed up and go to dinner—pretend it's been a great day."

Sophia and Carl passed on Lydia's dinner invitation. No surprise.

Walter's assistant had left, but Walter and Billy accepted Lydia's invitation.

Lydia selected a strapless sheath in crimson red silk. My black dress from Kalambaka didn't look too shabby either. My bruises had faded to yellow-green, concealed by makeup. I brushed out my hair to help camouflage the damage and put on chunky bracelets to distract from my scraped knuckles and broken fingernails.

Billy and Walter gawked when Lydia and I made our entrance. Before we could get out the door, Lydia's phone rang.

"Hello, I was hopin' you'd call." Lydia pointed to the phone and mouthed silently, "The University president."

She nodded a few times.

"No, I just wanted to confirm that y'all won't have classes here in the fall." Lydia winked at us. "Our scholars have made a rather nice discovery. We need the facilities for researchers and a documentary film crew."

She listened some more.

"We were leaving for dinner. I'll talk to you next week. We'll send a shipping container with all the university's equipment after the summer session. Bye now."

I laughed. "Would you really do that?"

Lydia raised her chin. "I'll have the rusted container dropped at his pompous front door if he doesn't stop playing games with me."

"What if he doesn't back down?" Billy asked.

"I guess I'll run a bed and breakfast in Athens. It is a prime neighborhood."

Lydia suggested the best restaurant in the Plaka. The owner hugged her and escorted us to the front table. Being Lydia's protégée did have benefits. Music and conversation wrapped us in warmth. *Tzatziki, dolmathes*, hummus and Mythos beer appeared.

Knowing that my attacker had been caught was liberating. No more worries about being stalked and assaulted. Now I could focus on my other problems, like learning Greek, returning the manuscript and getting back into graduate school. Tonight, though, I would celebrate.

Lydia raised her glass. "To you, Billy, and your success tomorrow."

Walter and I joined in the chorus of "To Billy" and "Success."

"We can't be too confident. It's still early. We haven't had independent review or scientific testing," Billy warned. "This could be either a forgery or a mystery that can't be pinned down. I've faced too many dead ends to count success yet."

Lydia rested her hand on his arm. "I feel good about this."

Walter nodded. "This discovery will clinch your appointment as head of the Nicene Foundation. You'll be a celebrity. This will put that pushy fundraiser back in his place."

I still hadn't figured out Billy's friend. "Mr. Smoot, tell me what you do."

"That makes me sound old. Call me Walter."

"Okay, Walter, tell me about yourself."

"I'm head of publishing for the Nicene Foundation. I also handle public relations and public policy. Billy is one of our top authors and speakers, so we work together."

"That sounds really challenging." I fluttered my eyelashes and smiled.

"It's important work, and very rewarding. We provide solid scholarship and support for traditional, orthodox Christianity based on the Old and New Testament."

"You promote the Greek Orthodox Church?"

"No, not Orthodox with a capital "O." Orthodox in its original meaning. Correct Belief. It's all too rare in today's society."

"You have a ring just like Billy's. Is it special?"

He stretched out his hand. "It's actually three interlocking rings, Borromean rings. The Borromean rings are an ancient symbol. Billy's books for the Nicene Foundation all have the three rings on the jacket."

Might be a nice factoid. "What does it mean?"

Our main course arrived. Mine was chicken baked with lemon and olive oil. I savored every bite as I listened to Walter.

"During the Nicene Council in A.D. 325, church leaders came together and affirmed the nature of the Trinity. The three rings represent the Trinity. These were made for the 25th anniversary of the Nicene Foundation."

"So are you a member of Billy's Early Christian club?"

"Yes, I work with them. They stage re-enactments for our annual conference and some of our videos. Several of our films feature Billy writing with a quill pen to illustrate lessons about the Bible."

Walter dug into his lamb, giving me a chance to get a word in.

"So what's your message?"

"Western Civilization was built on Christianity and the Ten Commandments. Today, though, society is losing its way. We've abandoned its foundation."

"What should we do differently?"

"It's simple. Acknowledge the sovereignty of God. Follow the Ten Commandments, the laws of Moses. Stop accepting every deviant behavior under the guise of 'diversity.'"

Billy joined in. "So many of our concepts of right and wrong, of justice, are based on the Ten Commandments. They're easy to understand, but hard to actually follow. Wouldn't life be better if we lived the Ten Commandments?"

"We do spend a lot of time coveting what other people have and scheming how to get it from them," Lydia said.

"Our government has totally lost focus," Walter said. "We're a Christian nation, but our judges and lawmakers have forgotten that. If we followed traditional Christian laws and values, we wouldn't need the other areas where government meddles in our lives."

"So do you have churches? Is this a denomination?" I asked.

"The Nicene Foundation is a think tank, a policy body. We provide resources to decision makers. We focus our attention on church and political leaders. We're going to turn society around, get it back on its traditional path under the rule of God," Walter explained.

"So you don't convert people, save souls?"

Billy shook his head, "Jesus saves souls through the work of the Holy Spirit. That's predestined. Our job is to encourage the world to follow God's universal laws."

The *bouzouki* player interrupted. He serenaded Lydia with slow seductive notes, drawing us into the Greek music. He turned to me as his fingers picked up speed and raced over the strings. The crisp bright notes reminded me of the rhythm of the Greek language.

The musician gestured Lydia to follow him. She tossed her red hair, then grabbed Billy. Soon, we were all winding between the tables holding the corners of napkins.

The Ten Commandments don't prohibit dancing.

64

Basil II

A.D. 989, Constantinople

"I won't do it. I told you 'No' before. I won't marry a barbarian," Anna the Purple-born said. "I'll go to a monastery instead."

Basil II was exasperated. His subjects should follow his orders. Still, she was his sister.

Basil had been 18 and Anna 13 when he became emperor. The past 13 years had been stormy, challenging.

The 18-year-old emperor grew up fast. He surprised everyone when he led an army to eastern Turkey and defeated a powerful general who wanted to usurp the crown. Now, another general was making a claim on the throne.

"You know, Anna, that our lives are not our own. We were born to serve the empire. We must do our duty."

Anna mumbled through tears. "Duty does not include sleeping with a barbarian."

"She's right, you know," said the chamberlain. "We must be careful whom we allow to form alliances with our noble family.

The young emperor bristled. The old eunuch bastard seemed to think that he ran the empire since he was part of the Lekapenos family.

He turned to Anna.

"Let me explain again. Vladimir of Kiev is sitting with *his* army in *our* city in the Crimea. I can't fight both Vladimir in the

Crimea and that usurper in Turkey. I need Vladimir as an ally. He will convert to Orthodox Christianity if you become his queen. The Rus' States will protect our northeast border and help us keep Armenia and eastern Turkey in the empire."

"Don't make me go," Anna cried. "I want to stay here."

"Staying here is not an option," her brother shouted. "You can become a queen in Kiev and lead the people to Christianity, or you can be killed when the usurper marches on Constantinople and seizes the throne. The death of the dynasty will be on your shoulders."

Anna bowed before the throne and left in tears.

"You know, there is a third option," the chamberlain said. "You could negotiate. Allow your challenger to marry Anna and become your co-emperor."

"Reward a traitor?" Basil asked.

"No, compromise."

Basil unclenched his fists as he watched him leave. The chamberlain had probably arranged for a nice payment from the opponent when he gained power.

Basil II looked forward to the military campaign. He loved living with the army. They were his real family. Their children were his children. He would take care of them and their lands.

Basil II never married, and did not allow his brother's daughters, Zoe and Theodora, to marry.

History labeled the emperor Basil the Bulgar-killer. But he didn't kill all of the Bulgars. The decisive battle came in 1014. Basil II and his general crushed the Bulgarians in the Battle of Kleidion. According to Basil's propaganda, they captured 15,000 enemy soldiers. They blinded 99 of every 100 men, leaving 150 one-eyed men to lead the defeated army back to their ruler.

With the defeat of the Bulgars, Basil pushed the borders of the empire to the Danube and absorbed the Bulgarian military leadership and aristocracy into Byzantine society.

Basil II ruled for 50 years. When he died in A.D. 1025, he left the empire with a full treasury and secure borders. He was the perhaps the greatest emperor of the Macedonian dynasty.

65

Athens

I hummed a Greek tune as we returned to the Institute. "Carl, are we going dancing tonight? I'm wearing the dress you picked in Kalambaka."

Carl put down his book. "I thought you'd never ask."

"Just don't stay out too late, kids," Lydia said. "We have a big day tomorrow."

"I will have her home by 1 a.m., *Frau* Jackson," Carl promised as he kissed Lydia's hand.

"I'll wait up for you."

"Oh, Aunt Lydia, I'm 23 years old."

"Just saying. I may still be up."

"We'll slip in quietly."

Carl hailed a cab and directed it to a club in Psiri. The Latin band was a nice change after the *bouzouki*. We even tried a tango. The place was just heating up as we left.

Carl snuggled close in the taxi. His hand worked its way around my shoulders as he whispered proposals.

"Quiet—what would my aunt think if I spent the night in your room instead of her apartment?"

Carl nuzzled my bare shoulder.

"She might like it the privacy—I caught the Rev. Billy creeping up the stairs early this morning. I think she had a guest last night while you were gone."

"Oh, he probably just joined her for breakfast coffee."

We giggled over the thought of romance among the older folks as Carl tried another avenue of attack.

"Actually, I do have something to show you. Can you keep a secret?" I confided.

"*Ja*, I love secrets."

"I don't know about this one—I've done something really bad."

"That's even better."

I found Lydia reading in bed.

"I'm going to visit with Carl a little longer."

"I don't know where you kids get all your energy," Lydia said. "I'm turning out the light pretty quick. I'll be snoring away."

Carl had grabbed a bottle of wine (German, of course) from the refrigerator. I made a detour, then appeared at his door clutching a pillow. A candle provided the only light. Carl's shirt was unbuttoned, revealing his golden tan. Cool night air drifted through the balcony doors, but Carl's checks were still flushed from the heat of the club.

Damn, he looked good. The helmet was right there on the bookcase.

Carl looked up from pouring liquid gold into goblets. "A slumber party? You decided to spend the night?"

I shut the door. "No. I want to show you this."

My wrapped bundle was hidden under a fluffy pillow. The smell of old leather escaped as I pulled the bundle out.

Carl plopped on the bed and took a sip of wine. "I'm ready."

I grasped the silver-faced boards protecting the precious parchment pages. As I pulled the codex out of Jim's pillowcase, flakes of parchment fell to the floor.

The book had survived 1,200 years. Then I stuffed it in a backpack and took a hike.

No reaction. Silence. Carl took a long swallow.

"You don't want to know what it is and where I got it?"

"No."

"It's the Constantine manuscript from Meteora."

"Don't tell me." Carl poured himself another glass of wine, swirled the glass and sniffed.

I waited. He sipped slowly.

"I took it. I didn't mean to. I just borrowed it to take some pictures, but then I couldn't put it back. The door was locked and the alarm went off so I had to bring it home with me."

Carl took the ancient codex from my arms and rested it on his desk.

"Sit down and think. On Monday, we'll consult an attorney. Perhaps we can return the manuscript anonymously through an intermediary."

"Well, Jim said he would sneak it back in. Unfortunately, I got upset and called him a Judas."

Carl looked at me and shook his head slowly.

"Maybe I need to be nice to him until he takes the manuscript back."

"You think?" Carl said.

Cool liquid tingled in my throat as I watched Carl don white gloves and cautiously open the cover, revealing the faded purple silk lining.

"Damn," he said. "I fantasized that you were going to show me your tattoo. A rose on your curvy little ass would be easier to keep secret than this."

"I wish a tattoo on my ass was my biggest problem."

Carl flipped on his desk light and blew out the candle.

"Have you damaged it?" he asked as he turned pages.

"No, it's been in that pillowcase since I left the monastery. Other than a few flakes falling off, it's the same."

He studied the final page.

"The last page has been torn out. It's missing," Carl said. "Did any pages come out while you were looking at it? Have you changed the order of the pages?"

"It's just like it was when I borrowed it."

"Boy, are you gutsy."

"Nah, I'm curious and impulsive."

"That, too." Carl smiled as he repackaged the manuscript.

He split the remains of the wine between our glasses. "Just don't do anything else impulsive. Besides getting a rose tattoo on your ass. That, I would approve."

The ominous bundle filled the room as we finished our wine. Having Constantine watch us from the desk chilled our hot feelings.

"Thank you for helping me."

I gave Carl a squeeze and a kiss on the cheek. I hoisted the bundle and left him pondering the chaotic state of my life.

And my lack of tattoos.

Lydia was asleep as I slid in beside her. Eating and dancing had been a nice diversion, but it hadn't solved my problems.

I had stopped the person who had pushed me over the edge and tried to steal Uncle Robert's chalice. But my graduate school situation was worse than ever. And a stolen manuscript was hidden in the building. Isn't there a commandment about stealing? The *Pantokrator* would surely send me to Hell now. After reading Revelation and studying pictures of judgment, I knew what it looked like.

I had come to Greece to find my way, but my life was a bigger mess than ever.

In two short hours, the *semantron* would call monks to morning prayers. I had to get some sleep. But I couldn't get the images out of my head. Something important was there. I just couldn't pull it into focus.

Prayers would have started at Meteora. The memory of Greek chants finally put me to sleep.

DAY EIGHT

"In the beginning was the Word, and the Word was with God, and the Word was God." John 1:1

Eight is the number of the Lord's Day, the day of the resurrection. Eight is the number of the New Creation.

It is the number of perfection. An eight on its side is the symbol for infinity.

Jesus gave eight beatitudes in the Sermon on the Mount. Ezekiel's temple had eight steps. Jesus was circumcised on the eighth day after his birth and received his name: Joshua, savior.

Eight people were saved in Noah's ark; eight people came through water into new life. Thus eight is the number of new life and of baptism.

The symbol for eight is the octagon. The Greek numeral for eight is the letter eta (H η).

67

Patmos

"My God, my God, why have you forsaken me? Why are you so far from helping me, from the words of my groaning? O my God, I cry by day but you do not answer: and by night, but find no rest." Psalm 22:1-2

The old man struggled up the rocky path. John had barely slept since the vision came to him a week ago. Still, he made the climb. He always came alone to the mountain top on the Lord's Day.

He raised his ink-stained hands in prayer to *El Shaddai*. All Strength. *Pantokrator*.

"Why do you bring such misery to Your chosen people? Why did You allow the destruction of your Holy Mountain? The children you have put under my care have begun to doubt Your promises."

Were such questions heresy? Job had questioned why God's children suffered. The Psalms cried for relief. Surely Jesus would answer.

"Lord, give me an answer for your children."

The elder stood in prayer. He heard waves against the rocky coast, thundering like hoof beats of charging war horses. Wind usually buffeted this rocky ridge; this day it was absent, as if angels held it back at the four corners of the earth. In the silence he heard a still, small voice.

"They will hunger no more, and thirst no more; the sun will not strike them, nor any scorching heat; for the Lamb at the center of the throne will be their shepherd, and he will guide them to springs of the water of life, and God will wipe away every tear from their eyes."

The stooped shoulders straightened. The tired figure stood taller.

He hurried down the path. He needed more lampblack ink.

68

Sunday, Athens

Aunt Lydia rose early, fretting about what she should wear for the presentation and how to get her apartment back in order.

I tried to snuggle back in with a pillow over my head. Instead, the events of the past week washed over me. I had arrived in Athens just a week ago filled with hope and anticipation. But that was before.

Before the Church of the Angry Jesus. Before Revelation. And images of souls being swallowed whole by the beast.

Before the trip to Meteora. And monks, prayers and manuscripts.

Before Sophia tried to send me home. And Lydia came to rescue me.

Before I learned of the Institute's struggle for survival. And the rivalries for Lydia's patronage.

Before I had ever heard of purple-born kings. Or stolen manuscripts.

Before graduate school kicked me out before I had even started.

Before Demetrius tried to kill me.

Naive innocence was gone, beaten back by a primal instinct for survival. Sleep was impossible.

Lydia, Billy and Walter were already at work in the conference room by the time I got dressed. We ran through the visuals again. Everything worked perfectly. It was only 8:30 a.m., a truly uncivilized hour.

Lydia suggested we relax over coffee in the library. Easier said than done. Billy fiddled with his notes.

"So, Amber, how are your Greek studies going?" Lydia asked. "Are you making progress translating Revelation?"

A feeble attempt at casual conversation. But I could play along.

"I'm finally comfortable with the letter forms and alphabet. Billy is right about the calligraphy writing. And seeing the original Greek words adds a dimension to studying the Biblical text."

I didn't explain that color coding made the difference, that Greek letters now had colors. I wasn't ready to announce to the world that I had synesthesia.

"Billy, Amber and I appreciate your help this summer," Lydia prodded.

Billy glanced up. "Least I could do for my favorite lady."

I set my laptop aside and joined the effort. "Billy, I have some questions about Revelation."

"Ask away, Amber."

"Some of the prophecy descriptions are dead-on for events in history. But others seem general. A person could apply them to almost any time and place. How do you know the prophecy is predicting specific events and not just rehashing language from the Biblical plagues of Egypt and the apocalyptic literature of the time?"

"That's why Revelation is so controversial and yet fascinating. People throughout the ages have seen signs for their lives."

"The dispensational 'Left Behind' view bothers me," I said. "When John wrote Revelation, Christians were suffering. They needed God's reassurance. Did God deny them an answer and instead send a vision for non-believers 2,000 years in the future?"

Lydia refilled coffee. Billy moved into our circle.

"That very question drew me to scholars who believe part of the prophecy has already been fulfilled," Billy said. "Interpreters have to defy logic to read that things will happen 'soon' and then assert that it doesn't happen for 2,000 years. And the pre-tribulation Rapture is an indefensible fantasy. It's absurd to think that God would write about something that won't apply to those who read His Word."

I summoned up my courage.

"What's to say that John didn't write this vision *after* the fall of Jerusalem to explain why God allowed Jerusalem to be defeated? Isn't that what scholars believe about the book of Daniel, that it was written about 160 B.C. as a coded message of hope during the persecution by the Syrian king Antiochus IV Epiphanes?"

Walter had arrived from the Hilton and joined the group in the library. "That's not a question a believer asks. You talk as if the Bible were a human creation. It's the Word of God."

Billy turned to Walter. "No, I don't mind questions. If we want to win hearts and minds in the modern world, we have to back our belief in the Word of God with scholarship and reason."

Billy took a sip of coffee.

"Amber, you're correct about most apocalyptic literature. It commented on current events in the pretense of a prophecy from a historic Biblical figure. That's what's different about Revelation. John doesn't pretend to be Enoch or Elijah. He doesn't claim the prophecy comes from the past. Sure, he draws language and imagery from the past, but he records his vision from Christ to current readers. Christ's letters to the seven churches are current. Then, John records Christ's three prophecies about the future."

I thought about that. "What about the coded references? Like 666 or the Great Whore of Babylon?"

"That's the traditional language of prophecy, natural during times of persecution."

Walter broke in again. "Besides, John didn't pick the languages or images. Jesus Christ picked the language and imagery, God chooses how to communicate with us."

I retrieved the photo of the New Jerusalem coming down from heaven.

"This is the good news," said Billy. "John sees a new heaven and a new earth, and the new Jerusalem."

"At least it's a joyful scene after all the death and destruction," I said. "Actually, that's not entirely accurate. I've made notes and charts. Revelation has a pattern. Each segment has a sequence of seven woes or judgments, followed by an eighth triumphal scene in heaven or on earth."

Billy scowled. "We've already talked about that. Seven is the key number in the book of Revelation."

"What does it mean when it says, 'there was no more sea,' in the final prophecy?" I said.

"Sea represents Gentile nations, so all nations will be Christian at the end," Walter said.

The doorbell broke the Sunday morning Bible study. A bleary-eyed Carl detoured from his journey to the coffeepot to answer the door.

Carl's side of the conversation floated in from the entry hall. "Hullo" ... "What the hell are you doing here?" ... "Does she know you're coming? Have you been invited?"

Carl slumped in, followed by Jim.

"This jerk claims you're expecting him, Amber."

What had I forgotten?

69

"I promised to take you to *Hosios Loukas* today," Jim announced.

I took a long sip of coffee.

"Remember?"

"You invited me for Sunday afternoon. But the presentation is this afternoon."

"That's why I came early."

Dang. That sad puppy look again. Those big brown eyes and long lashes could look so mournful. And I did need him to return my borrowed manuscript.

Lydia broke the silence. "Why don't you introduce us to your friend, Amber?"

"Aunt Lydia, everyone, this is Jim Sampras."

"Jim, this is my aunt, Lydia Jackson." I went around the room. "You may know Carl Helman, Rev. Dr. Billy Sullivan and Dr. Sophia Wright. Walter Smoot from the Nicene Foundation."

Billy rose to shake Jim's hand.

"You look familiar. Have we met before?"

"Perhaps. I'm at Meteora this summer. And, I was a student in Atlanta when you were a faculty member there."

Talk about half-truths!

"Despite all my time in Greece, I've never seen *Hosios Loukas*," Lydia said as she handed Jim a cup of coffee. "Tell me about it."

"It's older than Daphni, Amber's Church of the Angry Jesus,"

Jim said. "It's an octagon like Daphni, one of the few Middle Byzantine churches left in Greece."

Jim turned to me. "It's only a couple of hours, so we could be back before the presentation this afternoon."

He lowered those long lashes. Darn.

"You're ready for the presentation, so you could go," Lydia said.

"The mosaics are totally unbelievable, and it has two churches with great architecture," Jim said.

"I suppose I'd better change." I tried to think. My modest monastery attire was limited. My church dress was torn and blood-stained from my fall on Tuesday, my batik skirt was somewhere on a mountainside and my black dress smelled like it had spent the night doing the tango.

"We're taking my motor scooter, so wear long pants and sleeves. If it has a dress code you can borrow one of their skirts."

"You look great," Jim said as I emerged in faded jeans.

"Oh, stop with the flattery."

"I'm serious. Your eyes reflect the colors you wear. Today your eyes are soft denim blue."

I ignored the compliment. "Did you tell Father Paulos about us?"

"Only that you seduced me."

Jim laughed at my horror-struck face. "Don't worry—I told him I had been talking to you. I needed to explain knowing about the fragment and the meeting today."

Jim retrieved a sack from the storage bin of a rusty old motor scooter. "A peace offering."

The aroma of baklava emerged as he opened the bag. He played dirty, but I had willpower. He shrugged and put it back in the bin, then handed me a helmet.

"Where did you get this piece of junk? Is it safe?"

"I spent 750 euros on it—good enough for getting around Greece for six months."

He climbed on and gestured to the spot behind him.

We skirted the Acropolis and caught E75 north out of Athens.

The scooter putted through a pass in the mountains that surround Athens. This seemed to be the standard route anywhere north or west of the Athenian peninsula. Gradually, the metropolitan density and traffic thinned.

We stopped at a scenic turnoff for rest and pictures.

"So, Jim, are you making any progress on your dissertation?"

"Well, I've learned that the monasteries couldn't survive without tourism money, but tourism changes the monasteries. Even with hired help, tourism turns the monks into caretakers and tour guides. I thought I could figure out how to balance spiritual practices and modern life with six months of study." He laughed. "Pretty pretentious."

I licked honey off my fingers.

"No more pretentious than my summer goal," I said. "I thought I could discover the Truth—with a capital T—about God by spending a few weeks looking at early Christian art. All I've learned is that everything I learned about Revelation is wrong."

The bakery sack was empty. Darn.

We left the mountains. The land was flat by Thebes, and less arid. We took the exit at Akrefnia and pulled over for a pit stop. We ate *gelato* standing beside the scooter in a dusty parking lot.

"What do you think about Revelation?"

Jim scratched his pathetic beard. "Truthfully? I never thought about it. Despite all the *Pantokrator* images, Revelation is not a big deal in the Orthodox Church. The book of Revelation was more popular in the West. The early church used images of the ultimate triumph of Christ, but interpreted it in a Greek allegorical way after getting burned by a couple of End Time predictions. Images of judgment and destruction came with the Crusaders. The monastery of St. John at Patmos wasn't even built until the eleventh century."

He passed me the rest of his *gelato*.

"So now that you've studied with Billy, what do you think about Revelation?" he asked.

"I respect Billy, and his theory is fascinating, but I just don't see Revelation as a history lesson or as a schedule of events. It seems more like the parables. It's a story that makes a point rather than a story that predicts events. Billy thinks the fragment he found is related to Revelation."

"Irenaeus is important," Jim said. "The monks just don't know where the fragment came from."

I shrugged. "The library had a box of loose pages. What's the mystery there?"

"Usually, the cache has several pages from the same manuscript. It's a book that's fallen apart. Or, it's a loose page from a book in the library. But there's nothing related to this. It's one page with no evidence of the rest of the manuscript. There are other books by the church fathers, but none of them have the same page size and writing style."

I savored the raspberry *gelato* as I visualized Billy's fragment. The top right corner was broken and stained a sort of pinky purple.

I licked cold raspberry pink goodness off the plastic spoon. Pink. *Pink.*

"Pink!"

Jim shot me a glance. "What?"

"Pink. I said *pink.*"

My mind raced. "I know where the fragment has been. It's been stored in the back of the Constantine manuscript all these centuries!"

Jim laughed.

"I'm not kidding. The front and back pages in the Constantine manuscript are stained pink from murex dye in the purple silk lining. The pink stain on Billy's fragment must be from that binding."

I waived the spoon of pink *ice cream*. "All we have to do is match the pink stain," I babbled. "That's how the Ireneaus page came to the monastery; it was tucked in the back of the Constantine manuscript."

I pulled out my phone and dialed. Darn voice mail.

"Billy, I know where your fragment came from. It was in the Constantine manuscript. Call me."

I dialed Carl.

"Carl, answer your phone. I think Billy's fragment is important. It's been hiding in the Constantine manuscript all these years."

I bounced and wiggled as we hopped back onto the scooter. "I am good; I am sooo good."

Jim shook his head.

A crazy quilt of agricultural fields blanketed the valleys and climbed the mountains. We passed almond and olive orchards. Just before we reached Steiri, Jim turned onto the final road. I wrapped my arms around him tighter as the scooter swung around the blind hairpin curves on Mount Helikon.

"Oh, truck!" he yelled. He hugged the shoulder as a truck swung wide around the curve.

We arrived at the monastery without further profanity.

70

Hosios Loukas

I expected a poor country ruin, but the walled monastic settlement rivaled big city churches. The massive exteriors blended stone, brick and marble into intricate patterns.

Jim walked ahead to the western entrance to the *katholikon*. Outside the simple arched doorway, he stopped.

"Close your eyes; I'll lead you in," he said.

"Why?"

"It looks dark if you come in from bright sunlight. If you close your eyes, it gives them time to adjust to the interior."

I complied. Jim took my arm and led me up the steps into the cool stone interior.

"Wait," he whispered as he positioned me where he wanted.

"Now!"

I faced three doors. The royal door, straight ahead, led into the *naos*, the main aisle of the church. But my eyes were drawn to the arch above the door. The *Pantokrator* glowed from the shimmering gold cubes of the mosaic background.

His warm brown eyes met mine with a look of acceptance, not condemnation.

"I've been looking for you," I whispered.

Other visitors bumped against us as we blocked the flow of people through the narthex. But I was transfixed.

"Can you read it?" Jim asked.

I looked at the open codex in Christ's left hand. The black squiggles sprang to life against the white mosaic cubes, glowing with a spectrum of colors like light from a prism.

"*EΓΩ* ... I. *EIHI* ... am. *TO* ... the. *ΦΩς* ... light," I began. I looked at the top of the second page. "*MH* ... never. *ΠEP* ... walk."

The colors fell together into a meaningful pattern.

"'I am the light of the world. The one following me will never walk in the darkness, but will have the light of life.' It's the invitation to discipleship from John 8:12!"

Jesus' right hand pointed inward, palm toward his chest. Did he point to himself or into the church?

This was the gesture that Andreus taught me. Was it an invitation to follow the way of Jesus, or to enter the fellowship? Maybe both. Maybe they're the same thing.

I flashed back to the scene of Christ casting souls down to Hell in the narthex at Meteora. This Christ invited worshipers into a life of light.

Jim turned my shoulders, leading me to the image on the left.

The artist had reduced the crucifixion to simple elements against a golden sky. Jesus' lifeless body slumped against the cross, held aloft by nails in his palms and arches. Golgotha was a simple mound marked by a skull.

Mary drew her dark blue cloak around hunched shoulders with her left hand as she lifted her right hand in prayer. John, the beloved disciple, supported his dejected head in his right palm as he, too, drew his cloak around himself.

In spite of their stoic faces, I could feel their cold chill of grief; I snuggled against Jim's shoulder as he drew me closer.

"Now the good news," he whispered as he directed me to the door on our right.

Christ's body, lifeless on the left, crackled with energy. Jesus raised the empty cross as a battle standard as he soared out of the black depths of Hades. The gates of death lay broken under his feet. His white cloak billowed with motion.

With his left hand, he pulled Adam and Eve from their tomb, lifting humanity to everlasting life.

On his right, King David and King Solomon (looking remarkably like Constantine the Purple-born and Romanos II) raised hands in wonder as they witnessed the fulfillment of their prophecies.

This was the Byzantine image of Easter, the *Anastasis*. The Greek word means standing up or rising. No ambiguous empty tombs here—Christ conquers death with a flourish. In the West, this is called the Harrowing of Hell. The Eastern name is better.

"I've seen lots of Byzantine images of these scenes, but none of them have this optimistic energy, this hope."

"Aren't you glad I made you come?" Jim coaxed.

A big hug and kiss on the cheek were his reward.

"We need to move on," Jim prodded.

The *katholikon* was a cross-in-square layout, but the central space was huge. Like Daphni, the central dome rested on an octagon of eight huge piers. The arms of the cross were open four stories high.

Light streamed in the east windows, flooding the apse and altar area with glory.

Mary, the God-bearer, reigned from a pillowed throne in the golden half dome above the altar. A miniature man holding the wisdom of the universe in his baby body sat regally on her lap.

Pentecost filled the ceiling above the altar. In the center, the dove of the Holy Spirit prepared the empty throne for the coming of Christ. Radiating flames fell on each of the 12 disciples.

Above the piers were four scenes. The Annunciation was missing, but the Nativity, Presentation at the Temple, and Baptism of Christ stood between the square floor of earth and the round dome above.

I looked up into the broad, soaring dome of heaven overhead, expecting glory. Ghostly frescoes of prophets flanked the windows under the dome, while faded archangels lifted a shadowy *Pantokrator* to the heights. At least he looked friendly.

"That's ugly," I muttered.

"The dome and mosaic were damaged in an earthquake about 500 years ago," Jim said. "It was replaced with this fresco. The church was much poorer after the Latin invasion."

"I wish I had been a pilgrim 800 years ago," I said. "The original must have been magnificent."

Marble panels covered the walls of the *katholikon* in soft grays, blues, greens and mauves. The muted hues served as a calm, elegant background for the brilliant gold and jewel tones of the mosaics. Carved stone borders marked the stories as the walls soared upward to heaven.

Throughout the structure, the *Pantokrator* looked to his right and raised his hand in blessing. No angry Jesus. No leftward glances to judgment and hell.

We found St. Luke's shrine where the *Panagia* church and the *katholikon* join together.

In the mosaic, St. Luke had a long, thin face, accentuated by his long pointed beard. He gazed from golden eternity with dark almond-shaped eyes as he raised his hands in the traditional prayer gesture for the pilgrims.

Jim explained the history. "In 941 AD, Loukas had pronounced that 'a Romanos will take over Crete' from the Saracen Turks. Not the current emperor, but another.

"The generals at Thebes started a church when Loukas was still alive. That's the smaller church we see next.

"After St. Luke's prophecy came true, the first church wasn't big enough to hold all the pilgrims who wanted to sleep beside his tomb. The bigger *katholikon* and this linking entry were built later. The mountain slopes down, so there's a crypt under the main church to make the floor in the new church level with the original church. Greek churches don't usually have crypts.

"After the Fourth Crusade, Orthodox monks were kicked out

and replaced by western monks. The bones of the *Hosios* disappeared. The relics turned up in Venice in the 14th century, supposedly saved by Franciscans from the invading Turks.

"In 1986, Loukas' bones finally came home to this place. It was a huge event to Greek believers."

In the smaller *Panagia*, walls had been stripped of marble panels and mosaics. The blank center dome soared far overhead. Light played on the rough stones, revealing elegant proportions. The *Panagia* showed signs of active worship, once again serving the community as a church.

We retraced our steps. Frescoes and mosaics filled all of the arches and side chapels in the *katholikon*. A decorative carved motif on one of the piers caught my eye. I tried to untangle letters. It was a monogram: *Ω Π H*.

"Jim, that's the same graffiti I saw on the mountainside at Meteora. Do you know what the abbreviation means?"

"*Omega Pi Eta*? That's a new one to me," Jim said. "But it's not graffiti here."

I snapped a quick picture, then circled the floor. Sure enough, *Ω Π H* was on each of the eight piers.

"Jim, remember how you told me that churches represent the coming together of heaven and earth?"

"Yes, that's a crucial concept of our worship."

"I think the symbolism is not just in images on the walls, it's built into the architecture and layout of the worship space. In a classic Greek church the square of the building is divided into a cross shape inside. Corners become chapels and tombs.

"Worshipers enter from the west and walk from the foot of the cross to the crossing of the arms. The main dome is over that central joining point. Further to the east, the head of the cross is set aside for the priests.

"Both here and at Daphni, the main floor area is a square, representing earth. But instead of four piers at the corners, there are two piers on each side of the square, forming an octagon. It strengthens the symbolism of square to octagon to the circular dome of heaven at the top. The octagon becomes the main structural support of the church. The church is literally built on the promise of a second chance, the new creation that God delivered in Christ."

Jim got dizzy looking around at the structure that soared above us.

"The square, symbolizing earth, is joined to the circle, symbolizing heaven. An octagon brings the two together, symbolizing baptism, new life and resurrection through Christ," I explained.

As we left the *katholikon*, I paused in the narthex for a final moment with the inviting *Pantokrator*. A mosaic of Jesus washing the feet of the disciples graced the north wall. Huh?

"Jim, I've never seen an image of washing the feet given such prominence."

"Now you see why I love this church. It takes a unique theologian to put servant leadership beside the crucifixion and the resurrection."

"The artist who did these mosaics in the narthex is wonderful. It's too bad artists didn't sign their work," I said.

"The donors were important, not the craftsmen," Jim said.

"Maybe *Ω Π H* are the initials of the donor."

I pulled a note pad and pen from my purse. I started to write. Purple ink? Ugh. Where did I get a purple pen? I wrote the letters. *Omega. Pi. Eta.* It offended my sensitivities. How could I write *Eta* with purple ink? *Eta* was a bright yellow letter. It looked all wrong. It should be white-purple-yellow instead of purple-purple-purple.

A purple H?

Jim looked back at me. As I ran to catch up, I got it. A purple H is not an *eta*. It's an eight. That's what my synesthesia was telling me.

"Jim, what's *Omega Pi Eta* in Greek numerals?"

"Oh, I have to write it out each time." He took my notepad and wrote the numbers, then wrote Greek letters under them. "*Eta* is 8. *Pi* is 80. *Omega* is 800. So it's 888."

Jim's eyes widened. "The crypt!"

71

The Crypt

Jim ran back toward the church. A sign blocked the crypt: "Closed for Restoration."

"Darn!" Jim muttered as he kicked the barricade. We sat on the stone floor and leaned against the wall as Jim scratched his hairy chin.

"What are we looking for?"

"I remember a fresco," Jim said. "I think I saw that same series of letters."

I glanced around, then scooted on my butt under the barricade. No guards that I could see.

"You are such a bad influence," Jim whispered as he slid under a sawhorse.

We found our way down the stairs and between the scaffolds and tarps.

Footsteps.

We slid behind a tarp. Jim held me as we waited for the guard to pass. I eased around the tarp to make sure the room was empty.

The crypt was decorated with frescos, the midnight blue ceiling covered with eight-pointed stars. Jim began searching for the fresco he remembered. Some of the frescoes were chalky ghosts. We tried squinting and glaring, standing close and stepping back.

I gave up and started back to the entrance.

"Wait," Jim whispered. "I think I found it. Don't know if we can read it. It's in really bad shape."

Jim scratched his beard. "Do you have a bottle of water?"

"Of course." I dug it out of my bag. "I'll even share."

"Oh, I'm not going to drink it," Jim said. "I'm going to pour it on the fresco."

I laughed. "I have a hard time knowing when you're joking."

"You think I'm joking?"

"You'd better be joking"

He wasn't.

"You'll ruin it!" I tried to grab the bottle of water back.

Stealing a manuscript was bad. Defacing art that's a thousand years old is worse.

Jim examined the surface then stepped back.

"I've seen this done in Crete. Water makes this chalky deposit on the surface more transparent and darkens the pigments."

"I don't believe it."

"Get your camera ready," Jim said. "Once the fresco is wet, start shooting. It dries quickly so you have to capture it right away."

Jim opened the bottle and approached the fresco. We both listened. No footsteps. No voices.

I cringed as he started pouring.

The water dripped down the fresco. Jim followed behind the drips, squirting dry spots and keeping the sheet of water moving down the image.

Colors emerged from the plaster fog.

I shot.

72

Zoe and Theodora

A.D. 1042, Constaninople

Empress Zoe peered into the polished silver mirror. She admired her profile in the mirror. At 64, she was still the most beautiful woman in the court.

Her uncle, Basil II, had refused a match to a Byzantine noble or general who might challenge him for the throne. Her three matches since Basil II's death had not gone well. At least Romanos III had funded the church at Hosios Loukas in honor of her grandfather, Romanos II.

A loud knock interrupted. Her sister stormed in.

"We were supposed to hear petitions this morning. You didn't come," Theodora said.

"I had more important things to do than hear complaints from bureaucrats and commoners."

"If you don't care, allow me do it alone."

"I am the senior empress. You cannot act on your own."

"Look, I didn't ask to be here. I was content at the monastery. But your advisers dragged me here to help you." Theodora glowered at her sister. "If I were a man, I'd be emperor without question. You don't care that the Turks are pushing at our borders and threatening the true faith."

Theodora stalked out.

Zoe smiled. Ruling with her sister the last four months had

been hell. In a few days, she would have a new husband. With an emperor at her side, she would be free of her pushy co-ruler.

Who would be a fitting emperor? She ran though the possibilities. She called for her chamberlain as she paced.

"Most high empress, what can your humble servant do to serve you?"

"Send for Monomachos. He is my next husband."

"Does he know yet?"

"I will persuade him."

73

To Athens

An image emerged from wet plaster. People were being sorted, saved to the right, damned to the left.

"Let's get the heck out of here," Jim whispered. "We can translate later."

We hurried between the scaffolds. Ah, the steps ahead. Almost out.

Footsteps!

We slid behind a tarp just before the guard came down the steps. We watched from the shadows as he walked into the crypt. The footsteps grew softer, then stopped.

We heard a voice.

"He's calling on his cell phone," Jim whispered. "He saw the wet fresco."

He grabbed my hand and jerked me up the stairs. Jim slid under the barricade, then pulled me through.

"People," he mouthed as he turned. He grabbed me and started making out.

The tourists laughed. Jim looked sheepish. He muttered an apology in Greek as we stopped the public display of affection and walked away.

"I'd rather they think we were hiding to grab a quick kiss than sneaking into the crypt," he whispered.

"I thought almost getting caught made you hot."

"Oh, I've been hot all day. I've wanted to kiss you ever since I saw you in that sexy outfit."

"Faded jeans and a denim jacket? Don't make fun of my outfit, or I'll tell the *Archimandrite* the truth about you."

We emerged breathless into the heat. "Are you up to more curves?" Jim asked. "There's a scenic way back. We have time."

"Any place to eat along the way?"

Why laugh? It was a legitimate question. I put on a helmet and checked to see if the baklava had miraculously multiplied.

"We'll stop at Thebes."

Several cars also took the scenic turnoff. Each curve provided a new vista. Almond and olive groves hugged the slopes as mountains fell away into the shimmering aqua Gulf of Corinth below.

The curves and exhaust fumes made me light-headed. My stomach protested. I felt bile in my throat.

I tapped Jim's chest and pointed to the side of the road.

He nodded, slowed and pulled over at the next turnoff.

"Are you all right?"

I hopped off. "I'm going to throw up."

I ran to the guard rail to toss my baklava.

I straightened. "I think I'm okay now. The motion and the exhaust fumes got to me."

Jim stood by the scooter. "It does smell hot. Normally I don't get that gasoline smell."

"You're not swaying on the back seat bathed in exhaust."

A small tan car pulled off behind us as Jim bent beside the scooter.

"No, I think I've got a gas leak here."

The car started to pull forward. I waved to indicate appreciation. The driver didn't crack a smile. I saw his hands grip the steering wheel as he accelerated straight toward us.

"Jump!"

Jim looked up as I threw myself backwards over the railing. I heard metal on metal as the car smashed into the scooter, sending it through the railing.

The scooter exploded. Heat and pressure rocked me as the fire-ball rolled down the mountainside.

I wrapped my arms around my head and pulled into a ball, rolling down the slope. A tree stopped me.

"Jim? Jim? Where are you?'

I couldn't hear my screams or any response. The explosion echoed in my ears. The pressure in my head made it difficult to stand. I crawled back up the slope.

Jim, can you hear me?"

As I paused to catch my breath, I heard a faint voice.

"Here. By the guardrail."

I pushed myself onto my feet and ran toward him. Jim had been thrown free and caught in the guardrail.

Tires spun gravel. The tan car was backing up, returning to fin-ish us off. I pulled the railing, trying to free Jim's leg. Vultures cir-cled overhead.

"Go. Leave me."

"No." I tugged harder. The car kept backing, gaining speed.

I grabbed Jim's shoulders. "Push as I pull."

"I can't."

"You'll be a sandwich if you don't!"

A red car pulled into the turnoff.

Brakes squealed. The tan car skidded to a stop just inches from us. Gravel pelted us as it sped back onto the road.

White-faced vultures circled closer. Were we road kill? Great —a dream come true.

The couple got out of the red car and stared at the burning scooter. "Wow! Did you have a wreck? How cool!"

"Help me get my friend loose."

The tourists complied.

Jim tested his body as he stood up.

"Okay?"

"Okay."

I extended a scraped hand to our gawkers. "Thanks for stopping to help."

"No problem. I guess we didn't need to, since that other car was coming back to help."

"Yeah, probably so."

The two were honeymooners from Missouri, happy to give a ride to neighbors from Texas.

"Do we need to stop in Thebes so you can make a police report?" the young man asked.

"I don't see any point," Jim said. "That old scooter doesn't have much value. I'll call a wrecker on Monday to junk it."

"I'd like to stop at a rest room so we could wash up."

"You got it," the man said. "What an awesome crash."

"It's Amber's fault," Jim said. "She's accident-prone."

"What makes you say I'm accident-prone?"

"Well, first you fell off the wall at Meteora."

"That wasn't my fault."

"Then you had a rather interesting visit to see me on Friday and an exciting hike on Saturday."

A rather artful description of that fiasco. "Okay, that maybe was my fault. But you made me come."

"Then today, we were almost killed crashing off the side of a mountain."

"This is so not my fault. You wanted to come here. You were driving!"

I fumed as I watched fields roll past. When we got out of the car at Thebes, I pulled my scruffy friend back.

"It wasn't my fault. I even have a picture proving I was pushed from the monastery."

That got his attention. "What does it show?"

"A shadow with an arm. Someone came up behind me just before I fell. It was Demetrius—he pushed me."

Jim whistled.

"Kyrie Iesou Christe, Yie tou Theou, eleison me ton hamartolon," he chanted quietly. "What are you in the middle of?"

"I've puzzled all week. But now I know."

"So what? Give it up."

"When I arrived Sunday, I found a Byzantine chalice that belonged to my Uncle Robert."

He caught his breath.

"So Monday I asked Andreus Mikos about it." I paused. "Demetrius overheard. He's been trying to kill me and steal it all week."

I tried to think how to explain. "So I made a fake, put a GPS tracker in it, and let it be stolen. Dr. Karmanos tracked it and discovered that his assistant had taken it."

In the silence, a nagging thought crept in. Demetrius had been caught. He and Karmanos thought the fake was the only chalice. So why puncture the gas line and run us off the road today?

"Demetrius?" Jim said. "You think Demetrius just tried to kill us?"

"We caught him with the fake chalice yesterday. I don't know. Maybe he was mad at me for getting him in trouble?"

"He didn't push you Monday."

"He was there."

"But he went to Karmanos' car during our break. I let him out the gate right after we finished in the men's room."

"No, it has to be Demetrius."

"Can't be."

I took a couple of aspirins as I cleaned up in the restroom. No wonder my head hurt.

Jim was on his cell when I returned to the car.

"We're late. I was supposed to meet Father Paulos at the Cathedral and walk together to the Institute. I suggested he take a cab. Do you want to let the Institute know we might be a few minutes late?"

"No!" The word boomed. "I mean, uh, I just don't want the killer to think he almost got me."

I felt the weight of his eyes on me.

"I'm not going to let anyone scare me anymore."

I took another bite of the chocolate bar. Huh. How did that get unwrapped and in my mouth?

I focused out the window as we traveled back to Athens. Jim was a friend. Maybe. Was he telling the truth about Demetrius?

Our new friends dropped us in the Plaka.

"I'll run to the Cathedral to change," Jim said. "See you in a few minutes."

I raced up the front steps. Sophia emerged from the kitchen with coffee.

"Oh, you're here," Sophia said. "I thought you were delayed. I told Lydia to start without you."

"Give me five minutes to change."

Lydia was putting the finishing touches on her makeup. She wore an ivory linen suit and a royal blue silk blouse. She glanced at my torn jeans and frowned.

I traded torn denim for black slacks and shirt, appropriate for the AV tech.

We charged upstairs. Lydia paused at the door, then swept into the room. All the men rose to their feet, kissing her hand and treating her like royalty. She could make an entrance.

Father Paulos was Lydia's only rival in magnificence. I hadn't seen him in full regalia before. His tall hat trailed a long black veil. Orthodox monks and priests gained additional layers of robes and capes as they moved up in rank. Paulos was a second-level monk plus a priest plus an abbot. His layers would clothe a third world village. I recognized the medieval cloisonné cross on his chest from the monastery treasury.

I joined Carl at the AV desk.

"I have it all set up. We thought you were going to be late, so Billy asked me to run the AV. He doesn't want to use the clicker since he talks with his hands."

How did Sophia and Carl know we would be late? Did they know about our road mishap?

Lydia made introductions. As she went around the table, the credentials swelled. I hadn't realized that Andreus had an academic background and consulted for museums.

Iakobos came in just as Lydia finished introducing *Archimandrite* Paulos. Iakobos had donned his cassock and unveiled *skoufos*, but left off the heavy eyeglasses he used at Meteora.

Lydia raised her eyebrows and paused, surprised at the transformation. Paulos took over.

"Many of you have met Brother Iakobos, my assistant this summer."

Billy glowered. He hadn't made the connection. Carl looked at me and clicked his tongue. Naughty, naughty.

Lydia transitioned to the project as I dimmed lights and began the graphics. Billy took over on cue. The show was on.

74

Presentation

Sunday Afternoon, the Conference Center

The experts relaxed as we began. When Billy explained dating, postures shifted. The guests sat up and leaned forward. Sophia moved her chair up to the table.

Dr. Karmanos and his paleography expert exchanged soft comments and took notes. They asked a few questions, but no big challenges.

Billy moved to translation. Abbot Paulos was in his element. He added suggestions on word derivations and translation. The translation expert joined in. Again, no major challenges.

Billy's delivery gained authority as he built his case.

The final segment: what was this fragment? Billy explained his conclusion. It was a Greek fragment from Iraenus, a section previously known only from Early Latin versions. In it, Iraenus reported the origins of Christian scriptures.

I brought up lights as guests applauded. Billy had hit a home run. (My graphics were darn good, too.)

Sophia refilled coffee as Billy took questions. The paleography expert asked about the material and condition of the fragment.

"It appears to be a traditional lampblack ink on the parchment. Because of the oily lanolin in the animal skin, the ink tends to sit on the surface and flake off. But this is in remarkably good shape. It may be reused parchment. It looks like some writing has been scraped off. Or that may just be a note or correction."

"Of course, we will do chemical analysis of the ink and parchment," the expert said.

"You must ask for permission to test," said Abbot Paulos.

"We can get testing expedited. Probably one or two months to do the basics," Karmanos told Billy. "You can continue your analysis while testing is underway."

"The fragment is property of monastery."

Karmanos glanced at the abbot. "Yes, yes. I'll send an expert tomorrow to pick it up."

"You will not! We do not give permission." He towered over the others as he stood tall in his regalia.

Everyone stiffened. Sweat broke out on Karmanos' bald head. "You had stacked it in an old box. We know how to take care of it. My conservationist will come tomorrow."

"You think I will give it up?" Paulos said. "Send soldiers. Search entire monastery."

Karmanos stood, planted his arms on the conference table, and leaned toward the priest. "You have no authority here."

The *archimandrite* rose to every inch of his ecclesiastical authority and glowered back. "You have no authority at my monastery."

Sophia broke it up. "We can work out those issues through proper channels. The Institute follows the highest standards of scholarship and protocol."

The petite scholar had guts. When had she changed her mind about staying out of this? Was she sold on the project or just grabbing power?

"This is important for Biblical scholarship," Walter complained. "Don't let your turf battles stop a major advance in understanding the Bible. When the Nicene Foundation publishes Dr. Sullivan's findings, it will change theology. The attention will benefit both the monastery and the Byzantine Museum."

Billy turned to Walter. "It's too soon to announce the interpretation of this fragment. We need to be cautious."

"Well, we can't reach any conclusions without seeing the fragment." Karmanos turned his rage on Billy. "You could at least give us a copy."

Lydia moved to the front of the room, taking charge.

"We will meet about details in the coming days. We thank you for sharing your expertise. Join us for cocktails downstairs."

Sophia picked up coffee cups. Karmanos and his cohorts muttered to each other. They were obviously not done. But the women indicated this event was over.

Andreus came to the rescue. "I have a special invitation for everyone this evening. The bishop and I have a little surprise at the Cathedral. Then, we have dinner to celebrate Dr. Sullivan's magnificent discovery."

Andreus escorted Karmanos down the stairs, pouring on flattery. "I was impressed with your article in the last journal. I must hear more about it." Andreus turned and winked at Lydia. I was watching a lesson in how to get things done in Greece.

Sophia and I carried coffee cups downstairs.

Carl followed me to the kitchen. "Naughty girl! I didn't realize you had a thing for men of the cloth."

I turned away. "Don't be ridiculous, Carl. He's not really a monk. He's just working there this summer."

I felt Carl's hand on my shoulders and smelled his shampoo as he leaned close. His warm breath tickled the back of my neck.

"Do the others know you are consorting with the enemy?"

I stacked coffee cups in the dishwasher silently.

"I must ask Iakobos for pointers, since my kindness and attention have gone unrewarded."

Heat rose up my neck and spread to my cheeks.

"Does your lover's boss know that you stole their manuscript?"

I slipped out of his grasp and escaped to the safety of the group in the library. Lydia's favorite restaurant had catered hors d'oeuvres and wine.

Lydia and Billy focused on the *Archimandrite* as Andreus worked on Karmanos. The sell job was on.

"You must understand—we protect our manuscripts," Paulos said. "Meteora is under Patriarch in Constantinople, not National Orthodox Church in Athens."

"I didn't know that," Lydia said.

"When the government tried to seize books for National Library, people of Kalambaka came to our aid. We turned away greedy thieves empty-handed."

"When was that?"

"Right after Independence. 1828, I think. We provide refuge for *klepts* and freedom fighters! Then government nationalizes church and takes lands and books."

These guys had long memories.

Jim shed his cassock and hat, freeing his bangs to flop into his eyes. He had the dubious honor of talking to pompous Walter.

"Do you go by Jim or Iakobos? You've been introduced both ways today," Walter said.

"I answer to either. James is Iakobos, Jacob, in Greek. So it's the same name."

"Jacob. The heel grabber, the trickster. Jacob steals his brother's birthright and tricks his blind father into giving him Esau's blessing. Good name for a student pretending to be a monk."

"It has been interesting to learn monastic life this summer."

Jim turned toward us. Carl draped his arm across my shoulder in a surge of testosterone. A cock fight. I escaped and joined Lydia's conversation circle. The discussion had turned to the collection at the monastery.

"We are puzzled," Father Paulos said. "How did this Irenaeus fragment come to library? We do not have codex that it has fallen out of. Most fragments come from book in library, or there are other pages from same book."

"I have a theory," I said. "I think it comes from the back of the

Constantine manuscript."

"Amber, don't interrupt!" Billy said. "You can barely read a Greek sentence and you've never seen a manuscript before this week."

His words hung in the silence of the room. I felt the red rising up my face as all the eyes turned to me.

"I ... I ..." I couldn't force the words past the lump in my throat. "I'm sorry. I didn't mean to ..."

"Just let the adults talk," Billy said. "We have business here."

I slunk into the hall, followed by Jim. He squeezed my hand.

"Amber, don't let him get to you. I warned you that he was cut-throat," Jim said.

"But I was trying to be helpful, to support Billy's document."

"Just let him talk and be the big man tonight."

I breathed ten times, forced a smile and walked back into the library. Jim delivered an encouraging pat..

75

"Irenaeus is an important early source," said Paulos. "From him we learn what first church leaders taught and believed."

"That's why this fragment caught my eye," Billy said. "It's crucial for dating the books of the New Testament. We may be able to push back the composition of Revelation by several decades."

"I agree. This is significant."

"Father Paulos," Lydia said. "How can the Institute help you so that Dr. Sullivan can complete his studies?"

"We will allow access if everyone agrees we are owner," Paulos said. "Perhaps we can become place for learning once more, not just tourists."

I scooped some *tzaziki* on my plate with a slice of pita bread. It looked disgusting. Food stuck in my throat. The accusing eyes of the olives stared at me.

The conversation swirled around me, but I couldn't follow. I had more bruises and scrapes than I could count. The stitches on my head itched.

If Demetrius hadn't tried to kill me, then it was someone in this room.

Aunt Lydia visited with Father Paulos and Billy Sullivan. Walter Smoot stood beside Billy. Lydia and Walter hadn't arrived until later—I could count them out. Same with the experts who came with Karmanos tonight.

Sophia Wright smiled as she visited with Andreus Mikos and

Georgios Karmanos. Sophia had been at Lydia and Robert's home the weekend Robert died. She hated me and Lydia. But she seemed too cold to attempt a hot crime like murder.

Carl joined Jim and me. Everyone was relaxed—eating, laughing, talking, drinking.

My eyes focused on his face. The clear blue eyes didn't show a care in the world.

"Jim, have you been to the Havana Club?" Carl asked.

"No, I haven't had time for Athenian night life."

"Amber and I went there last night. Great Latin band. We set the dance floor on fire. She even swooped very gracefully into my arms when she tripped doing the tango."

Carl smiled over the top of his wine glass.

"I'll have to go some time," Jim said. "Maybe Amber can teach me salsa dancing."

"What do you think of this retsina, Amber? Greek wine is not as good as the German wine we shared in my room last night. Actually, it was this morning."

Those blue eyes were definitely teasing. And taunting. But were they a killer's eyes?

He spoke softly: "Have you seen the rose tattoo on her ass, Jim?"

I gasped. "What did you say?"

"I was telling Jim about the rose tattoo you showed me last night. Everyone would be interested in that, no?"

I couldn't breathe. Would Carl really tell everyone that I had stolen the manuscript?

He smiled.

I ran upstairs. It had been stupid to show Carl the Constantine manuscript. And stupid to take the manuscript. I should have left it at the library door when the alarm went off.

Run away, the voice in my head said.

Running away had brought me to Greece this summer. Running away had gotten me a stolen manuscript. Running away was easy, but it didn't work. Maybe it was time to stop running and confront my problems.

Just confess and give the manuscript back.

The simple thought squeezed the breath out of my chest.

Don't panic. Think. Surely I could come up with an easier way out.

I entered the first student bedroom. Who would suspect the plump mounds on the beds as a hiding place? I scooped up the pillow, bracing for the weight of the manuscript.

It was light as feathers.

Still, I looked inside. Not there. Where? I checked the other bed. The other unoccupied bedrooms. Back to the original room. Surely it was here.

It wasn't. My borrowed manuscript had been stolen.

76

End of the Macedonian Dynasty

January, A.D. 1055, Constantinople

Theodora rushed with her loyal guards to the Great Palace.

Would the senators heed her call to convene? Would others in the imperial guard allow senators to gather inside the palace complex?

Would the Senate still remember her? After her sister shoved her out, she had retired quietly to a convent on the western edge of Constantinople. But it was hard to watch Constantine IX's disastrous leadership. Surely the senate would not allow the dying emperor to hand over the crown to the Duke of Bulgaria.

She paused at the Chalke Gate. The people in the square outside *Hagia Sophia* bowed before her. Her family had passed through this gate to worship for 200 years.

Representatives of the powerful families greeted her inside the gate and escorted her. The senators rose as she entered the chamber and walked to the dais.

"She doesn't belong here. Get her out," one shouted.

Theodora raised her head higher. Imperial guards stood steady by her side. The rumblings quieted.

"You have come today not for me, but in concern for the Empire," Theodora began.

"I will not speak of the deeds of Basil the Macedonian, Leo the Wise or Constantine the Purple-born. I will speak of the last great emperor, my uncle, Basil the Bulgar-slayer."

A chant went up from the gathering. "Hear, hear. To Basil."

"Remember the Empire 30 years ago. Borders were secure. The army and navy were strong. The treasury was full. The church was united. Our empire was great."

Theodora paused as nods of agreement rippled through the room.

"Emperor Basil cared not for fancy buildings nor a comfortable life for himself. He cared for the people."

"Since he died, we have been led by men who cared more about their own glory than the glory of God and of the Empire. Instead of building safe borders, they built tributes to themselves.

"They put ego and power ahead of the unity of the True Belief. Last year, the church in the East and in the West split apart. That schism may never be healed. Why fight fellow Christians when we should join together against the forces of Mohammed?

"And now, you would let that pretender, who doesn't deserve the name Constantine, to pass the crown to a Bulgarian? The Bulgar-killer would rise from his grave at that outrage."

She paused, waiting for her supporters.

"Long live Empress Theodora."

She smiled to herself. All was going as planned.

The sole shout became a chorus. "Long live Empress Theodora."

Theodora ruled for 17 months. But the seventy-four-year-old empress could not undo the damage. The death spiral had begun for the Eastern Roman Empire

The Great Schism of 1054 had increased tension between Eastern and Western Europe.

Just forty years later, the First Crusade would expose leaders from the West to the culture, architectural wonders and opulence of the Eastern Empire. Jealous Western leaders responded by building great Gothic cathedrals to outshine the magnificence of *Hagia Sophia* and the Church of the Holy Apostles.

Tensions boiled over during the Fourth Crusade in A.D. 1204. Frustrated Crusaders sacked Constantinople. They looted relics, chalices, crowns, tapestries, jewelry, ivory panels and icons as spoils of war and to pay the Venetians for transporting the troops to the Holy Lands. Most of the creations of the Macedonian Renaissance ended in Venice and Rome, or in the hands of the kingdoms and noble families of Western Europe.

Books stolen from the Imperial Library of Constantinople spread knowledge across Europe, sparking the Renaissance in the West.

A few precious items were hidden in monasteries, awaiting the return of Greek sovereignty.

77

Sunday evening

I sat in the dark, fingering Gabriel's prayer rope.

A tall figure appeared in the door. "Are you looking for something?"

"Carl, what have you done with it? First you try to kill me, and now you've stolen my manuscript."

"You bitch!" He tried to grab me. I slipped his grasp as he fell on the bed.

I positioned myself in the doorway, ready for a quick escape. "Stay back. Don't touch me."

"I moved your manuscript to a safer place. How can you accuse me of trying to kill you?"

"You were there on Monday when I was pushed. You were the first person to look over the wall. And you knew where we went today," I accused.

"You fell on Monday. What are you talking about, today?"

"Don't play dumb with me. I know you tried to run us off the road."

Carl stared at me.

"You're the one who always drives. It must have been you."

"I went hiking to clear my hangover and get away from your aunt's crazy friends after you abandoned me to run off with that fake monk. Get real. You're attractive in a helpless schoolgirl way, but not enough to drive me to a jealous, murderous passion."

A likely excuse. No witnesses, I bet.

"Was it fun pushing me off the wall at Meteora? I bet you were surprised when you looked over and saw me still alive."

"Amber, Amber, Amber. I'm the only one here who is your friend. How could you think this?"

"I've been naive to not figure it out before. First someone pushed me off the wall, and then today someone ran us off the road. And now you've stolen my manuscript."

Carl held his hands out as he stood up.

"Let's get the manuscript. I'm not trying to hurt you."

"Walk ahead of me," I told Carl. "I'm not turning my back on you."

I followed Carl toward his room.

"I've always looked out for you, Amber. Sophia just puts up with you so that she can keep Lydia's money for the Institute. Billy is using you to catch a rich widow. I don't know if Jim is spying on us or lusting after your body—probably both. And your precious Lydia wants you to take some of the burden since she lost your uncle."

"Keep walking."

"I'm the only one who has nothing to gain. I'm your friend. I have no motive to do you any harm."

Carl disappeared into his closet. I stayed in the doorway in case he came out with a knife. Or worse.

The wrapped manuscript appeared, followed by Carl.

"I'm sorry. I shouldn't have moved it without telling you."

I took it and headed back downstairs.

"What are you going to do?"

"Give it back."

"Don't be crazy! I won't tell."

"You just threatened that you would."

"You could go to prison. You're already on the list of trouble-makers with the police."

Worse, I could be sent home to face my parents. Their disappointment could be harder to take than jail. Still, I had taken the manuscript. I needed to do the right thing.

I stopped outside the library door. Run away or tell the truth.

Gathered my courage. Stepped into the room.

Jim looked up and saw what I was carrying. The color left his face.

I could turn and run.

"Father Paulos, I need to return something that I borrowed."

"What is that, my daughter?" he asked as he rose.

He really did look imposing with all that regalia. I hesitated. Jim shook his head NO. I silently chanted a quick *Kyrie*.

"I borrowed the Constantine manuscript to take pictures of it." My voice quivered. Paulos leaned closer, straining to hear. "I'd like to give it back to you."

Paulos accepted the heavy burden, then stared at me in silence. I waited for my punishment. Pulse raced through my body and pounded in my head. I didn't dare breathe.

"Thank you for returning it," he finally said.

I sucked in fresh air.

Where was the wrath of God that I had earned? Is this mercy?

He cleared a spot and pulled the manuscript from its pillowcase.

"Mrs. Jackson, perhaps you have not seen this," Paulos said. "It is a masterpiece."

Sophia rushed to the table, then glowered at me. "What are you doing with this? I knew you were an idiot, but are you totally insane?"

Lydia bent over the codex with Paulos.

The bishop is waiting for us," Billy told Lydia and Father Paulos. "We can look at this later."

Lydia didn't hear anything. The manuscript captivated her.

Carl leaned close. "I can't believe you got by with that."

Jim joined us. "Why did you give it to Abbot Paulos? I told you I would sneak it back into the library. Don't you trust me?"

"Carl was going to tell."

"Where did you get that idea?" Carl said.

"You made that wisecrack about the rose on my ass. That's what we were calling my secret last night. You were threatening to expose my ass—the manuscript."

Carl rolled his eyes. "You imagine the craziest things."

Carl and Jim looked at each other. Jim shook his head.

"How are we going to protect this one?" Carl asked.

"It's hard," Jim said. "She's accident-prone."

Lydia called me back to the table.

"I see the pink stain," Lydia said. "You may be right. Either the fragment was stored inside this book, or in another binding with purple murex dye on the end pages or inside cover."

She turned to the front page. "Billy, have you seen the pink stain in this book?"

"I've never seen this manuscript," Billy said. "Amber told me about it when we got back to Athens. I certainly didn't know she had stolen it."

He rested his hand on Lydia's shoulder as he looked over.

"You've got a murex stain on your fragment," Lydia said.

"That's possible," Billy said. "Some parchment pages were dyed purple, then written with silver ink for members of the royal family. It could have been stored against one of those purple pages at some point in its life."

I found myself drawn to the manuscript despite my embarrassment. "Emperor Constantine VII wrote this Psalter for his son, Romanos II. It includes notes about being a good king. Constantine is known as the scholar king. He was a writer, artist and historian."

Lydia and Paulos reached the end of the masterpiece.

"It's missing the last page," Paulos said. "It had a blank page with messages from the monks written on it."

He leaned closer and studied the codex, then looked at me with piercing eyes. "Where is the last page?"

Oh, Hell. I wasn't going to slip through with the sheep. I had just been sorted into the goats.

Jim examined the codex with Paulos. I couldn't follow the rapid Greek. They seemed to be arguing.

Billy turned, grabbed my shoulders and shook me.

"How could you embarrass your aunt this way? It's going to be damn hard to get access to the monastery's fragment after you've stolen their manuscript and damaged it."

I jerked away. "Get your hands off me."

"I told Lydia she should be sent home," Sophia said. "It's been one disaster after another with her here this summer. We'll be lucky if the Institute survives this scandal."

I raised my voice. "Wait a minute. I did *not* remove the last page, and I did *not* damage the manuscript."

Sophia managed to look down her nose at me. "How can we trust anything you say?"

I looked around for support. Carl and Walter had disappeared.

Jim turned to me. "Amber, do you have the pictures we took of the manuscript at the monastery?"

What a relief. Finally, a friend.

"Yes, on my laptop. They'll show that there was no back page on Friday."

I found my laptop stuck aside on a side table and lifted the lid. Black coffee dripped out of it.

78

I knew better than to power up my laptop. I pulled the battery as Jim grabbed napkins. We blotted dry what we could, then propped it up to allow more coffee to drip out.

"It will need to dry for a day or two before I turn it on."

"See. She's a menace," Sophia told Lydia.

"This isn't my coffee. I drink it with cream and sugar. This is black. Someone else spilled this on purpose."

"Maybe you should have put it away instead of leaving it out and whining about the consequences," Sophia said. "That would be a novel idea for you."

Lydia turned to *Archimandrite* Paulos. "What can we do to make this right? This is not the usual way we operate."

"We need to keep our fragment research on track," Billy said. "We can't let a foolish act of vandalism by an ignorant student disrupt the most important discovery of my career."

Andreus and Paulos were the only calm people.

Paulos rose. "I will take the codex, and we will talk tomorrow. Rev. Sullivan is correct—we should not keep bishop waiting. He and Mr. Mikos plan something magnificent."

He gathered up his dignity and spoke in Greek to Iakobos. Jim wrapped the codex and carried it. I stuffed a black lace scarf for the cathedral in my purse and followed them out the door.

"We'll talk later," Jim whispered to me.

The *Archimandrite* paused. "My daughter, the *Gheronda* says the *Hodegitria* saved you for a reason. I do not always understand the ways of God. But I do expect you and Brother Iakobos to be honest with me. No more lies and secrets."

Jim and Paulos led our unlikely procession a few blocks to the *Mitrópoli*. The cathedral was the seat of the bishop of Athens. Karmanos bitched all the way that we should have called for cars.

I brought up the rear alone. I was too angry to chitchat. Why had I thought I should return the manuscript openly? My honesty could cost me my academic career. I'd be lucky to get a job as a school teacher after this.

The sun had left the sky. Trees surrounded the *Mikrí Mitropolí*, cloaking the little old Byzantine chapel in darkness. We walked from shadows around the mini metropolitan chapel into the lighted plaza in front of the big metropolitan cathedral, where the bishop waited to greet us.

A hot, acrid wind brushed my left shoulder. Glass shattered, spreading flames and shards in front of me.

79

Athens Cathedral

Another protest with Molotov cocktails? Why would they target the bishop?

Lydia and Billy were almost to the cathedral porch. She turned at the explosion.

"Get down, get down," I yelled. I ran through puddles of flame, smoke and broken glass toward her.

Another Molotov cocktail shattered between us. Lydia collapsed and screamed as the incendiary liquid sprayed her bare legs. Blood spurted where a shard of glass pierced her arm.

Another explosion behind me. Why would they target me?

I zagged the other direction—the last thing I wanted was to draw fire toward my friends.

Members of our group rushed toward Lydia as I stumbled across the Plaza in the thick smoke. Glass projectiles exploded around us. Shards embedded in the soles of my shoes.

The bishop screamed as his robes caught fire.

Jim dropped the manuscript as he and the abbot ran toward the bishop. They pushed him to the ground to snuff out the flames.

We were doomed in the light. I lunged back toward the darkness on the north side of the *Mikrí Mitropolí*.

My change in direction must have surprised the rioters. There was a pause, then a bottle smashed beside me.

At last, darkness. The shadows allowed me to catch my breath as my eyes adjusted. My black clothes blended into the darkness. I kicked off the glass-studded shoes and threw the black lace scarf over my face and hair. I might be able to avoid detection.

I hadn't seen anyone when we walked past the grove. The attacker must be hidden in the trees or up against the chapel itself. I visualized the trajectory ... he must be tucked in a doorway or niche.

The trees provided cover for creeping around the chapel. The attacker had seen me dash this direction. If I could come around to the other side, I might just surprise him.

Sirens echoed across the plaza.

What could I use as a weapon? All I had was a purse and the camera around my neck.

Gabriel's prayer rope as a garrote? Banish the thought.

I slid toward the back side of the chapel. A figure was flattened against the ancient stones, peering around to the north.

My new SLR camera was my best bet for a weapon, even if it meant ruining a second expensive camera this week. I threw my purse aside, wrapped the camera strap around my right hand and swung it in a test arc, like David and Goliath.

Now or never. I ran toward him, swinging the camera backwards. I brought it forward with as much force as I could. The thud against the side of his head produced American profanity as he knelt, clutching his right ear.

I retreated on my bleeding bare feet around the south side of the chapel to summon help.

A lighter clicked, breaking the darkness.

I froze.

A steady hand moved the flame, illuminating a bottle of pale liquid in his other hand. The dancing blue flame reflected off his braided ring and dark eyes.

He leaned the bottle closer, dangling the fabric wick closer to the lighter.

My lungs finally returned to work, sucking in air.

Think. He would have to light the wick and throw the bottle

hard enough to break glass and unite flame and fuel. About 20 feet separated us. Which way should I run?

The blue flame stretched up to the wick, sending golden fire and black smoke creeping up the fabric.

Firelight glinted off white teeth aligned in a wicked smile as he held the future explosion. He cocked his arm back.

Our eyes locked.

As the flame swung forward, I ducked and ran.

I smelled singed hair as the bottle flew over my head. Hot stings pelted my back as the force of the mini-explosion pushed me forward. I closed the gap between us and dove against his legs as he scrambled for another bottle.

Hah. That wouldn't do any good in these close quarters, other than to perhaps hit me over the head. I rolled on my side and swung the camera, delivering a thud on his back.

He grabbed my arm and twisted it. "You will be utterly burned with fire, for strong is the Lord God who judges the harlot."

Words from Revelation. I kneed his crotch. "Ready for a circumcision of the heart?"

His weight fell on me as he doubled over.

"I'm not some stupid little college girl you guys can jerk around." I squirmed to try to push him off me.

"You're the harlot, and God will get you!" He tried to control my arms.

An engine revved in the alley.

"Let's go," a voice yelled.

The rioter untangled himself and ran. The small tan car left a trail of rubber as it roared out of the alley.

As the adrenaline rush subsided, pain in my feet and body crushed me. I was too weak to rise off the ground. The flames and glass hadn't rained down from heaven, but they were as much as I wanted to experience. Enough of these dreams come true.

Flashlights flickered through the trees. Suddenly, police officers and people filled the grove.

Carl found me.

"Amber, are you okay? Amber?" He grabbed me by both arms and shook.

"Aooow, let go."

"You're hurt?"

"Of course it hurts. I've been bruised and battered all week."

He laughed. "Not so bad, I see. The police and ambulance are in the plaza." He yelled, "Over here. I found her."

"What about Lydia? And the bishop?"

"Already on their way to the hospital. We are searching for you."

"The bad guys got away."

"Don't worry about that now."

Jim was out of breath when he reached us. He gave me a big hug and was rewarded with a shriek. His hands were bloody when he pulled away.

He yelled to the medics to bring a gurney.

"My purse ... it's over there somewhere."

Carl and a police officer with a flashlight located it. Jim walked beside me as medics wheeled me around blackened pavement and broken glass to the ambulance.

"Now do you believe someone is trying to kill me?"

80

Athens Medical Center

A grim-faced group met me in the waiting room.

"Is Aunt Lydia okay?"

Sophia looked up from her conversation with Billy. "They've given her a light anesthetic while they remove the glass, stitch the wound in her arm and treat the burns. She may have some burn scars, but she'll be okay. They'll keep her for a few days." She scowled at me. "And you?"

"Just a few cuts in my feet and burns here and there. The nurse cleaned me up and glued the skin back together in a few places. I'll need a haircut to get rid of the singed places."

I plopped next to Andreus. Billy and Sophia huddled in the corner. Karmanos talked to a police officer in the hall. Carl and Jim both focused on their cell phones. Father Paulos stood with hands out, praying quietly.

"The bishop?"

"Hands and legs are burned," Andreus said.

"Can I see Aunt Lydia?"

"You have done quite enough already," Sophia said.

Lydia's scream echoed in my memory. Was this my fault? I just wanted to study art. What had I done that was so bad?

I ran through the events of the week. The package with the chalice—I was nosy, but did unwrapping it really set off all this?

Monday at the monastery I took photographs and enjoyed the view. What could be wrong about that? And what happened to the missing manuscript page?

I retrieved my phone and connected to the wi-fi. A few keystrokes and photos streamed from my online backup.

"Jim, look at this."

I flipped through images to the last page of the codex. It ended with a commentary on Psalm 88. Facing the parchment page was the faded purple silk that lined the back board.

"See, the original consecutive numbers are on the pictures. The time stamp is embedded in the file. This is how we found it."

"That's what I told Father Paulos," Jim said. "A conservationist photographed and evaluated the manuscript a few years ago. It had the last page then."

He interrupted Paulos' prayers. We showed him the sequence. Sophia and Billy looked over our shoulders.

"A mystery," Paulos said. "I will speak to conservationist tomorrow. We will look in library for missing page."

"What was on the last page?" Sophia asked.

"Nothing on front," Paulos said. "Back had a note across top written by scribe later."

Jim glanced at me, then back at Paulos. "What did the note say?"

"Only nonsense. It said, 'Key of Theodora is not here. Latinos took cup of Constantine.'"

Sophia touched my shoulder. "Amber, come talk to me."

Sophia, Billy and I gathered in the little conference room that doctors use to give patients bad news.

"You should return home tomorrow," Sophia said.

"But I haven't finished here."

"You must get out of Greece. Someone took the manuscript from the riot scene tonight. If Abbot Paulos or Dr. Karmanos press charges against you for the theft and destruction of the manuscript, they would have to go through extradition. You would be protected by the American courts."

Sophia stood. "Pack your bags tonight. Carl will put you on the first flight tomorrow morning."

"Wait a minute. I have something to say about this."

Sophia shook her head no. "Billy and I have come to a consensus. We think Lydia would want us to keep you safe."

"I won't leave without talking to my aunt," I said.

"Look, I'll let you see her tonight. But do not entangle her in your problems. Just see that she is okay. Then Carl will take you back to the Institute to pack."

When we returned to the waiting room, Carl put an arm around my shoulder. "It's been fun having you here. Crazy but fun."

I sagged against him. MacGyver would have helped me. But MacGyver is fiction. And I did accuse Carl of attempted murder earlier this evening.

"I'm sorry your time here didn't go well. You have the worst luck. I'll miss you."

"Before I came, my big fear had been going home to live with my parents," I whispered. "In just one week, I've been rejected by grad school, stolen a manuscript and gotten Aunt Lydia injured. I'll be lucky to stay out of prison."

"I think that sums it up."

I straightened my shoulders and pulled away. "I will not be defeated. I don't know what's going on, but I will stop it."

Wiki-head would not be outsmarted again.

As long as images swirled in my head, it was hard to read the pattern. I started through my photos, selecting key images. A shadow with a hand. A fragment. Our group at Meteora. Three interlocking rings. I added a few more pictures from today.

The images seemed more detailed, more real, when pulled together. The pictures spoke to me. What they said was not good. In fact, it was downright evil.

We had been together only eight days, but we were colleagues, friends even. I had come to appreciate hottie Carl, preachy Billy, snooty Sophia, and gentlemanly Andreus. Abbot Paulos, Brother Iakobos and Elder Gabriel were almost saintly. Even officious Karmanos wasn't so bad. My stomach felt like a ball of lead. Maybe I was wrong.

I flipped through again. No wonder I had missed it—I hadn't wanted to see the truth.

God, what should I do? I have to ruin a friend to save myself.

I fortified myself with a chocolate bar. I needed to talk to someone.

"Billy, I need your advice."

81

Denouement

I propped my phone on a small desk in the conference room so we could both see the images on the little screen.

"I have a theory about what's going on. I think you might have some insight."

"Glad to help"

The first photograph was the Angry Jesus, clutching the book of judgment to his chest.

I pushed words past the lump in my throat. "What would make Jesus angry?"

I had wondered at the time. Now, eight days later, I had seen things that might make Jesus angry.

A photo of Sophia, Carl, Billy and I eating dinner in the Plaka showed us smiling, looking at Billy's calligraphy, and anticipating our trip to Meteora.

"I'm totally clueless as to what you're trying to show me."

The next sequence was Meteora. I started with the group picture I shot in the courtyard, then showed Abbot Paulos accepting an autographed copy of Billy's book.

Next, Billy examined a silver-studded manuscript in the stacks under the prophet David on the wall above.

"I've had enough of these pointless vacation pictures. I'm not going to waste any more time here."

"Don't you want to know what else I have?"

Billy crossed his arms and sighed.

The view from the parapet overlooking the valley below.

My shadow against the railing.

Two shadows against the railing.

The shadowy arm reaching out toward me.

"So you really were pushed," Billy said. "I didn't believe you. That's an interesting conclusion"

"I'm not finished. There's more."

The next sequence was the monastery library and cache.

A picture showed the work tables in the monastery library, piled with my backpack and camera gear, Billy's reference books and all the other items that had been hauled in for our work.

Then Billy's manuscript fragment. Front and back.

The edges were frayed. The upper corner was broken back almost to the start of the lettering.

"Delete all photos of the parchment from your files," Billy said. "You're violating my confidentiality."

"Nope."

I moved the image of the fragment to the right side of the display.

The final existing page of the Constantine manuscript appeared on the left side of screen. The edges and tones matched.

"Your pink stain theory may be right," Billy said. "It looks like the fragment was stored in the back of this book at some point. That's uncanny. So you've proved your little theory about where the fragment was stored. What a waste of time."

"You haven't seen the conclusion yet."

I quickly showed the smoldering motor scooter.

"Someone punched a hole in Jim's gas tank while we were at St. Luke's. Then, we were run off the road. That endangered Jim as well as me. Tonight was another attempt to silence me. But two innocent people were injured. That's unacceptable."

I flipped to a close up of a book cover and a hand.

"Tonight, I saw the ring worn by a rioter. I just placed it. The fraud is over. I know who's behind this!"

Billy exploded from his seat and slapped me. My head snapped as the blow rocked my chair and head against the wall.

"You Jezebel. After all I've done for you, you make up this garbage."

I stared Billy in the eye. "You talk all high and righteous about following the Ten Commandments, but you lie and steal and try to kill people."

Billy's face turned red. "You don't even understand what the Ten Commandments say, little girl."

"The Commandments say you shouldn't lie. Well, I have a picture of you looking at the Constantine manuscript on Monday, just before I was pushed. You can't deny it now."

"You probably altered the photograph."

"What about forging that fragment? You're lying about history and theology."

"Wrong. The Bible says you shouldn't bear false witness. I've always given true witness to the Word of God. I'm not saying I forged the writing from Ireneus. But prophets of God have written what God told them, corrected mistakes and explained history for two millennia."

"How about stealing?"

Billy sneered. "*My* parchment fragment isn't missing. The only thing gone is the book *you* stole. And since the rioters grabbed it, there's no way to compare the DNA of the parchments."

"You pushed me to provide a distraction so you could steal the fragment and make your forgery overnight. You intended to kill me. Isn't that the Fifth Commandment?"

"The Commandment says, 'Thou shalt not commit *murder*.' You can't even quote it right. Believers have always been allowed to defend the faith. That's why we have wars and executions, to deliver justice. You stumbled off a balcony, fell in a garden and bumped your head. Your life is in God's hand, not mine. You're lucky he saved you."

What other proof did I have? I remembered the rings.

"You wear the same Trinity ring as the rioter."

"Oh, get real. You can buy Borromean rings for $20 online."

I poked Billy in the chest. "You covet. You want money and fame so you can be big dog at the Nicene Foundation and the voice of the Christian Reconstruction."

"God wants us to have resources and a voice. Your aunt is a good Christian. But you're as bad a heretic as your uncle. Don't slander or libel me with these accusations, or I'll ruin you."

"The truth speaks for itself."

"Our hungry young Christian lawyers will tear you to shreds. You'll be lucky to get a job at McDonald's when we're through attacking your academic credentials and spreading your heresy on Twitter and Facebook. Just wait until we're through with you."

Billy pushed me away and strode out of the room.

82

The hospital

"Amber's concussion was worse than we thought. That girl is totally confused," Billy told the others in the waiting room. "I'm leaving this loony bin."

He turned to Sophia. "This is the greatest Biblical discovery since the Dead Sea Scrolls. Don't let a confused child ruin it. Call me at the Hilton after she's gone tomorrow."

All eyes focused on me as he stomped off.

"What was that? Carl asked.

"Oh, I just accused Dr. Sullivan of pushing me off the balcony, forging the writing on the parchment fragment and ordering his holy band to distract or destroy me today. Plus stealing the Constantine manuscript."

"I knew we shouldn't trust those charlatans," Carl said. "Your brilliant author is a shitbag, a forger and a fraud."

"Hold on," Sophia said. "Do you have any proof? Stop and build your case from the beginning."

"On Monday, Billy pushed me off the balcony to create a distraction, then stole the back page of the Constantine manuscript. He took it out of the monastery in my backpack. He must have forged his Irenaeus passage onto the old parchment Monday night when he skipped dinner. He smuggled it back in with his reference books on Tuesday so he could 'discover' it."

"Proof. Proof."

"I can't prove that he's the one who pushed me, just that I was pushed. But Billy lied when he said he never saw the Constantine manuscript. My picture showed him looking at it on Monday in the library. Abbot Paulos, did the conservationist take pictures of the manuscript pages?"

Paulos nodded. "Yes, many."

"We can match my picture of Billy's fragment to the conservationist's picture of the missing back page. And we can see if the parchment fragment has the scraped-off message from the monks."

"I respect Dr. Sullivan. This is hard to believe," Paulos said.

"Will you let us check the pictures to see if they match?" Sophia asked.

Paulos paused, then nodded.

Sophia turned to me. "I misjudged you," she said. "You are a klutz, but you are not stupid. You just might succeed in academia after all."

Was that an apology? Good enough for me.

"How's the forgery related to our motor scooter wreck and the attack tonight?" Jim asked. "Why would Billy attack you again? Besides, he was with us tonight. We know he didn't throw Molotov cocktails at us."

I paused. This got speculative.

"I recognized the pink stains. I called him this morning and told him his fragment came from the Constantine manuscript. I meant it had been stored in the book, but he must have thought I had detected the forgery."

"Yes, you called me, too," Carl said. "But that doesn't tie him to these would-be assassins. You're the one who provoked the rioters on Wednesday by taking photos of them."

"One of the rioters' ring. It was the interlocking Borromean rings in three colors of gold, Billy belongs to. And it's the logo for the Nicene Foundation. He called Walter and his assistant to help with this project. Then, he decided to get me out of the way. They had to improvise."

Carl said, "No one else saw the ring on the rioter. That won't stand up as proof."

"What about the license plate on the get-away car?"

"You saw?" Andreus asked. "You remember? Why did you not say so?"

As he went to find Karmanos, I shrugged. "No one asked me about it."

Abbot Paulos stood slowly. "I go pray with bishop, then I return to rectory. I have been up since morning prayers at 4 a.m."

His shoulders and head drooped as he walked away.

Jim looked at me. "I'd better go with him."

I focused on my memory of the license plate.

I typed combinations on my phone. Z8K-4683. Cocoa Brown, Purple, Teal – Bright Yellow, Dark Red, Purple, Grass Green.

Not quite right. I visualized the car as it backed toward us on the road to *Hosios Loukas*. And as it sped away from the cathedral. Bright Yellow, Dark Red, Purple, Royal Blue. The last number was a 5.

Z8K-4685. That looked right. Synesthesia did come in handy.

Two police officers found me. "Mr. Mikos says you see license plate?"

"Yes, it was Z8K-4685."

"Not right. Three letters, four numbers."

I looked again. "Oh, I was translating *eta* as an eight ... like in Greek numerals instead of Arabic."

The officers looked at me like I was crazy.

"Try ZHK-4685. The car will have damage on the right front bumper or fender. You'll want to check the parking at the Hilton."

"That is Athens registration," the officer said. They turned.

"I also saw a ring on the guy with the Molotov cocktails."

They turned back.

"It was three interlocked rings of gold—white, yellow, and pink—Borromean rings."

Carl laughed and spoke Greek to the officers. One handed him the report pad. Carl sketched the medieval Trinity symbol. They nodded and laughed as Carl spoke.

"Language barrier," he explained.

Andreus joined us. "Doctor says you may see aunt for few minutes. Would you like to see her?"

I nodded my head, blinking back tears.

"I feel horrible about what I've put her through."

"No, no, do not feel this way," Andreus said as he led me through the hospital maze. "But do not tell her about Rev. Sullivan. Time for that later."

Lydia sat in bed drinking a cup of tea with her left hand. Her bandaged right shoulder was stabilized in a sling.

"Can you smuggle in some brandy?" she asked. "I think I've earned it."

I hugged her gently. "How 'ya doin?"

"The doctors say the glass didn't pierce any crucial nerves or blood vessels. So I just need to give those muscles time to heal and keep it from getting infected. That's why I have this IV drip, for the antibiotics."

"I could ask them to slip you a little morphine in the drip."

"Oh, I think they did earlier." Lydia giggled. "Wasn't that the craziest thing? Getting caught up with protestors in downtown Athens? Was it an attack on the bishop?"

I glanced at Andreus.

"Police are working. Do not worry tonight," he said. He lifted a fat briefcase. "I have something for you."

He unzipped the case on the foot of her bed, reached in, then paused. "This was the surprise at *Mitrópoli*."

Andreus smiled at me. I grinned back.

"Okay, so show me," Lydia said.

"Robert got this for your anniversary. Amber, you give it."

I unwrapped the chalice. It shimmered in the harsh hospital light.

"You've been gone a long time," I told the chalice.

Andreus nodded. "Too long."

I held it, allowing light to shine through the translucent sardonyx. The silver glowed with a warm patina.

"It's gorgeous," Lydia said. She wiped away tears.

"How did you get it fixed so quickly?" I whispered.

"Restorers from my shop worked all night and today. The bishop allowed experts of his to assist. Temporary glue. They do more later."

I turned to Lydia. "It's a royal chalice from the Macedonian Dynasty, about twelve hundred years old. It's for the Divine Liturgy, serving the wine at communion."

I glanced at Andreus. He nodded agreement.

"It was designed by Constantine Purple-born. It symbolizes baptism, resurrection and new life." I pointed to its features. "The base is an octagon, like a baptistery. The design carries up to an eight-pointed incarnation star carved into the sardonyx bowl of the chalice."

Andreus stroked the silver rim with its embossed palm border, symbolizing paradise.

"Crusaders took it to Burgundy—in France—where Uncle Robert found it. He had studied the Macedonian Renaissance."

Lydia picked up the goblet and examined the details. "That's right. In fact, he and Billy had a lively debate about ecumenical church councils that weekend before he died. He told Billy that Constantine ruined Christianity by calling the Nicene Council and forcing everyone to agree. Robert loved to play Devil's advocate.

"You'd better keep this safe until I blow this joint." She handed the chalice to Andreus. "Today was our wedding anniversary. You couldn't have given me a better gift."

83

The Institute

I plopped in a leather chair in the library and stretched my sore feet on a coffee table. "I assume I'm not going home tomorrow."

"Sophia, shall I pack Billy's things?" Carl said.

"Don't touch them," I said. "The police will want to search."

Sophia and Carl both looked at me.

"I suspect you are correct about the forgery," Sophia said. "But this conspiracy theory that Billy would try to kill you—I'm incredulous."

"Oh, it's way worse than that." I picked up a bottle of wine left from earlier, poured a glass, and chugged it.

Carl poured himself one as we sprawled in exhaustion.

I pulled out my phone. "Let me show you a video."

Carl and Sophia gathered close as my encounter with Billy replayed. Sophia's body stiffened. Carl leaned closer and shook his head.

I poured another glass. "I didn't get a confession, but I learned something from that confrontation. That slimy leach murdered Uncle Robert."

"What?" Sophia grabbed the phone to replay the video.

"Who gets bees in their house in February? And why was the EpiPen on the other side of the room under the bookcase?"

I scavenged some Kalamata olives from the hors d'oeuvres tray.

"Sophia, you saw Billy there that weekend. Lydia said he and Robert argued about theology. He saw that Uncle Robert wasn't buying his shit. He killed Robert to get Lydia's money. He must have planted the bees and hidden the EpiPen under the bookcase."

I looked at Sophia. "Uncle Robert didn't write, 'Be Careful Bees.' He wrote 'Be Careful Billy S.'"

Her face went white. Her body sagged.

"You know the worst? Unless they catch the so-called rioters and recover the manuscript, he'll get away with murder."

Sophia cradled her head in her hands. "Robert could have been my soul mate... I resented Lydia because she met him first."

She stood. "I wish I believed in Hell and damnation. If anyone deserves it, that man does. I will devote my life to proving his guilt."

"I'll let you prod Karmanos and the police about the car tag, the missing manuscript and checking Billy's things. That would be better coming from you than me."

"Most certainly."

"Do bees have distinct DNA?"

Sophia stared at me. "I'm a classicist, not a biologist. Why do you ask?"

"I intend to find a dead bee from Uncle Robert's office then match it to the source bees. I bet his re-enactment buddy who makes candles raises bees. I'll call my dad and get him started with the police."

Sophia raised her eyebrows. "Remind me to call about your readmission to graduate school. It seems we will be working together."

She selected a bottle of wine and marched up the stairs.

I breathed in and out twice, then picked up the phone.

"Dad, can you talk?"

"Sure, what's up?"

"Uncle Robert was murdered, and I know who did it."

"Oh, my God!" I heard a sob and labored breathing.

"How do you know? And don't be joking with me."

"No, Dad. Uncle Robert didn't write, 'Be Careful Bees," he wrote "Be Careful Billy S.' He was trying to identify who killed him."

"My precious older brother? I looked up to him forever. It's been tough to deal with that hole in my life, but you think he was murdered?"

"Yes, and you need to call the Fort Worth police."

I explained my theory. At first, he just sobbed. Finally he got mad and started taking notes. I admit, my theory was mostly circumstantial. But who could argue against a death scene accusation?

"I'm calling my friends at the Texas Rangers tonight. Call me back tomorrow on what Athens authorities are doing and if they've arrested that snake."

"Can do. Love you, Dad!"

His voice caught. "Love you too, sweetie."

Carl and I stared at each other. Thoughts churned in my head.

My stomach growled. I gathered a plate of abandoned hors d'oeuvres.

"Want to share my late dinner?" I asked Carl.

He wrinkled his nose. "I pass."

"It won't be bad once I nuke it."

I hauled the feast to Lydia's apartment. I cued a few pictures to the printer while trying to fill the hole in my gut with food. How could God let horrible things like this happen?

My phone buzzed... a certain shaggy monk was at the front door.

84

The Key

He was waiting when I unbolted it. "Isn't it a little late for a social call?"

"I talked to Father Paulos. I want to tell you about that. Plus I have something to give you."

"Okay, shoot."

A voice floated down. "I can hear everything you say."

We looked up.

Carl waved from his balcony. "Don't do anything I wouldn't do."

"You have a dirty mind." I let Jim in and re-bolted the door.

Jim accepted a glass of wine as we dug into the leftovers.

"So, I confessed almost everything to Father Paulos," Jim said. "By catching the forgery, you saved the monastery from embarrassment. That wouldn't have been possible if you hadn't taken the manuscript."

"I'm okay? I won't get deported?"

"If we recover the manuscript. In fact, Father says the *Hodegitria* chose you to show the way since he was distracted by pride."

"Maybe she did. Or maybe it's serendipity.... I found the key to Revelation today."

"Are you serious?"

"The monks were looking for Theodora's key. They should have looked for Stephen's key."

"Stephen? We've got a lot of Stephens in church history."

"Patriarch Stephen, Constantine Purple-born's uncle.

"Constantine used comments on the Psalms from his uncle. Can I get you to translate the comments on Psalm 8 and Psalm 88?"

"Okay. Send me photos of those pages and I'll see if Father Paulos or Father Gabriel will help me. So where is Stephen's key?"

"Not where. What. It's eight, the number eight. The number seven dominates Revelation symbolism. John *veiled* the One who comes after seven. Remember the first chapter. John saw seven lamp stands of the churches, standing in the world. But Jesus stood with them. Seven plus one equals eight."

"Maybe you're right. We've seen a lot of eight-pointed stars and octagon baptisteries."

"In the parables, Jesus taught that the kingdom of God was at hand. John delivered the same message using visual images. And he did it eight times in the prophecy."

Jim gave me a high-five. "Congratulations"

"This may be my first Wiki-pedia article. Maybe my master's thesis."

I retrieved a picture of the wet fresco from the printer and sat down next to Jim. "You were right about the fresco. Here's our *omega pi eta* monogram above the people who are saved."

Jim pointed "There's another monogram, X Ξ F, above the followers of the beast."

I jotted a note in the margin.

X Ξ F = mark of the beast.

Ω Π H = followers of I H Σ O Y Σ (Jesus).

The black numbers glowed with color. The translation emerged:

600 60 6 = mark of the beast.

800 80 8 = followers of 10 8 200 70 400 200.

Jim looked at my scratching. "What are you doing?"

"It's a Byzantine riddle."

I checked the math.

$800 + 80 + 8 = 10 + 8 + 200 + 70 + 200 + 400$.

888, the sum of Jesus' name, was the mark of believers, the family of the new creation. The scripture was literally titled "Revelation of 888" in Greek.

85

Jim scratched his beard as he looked at the riddle.

"I'll have to think on this tomorrow. So do you really think those rioters were after you instead of the bishop?"

"Yup. They spoke English and called me the Harlot. They have to be cohorts of Beast Billy. I'm going to calculate his number."

After we polished off the leftovers, Jim got up to leave. He folded the riddle and stuck it in his pocket.

"Oh, that reminds me. I want to give this to you."

He handed me a candy bar from his pocket. The wrapper had been taped back together.

I undid the tape. A condom packet fell out as I removed the paper wrapper from the foil-covered chocolate. "I owe you one seduction," was printed on the inside of the wrapper. My writing.

"I found this under my pillow after you left the monastery," Jim said in a low, husky voice.

I stared. "Tonight? You want to collect tonight? Is that all men think about?"

I couldn't hold my MacGyver calm any more. I grabbed a handful of tissues.

Jim picked up the candy wrapper and tore it in half. Again. And again. Soon, it was in tiny shreds.

"I came to return it to you. When we make love, it won't be a test, or an obligation. You're free of this IOU."

I blew my nose again and wiped away tears as he stood to go. Maybe there were one or two decent men left in the world.

"*When* we make love?" I asked. "That sounds pretty confident."

"No, optimistic."

As I let him out the door, he gave me a hug and whispered in my ear.

"Save that condom for me." His beard brushed against my cheek.

"When does the scruffy beard come off?"

"*When* does it come off?" he asked. "I might keep it."

"I might keep the condom."

His farewell kiss did its best to answer that threat.

I bolted the door and glanced up the stairs.

Gorgeous Carl in an Athenian helmet? Or Shaggy Jim in forbidden black?

Justice for Uncle Robert. New research. Hope for graduate school. Maybe a job with Aunt Lydia's foundation. I glanced down —the marble tiles were octagons. Eight.

Tomorrow. A new day, a new beginning. Life was full of possibilities.

Author's Notes

The Scripture quotations contained herein are from the New Revised Standard Version Bible, copyright 1989, by the Division of Christian Education of the National Council of the Churches of Christ in the U.S.A Used by permission. All Rights reserved.

"The Jewish War" by Josephus is not covered by copyright.

One of the reference books on interpretation of Revelation was "Revelation, Four Views: A Parallel Commentary" by Steve Gregg. Copyright 1997 published by Thomas Nelson, Inc.

Among the numerous sources on Biblical numerology is an article by David H. van Daalen in the "Oxford Guide to the Bible."

This novel's interpretation of the Book of Revelation is solely that of the author. The explanation of other interpretations is again solely the opinion of the author.

The Omega Pi Eta monogram is designed and copyrighted by the author.

Constantinople is now known as Istanbul, Turkey. Hagia Sophia (Holy Wisdom) is now a museum. It was used as a mosque for about 500 years.

All modern-day characters in this book are fictitious. Any resemblance to actual persons, living or dead, is purely coincidental.

The photograph of Varlaam Monastery on the front cover is courtesy of Visit Meteora.

Want to know more? See the website to learn what's real and what's fictional in the locations, manuscripts and works of art described in this novel. It also offers a timeline of the Macedonian Dynasty.

www.RevelationKey.com

F.L. Wylie

Acknowledgments

Thank you to my husband, John, who always believes in me. He taught me how to write and is a great journalist, editor, publisher and teacher. My son, James, traveled to Greece with me and offered great suggestions for this mystery.

I started my novel with little understanding of the difference between writing news and a fiction novel. Author William Bernhardt straightened me out in an intense writing seminar. I continue to depend on him and on my writing classmates, Betty Ridge, Lara Bernhardt and Elton Williams, for feedback and advice.

I also thank my family members, co-workers and friends who encouraged me through the writing and editing process. Some of my beta readers stood with me through countless drafts.

Special thanks to Dawn Kester, Carolyn Estes, Tim Carman, Vickie Hefner, Dana Carr and Ellen Blank.

A final acknowledgment must go to my cancer doctors, support teams, family, and friends who helped me beat the odds.

F.L. Wylie

F.L. Wylie

About the Author
F.L. Wylie

Faith Lubben Wylie is an award-winning author, publisher and graphic designer who recently retired after 33 years as publisher/ owner of a community newspaper. Her newspaper columns won state, national and international honors. She is a member of the Oklahoma Journalism Hall of Fame.

The Revelation Key was inspired by a trip to Meteora, Greece.

She and her husband live on Oologah Lake, Oklahoma with their cat, Frank Sinatra.

.

95142687R00178

Made in the USA
Columbia, SC
06 May 2018